HER BEAUTY WAS
SHOCKINGLY UNEXPECTED

Arched eyebrows over large brown eyes, flawless golden skin, and a sharp jaw line with prominent cheekbones. Her skin was silky soft, and, underneath him, her petite body cushioned his muscular frame. He fit into her grooves perfectly. She was flower petals, wicked cars, and perfumed sheets made sweaty by the twisting of lovers' bodies. Every one of his senses keyed in on her, his body's response so fierce it took him a long moment to speak.

"Well," he inhaled deeply, "it looks like I've been captured by an angel."

The woman's breathing slowed, her body lost its rigidity, and she stopped trying to wiggle away from him. He released one of her wrists, testing her reaction.

The woman whimpered. Fear distorted the beautiful features of her face.

She needed protecting.

ALL THE WAY

KIMBERLEY WHITE

KENSINGTON PUBLISHING CORP.

http://www.kensingtonbooks.com

DAFINA BOOKS are published by

Kensington Publishing Corp.
850 Third Avenue
New York, NY 10022

All Kensington titles, imprints, and distributed lines are available at special quantity discounts for bulk purchases for sales promotion, premiums, fund-raising, educational, or institutional use.

Special book excerpts or customized printings can also be created to fit specific needs. For details, write or phone the office of the Kensington Special Sales Manager: Attn. Special Sales Department. Kensington Publishing Corp., 850 Third Avenue, New York, NY 10022. Phone: 1-800-221-2647.

Dafina and the Dafina logo Reg. U.S. Pat. & TM Off.

ISBN-13: 978-0-7582-2209-1
ISBN-10: 0-7582-2209-2

First Printing: December 2008
10 9 8 7 6 5 4 3 2 1

Printed in the United States of America

For Sha-Shana Crichton—
she just keeps on pushing me to do better.

And for Christopher,
who always helps me figure out what cars
best reflect my characters' personality.

Dear Readers,

You have stuck with me since the first book and all these many novels later you continue to send me ideas to stimulate my creative flow. I hope this book lives up to your standards. Please continue to write and visit my Web site.

P.O. Box 672
Novi, MI 48376

Email: kwhite_writer@hotmail.com
Web site: www.kwhitewriter.com

Chapter 1

"Ms. Vaughn! Get up!" The door of the suite flew open and a breathless female detective rushed in, locking the door behind her.

Payton bolted upright, instinctively reaching for the bedside lamp.

The lady detective rushed over. "Don't turn on the light!" Breathing hard, she grabbed Payton by the arm with a grip too strong for the slightly built lady and pulled her from bed. "They've found you. There are three, maybe four men out there."

Payton felt disoriented, confused. With her number of sleepless nights growing by the day, she wasn't her sharpest at the rude awakening. She'd been removed so abruptly from her home she wasn't even sure what hotel they were housing her in.

How long had she been asleep? What was this frantic detective's name? There had only been a few, but they weren't protecting her because she remembered names. It was the other information they wanted. She shook herself from her drowsy state, still befuddled, but the detective's message was clear: Her life was in danger.

The bathroom light illuminated a look of ghastly terror on

the detective's face. "At least one officer is down. I don't know how long we can hold them off." She kept her revolver trained on the bedroom door while pulling Payton to the oversized window.

Payton realized her life could end within the next few minutes. It had never felt like a true possibility before, even with the warnings from the authorities. Her mouth hung open as she reeled from the unbridled fright in her protector's eyes. *He* had found her, and he wanted the only witness to his crime dead.

Muffled gunshots sounded in the outer room of the hotel suite.

"Go out this window. Move along the ledge to the adjoining room, where the officers sleep. They'll help you out of the hotel to safety."

"What about you?"

"I'll hold the shooters off until you make it across the ledge."

Something in the detective's voice told Payton she would not follow. She would sacrifice her life to save the witness.

The detective placed her revolver on the ledge long enough to fling the window open. Payton stuck her head out. Below awaited the black asphalt parking lot crammed with cars. She had prayed there would be an awning or at least grass. She turned to reason with the panic-stricken detective. "There has to be another way out."

Having reclaimed the revolver, the detective lowered her arm from its ready-to-fire stance. "This is the only way."

"But—"

Payton looked out the window—ten stories down. The height took her breath away. She couldn't climb out onto a ledge in the middle of the night—

Ping!

The bedroom door split near the top.

Ping!

Another slither of wood near the lock flew away.

Payton's options became as terrifyingly clear as the horror on the detective's face. The tiny bit of steak she'd managed to eat at dinner burned the back of her throat as it threatened to come up. She crisscrossed her hands over her mouth to hold it back.

"Get it together!" the detective shouted, shaking her hard.

Gruff voices slithered underneath the door. Payton hoped the voices belonged to the police guarding her, but the lady detective's stiffening trigger finger discounted that theory.

"Ms. Vaughn, you have to go! Now!"

"Where are my clothes?"

The detective shoved her toward the window. "There's no time for that."

"But—"

"Hurry up!" the detective yelled, crouching and preparing to return fire.

Determined not to lose her life without one hell of a fight, Payton stepped out onto the ledge.

The window closed soundlessly behind her. *No turning back.*

A pit of darkness waited below. A car's headlights eerily illuminated the asphalt of the parking lot at the rear of the hotel. Envisioning herself splayed on the ground with strangers shielding their eyes from her mangled corpse, Payton pressed her body against the rough brick wall of the building.

It was a temperate night with a clear black sky, but the night breeze felt like an arctic wind as it pummeled Payton's exposed limbs. Her teeth chattered as she moved sideways one small step at a time toward the open window. Tiny rocks scattered along the ledge bit into the soles of her bare feet. The wind whipped at her ankles, raising the hem of her nightgown. The resulting chill permeated her down to the bone.

Fear of falling made her pant rapidly with every step. Her chest heaved. She was breathing too fast. She stopped to catch her breath. All she needed was to get lightheaded and fall. She concentrated on remembering how badly she wanted to live and calmed her breathing to a slow, steady rate.

Payton looked down. Her head began to swirl. She pressed her back against the wall with a whimper. How had her life been destroyed by her ambition?

A flash of bright light burst from her suite. Then everything went dark.

"Oh God." She fought against the internal shiver that cooled her and worked methodically to reach safety.

Payton climbed through the open window. She braced the ledge with both hands. With a new fear of heights, she vowed never again to allow her feet to leave the ground. She forced deep, soothing breaths into her lungs. *Safe.* She had made it across the ledge, and the window had been open wide enough for her to climb through—just as the detective had promised.

You're safe. Calm down. Pull yourself together.

Quiet.

The unnatural silence in the hotel room exploded in Payton's head. She couldn't hear the gunshots from next door. *That's explainable,* she told herself. *The upscale hotel has soundproof walls. But there are no sounds in* this *room.* No one rushed to retrieve her from the ledge. The cavalry wasn't there to rescue her.

Quiet.

Still.

Uncanny quiet mixed with ghostly stillness.

Payton's body trembled. An instant freeze covered her fingers and the tips of her toes.

"Ohmigod," she mumbled. She turned, slowly, in a full circle.

Bloody bodies. The mangled corpses were scattered near the entrance of the room. If there was ever any doubt about the seriousness of her situation, it vanished with the three lifeless policemen wearing blood-splattered uniforms, revolvers still in their grasp.

Violent spasms racked Payton's body. The sharp metallic

scent of blood mixed with the intense stink of fear. She clamped her hand over her nose.

Safety. Get to safety.

The hotel was no longer a "safe house." It had become a death house.

Get to safety, her mind screamed. *Safety is out of this hotel.*

Unable to stop and mourn and still save her own life, she tiptoed around the dead officers to the door.

Oh God. Oh God. Oh God.

Where would she go?

She could hear police sirens in the distance, but were they coming to her aid or racing to deliver the sick to the nearby hospital? If she hid in a closet, could they reach the hotel before the assassins found her?

She edged along the wall to the door, careful not to step in a bloody puddle. The stench fogging the room caused her to heave. Her hand covered her nose and mouth again, but she kept moving.

Slowly, carefully, she opened the door to the hallway. Gunshots rang out: two rapidly firing together, then one returning the shots. She could only guess who remained alive in her suite, or how many hit men were on the scene. She chanced looking out in the hallway. The corridor appeared to be another casualty of war. Debris was scattered across the carpet. Guest room doors stood wide open.

The sirens were closing in. The hired killers would hurry to make their escape. Or they would complete a suicide mission to eliminate her. She couldn't gamble on knowing what made a killer's mind work. No matter what they did, she had to get out of the hotel to safety.

She remembered her brief tour of the exits. "In case of an emergency," the detective had said.

To the exits. Get out to safety. Crouching low, she darted down the hall to the stairwell.

Chapter 2

"Jake, are you almost done?"

"There's something going on inside the hotel." A pause on the phone line, then animated voices colored the background. "People are pouring out of the elevators and stairwells. There are tons of police cars out front. I'm going to check it out."

"I'm on the way." Securing the cell phone to his ear with the use of his shoulder, Adriano reached for the door handle.

"No. I'll check it out. I don't want to scare off the informant. Wait fifteen minutes, and if I'm not out, I'll meet you at the hotel."

"Are you sure?"

"It's okay." Jake ended the call.

Adriano put away his cell phone. He ducked his head, inspecting the rear parking lot of the hotel. Nothing suspicious—only a guest here and there, coming and going. Pretty quiet considering the action Jake described. Whatever had the guests upset inside hadn't spilled out into the parking lot. Not yet. He decided to drive around front to check things out, but quickly reconsidered. If Jake ran into trouble, he'd come to the back parking lot, where he knew Adriano was waiting.

Intuition made the hairs on Adriano's neck wave. He noted the time. Maybe he should go inside to check things out. He never liked to meet with unknown informants—too dangerous—but this had been Jake's call. Certainly, the informant had selected the meeting place knowing it would be rumbling with activity. The Adam's Mark Hotel was one of the most prestigious inns located in Uptown Charlotte.

Adriano watched the door, searching for his partner. Despite their radically different personalities, Jake was the best partner he'd ever worked with at the *Chicago City* newspaper. Adriano got off on the action. Jake liked to meticulously analyze information. Together they investigated stories no other reporters even considered pitching because of the danger involved. With Jake's detecting skills and Adriano's fearless prowess, they were unstoppable.

Their latest story involved a big-shot gangster suspected of having ties with Mexican drug smugglers. The gangster resided in Charlotte, but had homes in all the best drug-trafficking cities: Miami, New York, Detroit, Chicago—no port was left unexploited by this thug. Only recently, Adriano and Jake had learned the gangster owned two homes in Charlotte, North Carolina. The story included all the usual elements attached to making illegal money: sex, drugs, and murder. Needing always to be stimulated by the new and exciting, Adriano placed his own spin on the investigation by keeping surveillance on the prime players and testing his newly acquired photography skills.

Grazicky had shielded himself with so many layers of people—drones—the authorities had never been able to obtain the evidence needed to connect him with any of his crimes. But Adriano and Jake were working with resources not available to the financially strapped prosecutor's office: time, money, and the offer of fame. Adriano and Jake were exclusively assigned to the Grazicky story. The *Chicago City* paper was willing to fund the venture as long as results were promised. The story offered the low-level drones their fifteen minutes of fame. Who in this business didn't want to be the next Deep Throat?

"C'mon, Jake," Adriano grumbled, more concerned than angry.

The back door of the *Chicago City* Land Cruiser was yanked open and then closed with a slam that rocked the huge SUV.

"About time." Adriano turned in his seat. "What—"

"Turn around!" a feminine voice commanded. The woman scrambled a bit then stuck a blunt object against the back of his head. She wrapped her other delicate arm around his neck with a grip he didn't expect.

"Hold on." He lifted his hands in surrender while trying to catch a glimpse of the woman in the rearview mirror.

"Put your hands on the wheel!" she shouted. "Are you an employee of the *Chicago City* newspaper?"

Adriano stole his first glance of the woman. Her eyebrows were arched, her brown eyes wide and afraid. "I'm an investigative reporter for the paper—my credentials are in my bag." He leaned forward to retrieve the camera case, but the sudden movement frightened the woman and she tightened her grip on his neck, making swallowing a challenge.

"Put your hands back on the wheel!"

Slow and easy, using every second to sum up the situation, he complied. "Okay. Check for yourself."

She didn't make a move toward the bag.

"What do you want?"

The woman's head swung around, checking their surroundings. "Why are you lurking in the parking lot?"

"I'm not 'lurking.' I'm waiting for my partner."

"Keep your hands on the wheel!"

Another glimpse of the woman provided more pieces to the puzzle of her physical makeup—clear complexion, creamy brown skin, confused expression.

"Listen, sweetheart—"

"Shut up." Her hand trembled as she watched several people exit the rear of the hotel. "Drive."

"Drive? Where to?"

"Drive." She poked the blunt object against the back of his head.

A flashlight? It would have been comical if the woman wasn't so afraid.

"Okay." He lowered his hands, placing one on the steering wheel and the other on the key dangling from the ignition. His next glimpse revealed golden brown shoulders scored by the spaghetti straps of a silky, cream-colored gown. *She'd left the hotel in a hurry, half-dressed.*

He complied with the woman's demands. Not out of fear; the woman would be no match for his large frame. He considered twisting around and wrestling her to the seat. He wasn't stupid. Whatever made her voice shake had her scared. Scared enough to hijack the news truck.

His craving for adventure grappled with his common sense as he pulled out into traffic. For now he'd see where this escapade would lead him. His keen investigative skills told him this might result in the next front-page story for the *Chicago City.* If the story was hot enough, it might be picked up by Court TV, MSNBC, and CNN. He could already imagine himself on the television screen explaining how he'd been dragged into the middle of the adventure by the frightened carjacker.

He snaked the SUV through a labyrinth of city streets. The one-way streets gave way when they left Uptown, becoming divided highways landscaped with lush green bushes and colorful flowers illuminated by discrete city lighting. As he navigated the light traffic flow, he tried to steal another peek at the woman taking him captive. The darkness shielded her features, but the passing streetlights gave him triangular flashes of her makeup. Beautiful brown eyes. Small. Fragile. Very afraid.

Two police cars with roaring sirens whizzed past them,

heading in the direction of the hotel. The flashing lights of an ambulance followed closely behind.

"What's going on at the hotel?" Adriano questioned, remembering he'd left Jake behind to check it out. "Did you have anything to do with what's going on?"

"Drive, and be quiet. Keep your eyes on the road."

He considered stopping the Land Cruiser and ending the woman's siege, but she had him at a disadvantage. Being behind him in the SUV put her just out of his reach. From the way her voice rattled and her hand shook, he didn't believe she would try to hurt him. She was frightened out of her mind. He didn't attribute her behavior to drugs—he'd seen enough strung-out victims of addiction while investigating his current story to know a druggie when he saw one.

Another police car and a fire truck sped by. Adriano thought of Jake again. If anyone could take care of himself, it was Jake. He hadn't sent a distress call. Knowing his partner, he was probably taking advantage of being the first reporter on the scene and copping two stories at once: the informant's tale, and whatever had the hotel buzzing with police and rescuers. Working on his own exclusive, Adriano would play this out with the anxious woman in the back seat.

He waited until they were outside the nucleus of tangled Uptown streets before he spoke again. "Where am I driving to?"

The woman tried, unsuccessfully, to steady her hand.

"You carjacked me for some purpose, I assume."

Her teeth chattered in response.

"Maybe I can help you."

The right side of her face moved into the light, and Adriano was able to make out more of her features: full lips, straight nose.

He tried another approach. "Do you want money? You could've asked for that without kidnapping me."

She didn't answer.

"You do know this is a marked news truck." The *Chicago City* newspaper logo was tattooed on both rear doors and the hatch. "Once my partner reports me missing, it won't take but a second for the police to track us down."

"Drive me to the airport."

"The airport?" Adriano's humor with the request tumbled past his lips in a deep laugh.

"What's funny?"

"Lady, if you plan to make a quick getaway by jumping on a plane, it won't happen tonight. The tropical storm in Florida is causing bad weather as far as Atlanta. And it's heading up the coast this way. All flights out of Charlotte have been delayed. It's supposed to be a hell of a storm."

She made a noise that resembled a desperate sob.

"Looks like you should've called ahead and checked."

The woman's grip on his neck slipped when he took a corner. All he needed to do was keep her talking, make a sharp turn, and then end this madness.

He kept talking, hoping to distract her. "Besides, the traffic in Charlotte is worse than in Chicago. How'd you think you'd outrun the police?"

No response.

He glanced in the rearview. "So you're running from the police. What did you do?" No response. "When women find out I've been kidnapped, they'll send the armed forces out to get me back."

"This isn't funny!" she shouted in his ear.

"Listen, lady—" Fed up with the flashlight bumping against his skull, Adriano turned the steering wheel hard to the right, bringing the SUV onto the side of the road. The woman flew in the opposite direction, landing with a thud against the door. He slammed on the brakes, cut the engine, and jumped into the back of the truck. Before the woman could right herself, he was wrestling her down in the backseat.

"Get off of me!" The woman fought him with all of her

strength, but once he pinned her small frame to the seat, she couldn't do anything more. He wrestled away her "gun," the flashlight rolling underneath the front passenger's seat.

"Stop it, lady. This is over."

"Let me go!"

"You tried to carjack me with a *flashlight?*"

"Get your hands off me!"

"Calm down." The frantic woman put up a good fight, but she couldn't win. Not against his brawn and lightning-quick moves. She was fiery; he'd give her that much. Not a woman who would cower in the corner and cry at the first sign of trouble. She'd have his back when he needed it. Rare to find this type of woman in his circle—most of the women he encountered wanted a hookup, doors opened into the industry.

"Calm down," he repeated. "I'm not going to hurt you."

He pinned his body against hers and waited until she exhausted herself. He worried his large frame would crush her if she didn't stop struggling. She wore a cream-colored nightgown, and he could feel every one of her dips and curves crash against his body. She twisted her hips, and his thigh slipped between her legs against the cushion of her soft thighs. Things below his waist awoke with a lazy yawn, but keen interest soon followed.

"Get off!" she shouted before collapsing.

"Have you had enough?"

She didn't answer. She breathed heavily, her breasts thrusting above the laced bodice of her gown.

Adriano lowered his face inches from hers in the semidarkness to see her features clearly. Her beauty was shockingly unexpected. Arched eyebrows over large brown eyes, flawless golden skin, and a sharp jaw line with prominent cheekbones. Her skin was silky soft, and, underneath him, her petite body cushioned his muscular frame. He fit into her grooves perfectly. She was flower petals, wicked cars, and perfumed sheets made sweaty by the twisting of lovers' bodies. Add her fiery spirit, and she was his next wet dream. Every one of his senses keyed in on her, his body's response so fierce it took him a long moment to speak.

"Well," he inhaled deeply, "it looks like I've been captured by an angel."

The woman's breathing slowed, her body lost its rigidity, and she stopped trying to wiggle away from him. He released one of her wrists, testing her reaction.

The woman whimpered. Fear distorted the beautiful features of her face.

She needed protecting.

"I'm going to let you up. No funny stuff." He cautiously lifted his body from hers.

She sat up and adjusted the crisscross straps of her gown.

Brushing his tongue over his top lip, Adriano appraised her. "You certainly don't look like any thug I've ever met. Why don't you explain to me what's going on?"

The woman's body remained still, but her eyes darted around, searching for a way out.

He pulled the door closed behind him. "Or I could turn you in to the police."

"No!"

"Finally, a reaction. Why don't you tell me why you jumped in my car and took me hostage?"

"Someone's after me."

"The police?"

"No."

Adriano studied the arching of her eyebrows as she rattled on. Completely unnerved, this woman was still gorgeous.

"I'm sorry. I don't know why I did something this stupid. If you could let me out—"

"Hold up. Who's after you?"

The woman dropped her head. "If I tell you, it'll put your life in danger."

"I live for danger."

"This isn't a game."

The Land Cruiser jerked forward with a loud crashing sound, accentuating her point. Adriano turned to see headlights advancing on them again. The woman screamed hysterically. The SUV suffered another hit. Someone was trying to push them over the embankment. Thinking quickly, he jumped over the seat and started the engine. The SUV jerked forward a third time.

"Hold on." Adriano pulled onto the dark highway. He hit the gas, and the SUV zoomed off with a screech of tires. He navigated with expertise. They bumped and bounced down the dark road. The woman hid behind his seat, yelling. He crossed terrain the other car could not handle, and he pressed the gas, propelling the SUV to dangerous speeds. The Land Cruiser gave him the power he needed to accelerate and escape the unidentified headlights following them.

Adriano's heart pumped wildly as he tried to decide if the noise he'd just heard was a car backfire or gunfire. The woman's shrill screams must have prohibited his clear interpretation, he tried to convince himself. He turned down the first abandoned, dirt-covered road he could find, losing the shooter. He wanted to jump over the seat and take the angel in his arms, comforting her until she stopped screaming, but he had to get them to safety.

He turned to the woman hiding on the floor of the backseat. "Be quiet," he ordered the woman as he shut off the engine and cut the lights. "Stop screaming. We're safe. They can't see us down this deserted back road."

The woman pressed her hands over her mouth, and her screams turned to loud whimpers.

Seconds passed before headlights crossed the path behind them.

"Who are you, angel? And who the hell is after you?"

Chapter 3

Sherman Grazicky was not the kind of man who appealed to women. He was short and ugly, and he'd quickly realized he'd never get a woman based on looks or physique, although it didn't stop him from wanting the prettiest woman wherever he went. So he concentrated on developing a charming personality. He became a woman's best friend and confidant, and when they least suspected it, they had fallen for him. He smiled over at his pretty, rich bitch of a wife, Cecily. His scheme had worked nicely on her.

A servant bent down to whisper into his ear.

"Excuse me a moment, gentlemen." He stood from his place of prominence at the head of the dinner table and kissed Cecily sweetly on her aging cheek. "Business. Please continue to enjoy your dinner."

The dinner guests acknowledged Sherman with a chorus of grunts, quickly returning to their dinner. Cecily was excellent at entertaining. He was sure she'd keep the guests occupied in his absence. She was the one who insisted on hosting these boring get-togethers. He'd much rather be down at the club, running things and being in charge. He liked his life best when he was the boss.

Sherman didn't acknowledge Hiram's bulky presence as

he passed him waiting in the foyer. He proceeded to his office with Hiram following in silence. As he walked down the long hall, his demeanor changed. The impeccably dressed, refined dinner host morphed into a ruthless businessman who didn't accept incompetence. Although physically short and stout, thanks to Cecily's money he wielded fierce power in the underworld. He strolled to the edge of his desk before he turned to the waiting man. "Your face tells me the news isn't good."

Hiram lifted his broad chest and widened his stance, ready to assume responsibility for the failure. "Payton got away."

His lips turned up into a sinister grin. "Payton got away," he mocked. He pounded his fist on the edge of the desk. "Payton got away? How did she get away when you assured me you could handle this job? And an easy job too. The woman is nothing more than a cup of tea. And the police couldn't protect my dogs."

Hiram removed his skullcap, twisting it between beefy hands. "We took the hotel, no problem. But when we checked the suite, she was nowhere in sight. It must have been a setup."

"Do you seriously believe the police have the resources for a decoy that elaborate? No. My source says she's been at the Adam's Mark for days. He was right when he fingered her as the prosecution's witness; he's right about this. She was there. The question is, where did she go?"

He bolted across the room and grabbed the taller Hiram by the collar. "And who I'm going to get to kill you."

"Mr. Grazicky"—sputum spewed from his mouth—"I can finish this job. Give me a chance to find her."

"Why? My time is running out. Why should I waste one more minute on you? You were supposed to bring Payton to me. You stormed the hotel like an amateur. It's all over the news. I tell you to be discreet, and you have a shoot-out at the Adam's Mark?"

"She was taken into custody before I could get to her,"

Hiram tried to explain. "I had to snatch her before they moved her someplace else and we lost her." The man wasn't the smartest, but he had a reputation of getting the job done Sherman knew to be true.

"People—policemen—are dead. More crimes to pin on me! The police won't let that go until someone hangs."

"Who knew the police would shoot first? These new rookies don't honor the code." Hiram cursed. "It should have been a simple snatch."

"Then you show up here—where there is a room full of witnesses to connect me to you. Exactly why should I let you live?"

"I have a lead."

Sherman's anger disappeared as quickly as it had surfaced. He released Hiram's collar and smoothed his rumpled clothing. He loved having the clout only money could buy to make big gorillas squirm. "Well, why didn't you say you had a lead?"

"My guys saw a half-dressed woman fitting Payton's description get into a *Chicago City* newspaper truck. That's why I thought it might be a setup. The police wouldn't allow Payton to give an interview if they were trying to hide her, but the news would try to get the story and find where Payton is really stashed."

"Like one of those *20/20* sting operations where a poor sucker is caught on hidden camera doing something stupid. Could the woman have been a decoy while they moved the real Payton?"

The puzzled expression on Hiram's face confirmed he'd never considered the possibility.

"I got the license-plate number of the SUV," Hiram told him.

"Good," he said absently. "Follow it up. Where would a woman with no real financial means go if she were on the run?" Sherman asked himself. "Assuming the woman you saw getting into the news truck was Payton, she has no money and no clothes and—"

"What?"

"Go to her apartment."

Hiram's dumb expression didn't fade, but he knew enough not to ask questions.

"See if she doubled back to her place for clothes, then follow up on the SUV." Sherman strolled over to the desk and perched his hip on the corner. "Let me make something very clear. I'm paying you good money to get this job done. I don't have a lot of time to play with here. Payton has to be stopped from testifying. I don't want the FBI to even get a chance to depose her. If Cecily finds out . . . if Payton talks . . . I go to jail . . . and you go to your grave."

"Don't talk," Sherman ordered the young woman in the hot tub next to him. "Be quiet and do what you do best."

He spread his arms wide across the rim of the hot tub while the woman stroked his naked, tanning-booth-browned body. Even this woman's skillful hands and hungry mouth could not distract him from his troubles. Managing an exclusive club that catered to the rich and famous had its privileges, but Cecily's money afforded him many pleasures, and the ability to have beautiful women twenty years younger than him had to be one of his favorites. Of course, if Cecily knew the VIP floor of Skye was where he "auditioned" the hostesses, she would have shut the club down and thrown him out of the house—if he was lucky. He let his head drop back and stared up through the skylight at the star-splattered sky. This suite of the club was his favorite—skylights, the scent of fresh cedar, and a private bedroom off the massage room.

He had made the same stupid mistake most men in his position make. He let himself fall for a beautiful woman. Sure, at first Payton was only eye candy. Gullible and eager to please, she had believed he was actually interested in her suggestions for running his Miami location of Skye. His interests were more focused on the reaction of his groin to her beautiful, exotic features. She kept politely rejecting him, but Sherman was certain it was only a matter of time before he had her in one of the hot tubs. Being able to buy almost any woman he wanted, the depth of his attraction to Payton even after she refused him was astonishing.

The woman in the hot tub straddled him, moaning her wanting of his body. All pretend. She was a pro. She knew what to do to get a man to take care of her. There was no simmering passion like he had seen so many times in Payton's eyes. He'd tried so hard to get her heat focused on him. If there were any way he could erase what Payton had seen that night, he would. If it meant he could have her, he'd travel back in time to correct his mistake.

Reliving the deadly scene of that night made him thrust upward in anger. The woman bounced on his lap, an Academy-Award performance well worth a minimum-wage hostess job. But the women who worked at Skye weren't there for the money. They were there to meet the rich and famous athlete who would marry them and lock them up in a fancy mansion. Or the politician who would make them respectable and erase their years as street whores. Or, his favorite, the women who wanted a chance to impress Diddy or Gordy or Face with their singing.

He pushed the bouncing hostess-wannabe off him the second he climaxed. "Get dressed and get out." He grabbed a towel and wrapped it around his waist before he stepped out of the tub.

Two mistakes had been made that night. One, believing Payton had the mental armor to be one of his mistresses. His heart had wrenched when he saw Payton standing in the doorway, speechless and crying, in shock from what she'd seen. And that had been his second mistake—letting her get away.

Chapter 4

"I'll tell you everything you want to know," Payton promised. "Later. When we're safe. We should go. Before they turn around."

Breathing heavily, the man watched her as he contemplated the situation. The eagerness in his eyes pulled at Payton's core. This was a man who devoured adrenalin and used it as an aphrodisiac. As soon as the chasing headlights had passed, he jumped into the backseat and pulled her, shivering, into his arms from her hiding place on the floor. He looked out the back window into the darkness. "I think we lost them, angel."

The endearment made her feel even more guilty about getting him involved, but she had to use every resource available to survive. Considering the circumstances, an apology would sound trite, but the truth wouldn't. "I'm really scared."

His arms tightened around her bare shoulders. This stranger had the ability to erase a measure of her panic with one reassuring look. He was the best parts of G. I. Joe and Ken in the flesh: ruggedly handsome with brazen cockiness tempered by underlying sensitivity. His long, silky hair was fastened in a ponytail that cascaded to his wide shoulders. His cheekbones ended in a V at the top of his heart-shaped lips. Stationed at the perimeter of his left eyebrow sat a fairy kiss—a black mole delineating the rugged handsomeness of his face.

"We'd better get going," he said, releasing her. He left the backseat of the SUV to get behind the wheel.

Payton climbed from the back and into the passenger seat, snapping the lap belt over her. "Where are you going?"

"I'm taking you to the nearest police station."

"I can't go to the police." She had to *get to safety,* and being with the police hadn't proved to be safe.

The man whipped the steering wheel, navigating the huge SUV with ease. The narrow dirt road gave him barely enough room to turn around, but he managed without chipping a branch. He glanced at her as he pulled to a stop at the intersection of the main road. "Where do you want to go?"

"I haven't figured out what to do next," she admitted.

Payton looked down at the tattered cream nightgown. In her haste to flee the suite, she hadn't even had the time to put on shoes. With gunshots splintering the door, it hadn't been a priority. Being safe for the moment allowed her to drop her guard and remember that Charlotte's spring temperatures still required clothing. Goose bumps stood at attention on her arms. She crossed one foot over the other for warmth and flinched at the damage done by the rock chips on the ledge.

"I need clothes." There was a sure thought. She could hang on to it until her mind stopped buzzing. Think in concrete terms: get clothes, find a place to hide, contact the authorities. "Can you drop me at my place? I'll decide what to do from there."

"Do you think it's safe to go home?"

Where *could* she go and have no fear of being harmed? She'd never imagined being in a situation like this. She had no idea how to handle it.

"Why don't you tell me why those men are chasing you, and I'll help you figure this thing out."

Her thought processes were as scattered as when the

female detective had woken her earlier, bullets flying. She had no money. She didn't have anyone in Charlotte to turn to. After the night's events, she didn't feel the police could adequately protect her. A sob choked her. She swallowed it and asked, "What's your name?"

"Adriano Norwood."

"I'm sorry about all of this. I really am, but I have to get . . . away from here. Take me home, and it'll be over for you."

Adriano's dark expression softened a bit. "What's your name?"

"Payton Vaughn."

Adriano's eyes widened with curiosity. "Payton Vaughn? I've heard your name before somewhere. Who are you?"

"I've told you my name. It's enough." The police had been diligent about keeping her identity out of the news, but Sherman's men had somehow discovered who she was.

He arched his fairy-kissed brow. "Who's chasing you?"

"Enough questions." She shivered when a cold wave passed over her. The less he knew, the better for him.

Mistaking her reaction for a response to the temperature, he reached over and cranked on the heat. "You need clothes, but going to your place isn't safe."

"Where do you live? How far is it?" He would have old clothes she could wear. A man this good-looking had a wife or girlfriend. If no significant other, he had to have a sister. Worse come to worst, she could borrow a pair of his sweats. She would change and be on her way. By the time he alerted the police, she'd be across the state line into South Carolina.

"Where do I live? Do you think I'm going to invite you over?" Adriano's voice dropped an octave. "Although, pretty lady, I might be persuaded to consider—"

"You sure are full of yourself. How far from here do you live?"

"About eight hundred miles."

"*What?*"

"Chicago."

"Chicago?" Payton's voice rang with alarm.

"What's wrong with Chicago?"

"The SUV has local plates."

"*Chicago City* has offices in every city. It's not unusual to borrow a truck when I'm on assignment."

"What assignment?"

"I'm not answering any more questions until you explain yourself. I want to know why you jumped into my Land Cruiser, tried to make me think a flashlight was a gun, and used me as a getaway car. Explain, Payton."

He would be the type to play hero and try wrestling her down in the seat again.

The cell phone tucked in the center console rang. He reached for it.

"Let it ring."

"No." He grabbed the phone and flipped it open. "Adriano."

She snatched the phone away from his ear and tossed it in the backseat.

"What's your problem? My partner is still at the hotel. You saw the ambulance and police cars. He might be in trouble."

A lump thickened in her throat at the memory of the slain officers. "Your partner's safe. The ambulances weren't for him." Remembering her circumstances, she tried to sound tough. "He'll call a taxi when he can't find you."

"You know who the ambulances were for?" He had nosy reporter written all over him. He detected a story and would do whatever he had to in order to get it. His nature might work in her favor; it might not.

"Listen, angel, playing this game with you has been— interesting—but I need to get back to *my* hotel tonight, so I can pack my bags. I have an early flight to Chicago. You don't want to tell me what's going on, fine. Tell me where to drop you. I have things to do."

His flippant attitude angered her. "Don't you understand how serious this is?"

"No, I don't. You haven't told me what's going on."

Payton watched him, trying to get a read on his trustworthiness. It was impossible. Even under duress, his eyes looked as if they danced with laughter. His tone roared with arrogance. He wanted to be in control. She wished she could relinquish it to him, relying on his strength to pull her through. The hardest part of everything she had suffered was going through it alone.

Adriano licked his lips and grinned devilishly, knowing he had gained the upper hand. "I'm waiting, Payton Vaughn."

She'd never forgive herself for what had happened to those police officers at the hotel. She couldn't endanger him. "Take me home."

She could see the wheels in his head churning, dangerously spinning ideas, but he only asked, "Where do you live?"

Adriano drove past Payton's apartment building three times. "This is a terrible idea, angel."

She *had* no ideas. What did a person do when bad men were trying to kill her and the police had failed in their attempt to protect her? She needed to settle her racing thoughts and come up with a viable plan. She needed to feel safe for just a moment to weigh her options and figure this whole thing out.

"I was hard on you before, but I mean it. This isn't a smart move." Adriano kept talking, taking the SUV for another tour around the block while he tried to convince her not to go home. "Do you have any family or friends you can go to?"

No way was she dragging her brother and his family or her elderly parents into this. She'd managed to keep them at a safe distance so far; she wouldn't chance them being used as leverage. "I appreciate your concern, but I need to change. I need money. I need time to think."

He continued to sweep the block, looking side-to-side as he drove, checking for anything suspicious.

"I'm going to go in and change, pack a few things, and then I'm leaving," she told him. "If I get this done I can be out in ten minutes. It'll take longer than that for those thugs to track down my address."

"You don't think they know where you live?" He snapped into reporter mode again. "How did you get mixed up with such dangerous people?"

"Please. Let me out."

He rolled to a slow stop in front of her building. "I don't like this."

She turned to apologize and thank him for all he'd done when he hopped out of the Land Cruiser and joined her on the sidewalk. "I'll make sure you get inside okay," he told her.

Everything had happened so quickly she'd never had a chance to unpack after her trip to Miami. She'd spent three days at the new Skye club in Miami, gathering ideas for the best way to operate the business. She was so excited by the trip she'd headed right over to Sherman's office from the airport after her return. She knew he'd be there, no matter how late. She had no idea what he would be doing when she arrived.

Becoming an unwilling witness, she'd gone straight to the police station. After hours of questioning, she was released. Shaken and exhausted, she collapsed into a fitful sleep until the next morning. Local news reports were covering the story by noon. The Skye club in Charlotte was closed down while the police searched for forensic evidence. Sherman was called in for questioning the next day. Twenty-four hours later he was posing for the cameras, smiling while he commended the police on their attempts to dole out swift justice. At dawn the next morning, Payton was being stuffed into the back of an unmarked police car "for her own protection."

Her apartment was as she'd left it: giant duffel bag consuming the entryway, correspondence lying on the floor under the mail slot, living room needing a good dusting, no lights left on to welcome her home.

She turned to Adriano. "Thank you."

"You realize you can't stay here."

She nodded. *Where would she go?*

He watched her, dark eyes blazing with unused energy. It pulsated off his hard chest, barely constrained by the black *Chicago City* newspaper T-shirt. He didn't want to go. And she didn't want to be alone.

"You promised to tell me who these guys are who are chasing you," he said.

The way she calculated it, she had twenty minutes tops to get changed and get out of her apartment. If the hit men were headed this way, it would take them no longer than that to find her address and weave their way through the maze of one-way streets leading to her apartment complex. She didn't have time to share her story. Nor did she want to.

"I can listen while you change," Adriano prompted. "Reporters have unlimited resources. You'd be surprised who I might know that could help you out of this jam."

A bump came from down the darkened hallway.

"Cat? Dog?" Adriano whispered, dragging her behind him. "Roommate?"

"No."

He stepped backward, pushing her toward the front door.

"Hold it right there."

Adriano's hands went up.

"You one of Sherman's men?" The body attached to the voice emerged from the shadows. Payton peered around Adriano's broad chest and saw the barrel of a gun.

"Sherman?" Adriano questioned.

"Who are you?"

"Adriano Norwood, *Chicago City* newspaper."

"What are you doing here?"

"Working the story," Adriano answered, but his voice was

strained, not the smooth cadence she'd heard before. "Are you police?"

"FBI," the man answered.

FBI. They'd stationed an officer at her apartment in case she showed up. She exhaled a long-held breath, releasing her tension with it. The FBI was expert at hiding witnesses and keeping them safe. Look at all the mobsters they'd protected over the years, offering them a new life in exchange for their testimony.

"Show me your credentials," Adriano said, "and I'll show you mine."

"Like I need to see 'em with you busting out of that T-shirt."

"Still, I'd like to see yours," Adriano pressed.

Payton interrupted the battle of wills. "Would you stop being macho? Officer, I'm Payton Vaughn."

She stepped out from behind Adriano's protective chest, but he grabbed her upper arm and yanked her back. She stumbled, smashing into his chest.

"Agent, isn't it?" Adriano asked the man.

"Honest mistake," the FBI man said with a kindly smile directed at Payton. "You're the one I've been waiting for."

Payton disentangled herself from Adriano. "If you could give me a minute to change, I'll be ready to go with you."

"No need to change," the agent said.

"What do you mean?"

"Why were you hiding in the bedroom?" Adriano asked, moving his body to partially block hers.

"Surveillance," the man answered without hesitation.

"In the dark? Alone? Where's your partner? There was no unmarked car out front."

"We wouldn't be very good at our jobs if you spotted the car, would we?" The edges of the man's smile curled downward a fraction.

Payton looked up at Adriano and realized he'd known from

the beginning what she was just now seeing. This man was not there to take her into protective custody. "Sherman sent you."

"Beautiful and smart!" the man exclaimed. "Now get over here."

"You're going to kill me."

"Sherman wants to see you. He needs to talk. That's all."

Adriano spoke to her, keeping his eyes on the man with the gun. "Please tell me Sherman is a jealous ex-boyfriend who doesn't understand what it means to end a relationship."

"Muscle-bound and dumb," the man answered. "Get over here, Payton."

If she went with the corrupt FBI man, she'd be killed—or worse—when Sherman got his hands on her. Refusing meant placing Adriano in danger. Either way, more innocents were going to be dragged into the middle of this mess. She wouldn't jeopardize Adriano, but she wouldn't go without a fight. "Let Adriano go."

"What?" Adriano and the FBI man asked simultaneously.

"You let a woman fight for you, Superman?" The FBI man laughed, directing the gun to the newspaper logo stretched across Adriano's chest.

"What are you doing?" Adriano asked her.

"My problem. My fight. Leave while you can."

"He's not going anywhere."

Adriano ignored the man and spoke to her. "Heroism is an admirable quality, but stupidity isn't."

"You're calling me stupid?" Indignation rang loudly in her voice.

"If you plan on giving yourself up, yes." He dropped his hands and turned to her, engaging her in a full-blown argument. "What makes you think I'd leave you here with this nut anyway?"

"Hey!" the FBI agent shouted.

Payton ignored the man and answered Adriano. "Thanks for the ride, but this doesn't involve you."

"It involved me the second you carjacked me."

"Melodramatic! You were never in any danger from me, and you knew it. If you hadn't been so distracted by staring at my breasts, you could have gotten me here before this man even showed up."

"Now this is my fault?"

"Shut up! Shut up! Shut up!" the crooked FBI agent shouted. "What's with you two? *I've* got the gun."

Payton and Adriano lifted their hands in perfect synchronicity.

"If you've been stuck with her mouth for more than ten minutes, it seems you'd be happy to have me shoot her."

"Listen—" Payton started.

"No. You listen. It's time to go."

"Where are we going?" Payton asked, stalling for time, hoping an idea would come to her. *Keep him talking.* She could feel Adriano's body coil as he hunted for a solution.

"You're going to see Sherman. I already told you."

"What are you going to do with Adriano?"

"It doesn't matter. Last time. *Get over here.*"

"No."

"No?" the FBI agent repeated. "I have a gun!"

"I won't go until you tell me what you're going to do with Adriano. I'm responsible for getting him mixed up in this mess. He has no idea what's going on. I can't let him get hurt because of me."

"And what do you suggest I do with Superman here?" the man asked sarcastically.

"You could tie him up so he can't follow us."

"I could, but it would take too long." He tapped his temple with the butt of the gun. "How about I just shoot him?"

When the FBI agent aimed the gun at Adriano, Payton saw the bloody policemen, dead at the Adam's Mark Hotel. She heard the frantic pleas of the female detective who had sacrificed her life for the safety of the witness. Propelled by the emotions this evoked, Payton charged the corrupt agent, kinetic energy building with every step until she gathered enough momentum to crash into the surprised agent. He staggered backward, losing the gun when he tried to break his fall. They landed hard on the floor, with Payton's full weight landing on his chest. She didn't weigh enough to break anything, but it did knock the wind out of him long enough for Adriano to jump into action.

Adriano crossed the room, shoved her aside and smashed the man in the face with her giant duffel bag. Two sickening thuds later, the man lay unconscious.

Her first trip to Miami hadn't only been about business. The bag was stuffed with souvenirs, including a stone replica of the Miami Beach coastal skyline.

Chapter 5

Adriano drove down Providence Road and made a right turn onto Tyvola. He fired questions at Payton, trying to slowly gather pieces of the mystery she refused to tell him. Minutes later, when he reached I-77, she had lapsed into complete silence.

"The less you know, the safer you'll be," she told him.

He studied her as she rested against the glass of her window, watching the scenery pass in the darkness. When he caught her eye, he saw a startling fear that made him want to take her in his arms. He stopped pushing for information. He was an investigative reporter, and one of the reasons he was successful was because he knew when to apply pressure and when to back off. As strong as Payton tried to appear, she was frightened. She had admitted it earlier, although he'd probably never get her to confess to it again.

"Head south," she said when the interstate signs appeared.

He worried about the force of storms coming from the south, but he complied without protest. When the weather changed, they needed to be inside.

"Take the first exit you see with hotels."

He cranked up the heat when he noticed Payton's body shiver. After knocking the FBI agent unconscious—possibly committing several felonies—they had fled her apartment without stopping for her to dress.

He drove by Carowinds Amusement Park before passing the sign marking their entrance into South Carolina. With the Confederate flag flying at the state capital, South Carolina was no place for a black man to be with a woman dressed in a ripped nightgown. He veered to the right and exited the freeway. Not far down the road he found a closed used-car lot. The tires of the Land Cruiser spat gravel as it came to a stop.

"Talk," he demanded.

She turned away, staring out the window into the darkness.

"That man was going to kill me back there. Tell me what's going on."

She tried the door handle, but it was locked. "Let me out."

He gawked at her. "You want to get out in the middle of nowhere? Clearly, the stress of today has been too much on you."

"The sign said there's a hotel just down the road."

"You'd rather walk down a dark, deserted road dressed in your nightgown than answer my questions?"

He couldn't figure this woman out. The women he knew would have been draped all over him, begging him to help and crying for him to save them. Payton Vaughn was so stubborn, she didn't even want to explain what this night had been all about.

What had her so afraid?

What could be scarier than what he'd already experienced tonight?

"The door," she said, refusing to look at him. "Please."

He handed her the bills from his wallet. "It's all I have." Two hundred dollars wouldn't get her very far. He never traveled with cash. *Chicago City* paid all his expenses.

Payton looked out into the darkness. Apprehension covered her face. "I wish I could tell you how sorry I am about all of this."

"You don't have to do this alone. Talk to me, angel. I'll help you in every way I can, but you have to tell me what I'm getting into."

She shook her head adamantly. "I can't." She was involved in something serious, and he couldn't jump into the middle of it when he didn't know what was going on.

"I was almost shot tonight—twice. I won't go into this blindly."

She found the correct button to release the locks. Her fingers wrapped around the door handle. Her knuckles were white. "I understand."

Adriano nodded, curious about whether she would actually step out into the deserted road. He had never questioned fear providing the motivation for her desperate getaway. She wasn't a vicious street thug out to "jack" him for the SUV. While she played the tough role, her voice trembled with fear.

She took in a huge breath that made her cleavage heave before pulling on the door handle. He watched as she started to jog away from the SUV. The gravel underneath her bare feet slowed her down to a hop-run-hop. Soon the darkness swallowed her, leaving only the outline of her cream nightgown to be seen moving down the road.

Jake would never believe this. Adriano didn't believe it himself. A gorgeous woman jumps into the SUV and takes him hostage, they're attacked by a crooked FBI agent, and then the woman demands to be let out on the side of a deserted road in backwoods South Carolina.

A woman without any money or clothes.

A woman so desperate to save herself she takes a man two times her size hostage with a flashlight.

She probably didn't even have any idea where she would go after tonight.

He stared after Payton. His headlights illuminated the cream-colored gown in the pitch-black darkness.

Police cars, ambulances, and fire trucks, racing to the Adam's Mark Hotel.

Hit men trying to run them off the road with gunfire.

A crazy FBI agent threatening to take her at gunpoint to see "Sherman."

Adriano knew of only one notable "Sherman," and there was no way in hell an angel like Payton would be mixed up with him.

He could no longer see the flashes of cream. As beautiful as she was—big brown eyes, pink puckered lips—a man would come along and help her out of her jam.

Or take advantage of a stranded woman wandering down the side of the road. He remembered the way she tackled the crooked FBI agent. She wasn't completely helpless. She could take care of herself. Or could she? He could have ended her siege within minutes if he had chosen to. Another man might not be as kind as he had been.

He pulled the SUV out onto the road. *Just call the police and let them handle it. Walk away,* he told himself. His gut said, *The lady is trouble.* The kind of trouble many men have died because of.

Sherman couldn't be the *Sherman* he knew; her Sherman must be an angry old flame. He could understand an ex-someone not wanting to let her pack and walk away. Payton Vaughn was prime real estate. Even as he tried to convince himself, he knew no ordinary ex-boyfriend would have the means to corrupt an FBI agent. *Payton Vaughn . . .* where did he know the name from?

The remembered sensation of her near-nude body trapped underneath his in a carnal struggle of wills when he wrestled her to the seat made him press down on the accelerator. He could picture night after night of wrestling her into submission. Hellcat that she was, she would be even more rambunctious with his unrestrained penetration. In the light of day, her beauty would make him the envy of every man who laid eyes on her pretty face and gorgeous body.

Temptation made him glance in the rearview mirror. The angelic creature in the cream nightgown had vanished. The surreal night was over for him. Why did he feel suddenly alone? He'd met Payton only a few hours ago, yet he felt the void of her not being there.

Back to the hotel. On the plane in the morning. Life back to normal. He recited the mantra over and over, believing it a little less each time. Somehow he knew his life would never be the same after meeting Payton.

Keep driving, he told himself as the SUV crept toward the highway.

He was back at the interstate sign when a clap of thunder announced the arrival of tiny raindrops.

Payton began to cry when the first streak of lightning illuminated the sky. A fine mist of rain coated her as she hurried down the dark road, praying to find the motel advertised on the interstate directional sign. Thank goodness she had held it together in front of Adriano. She hated women who cried.

Thunder rumbled, and another streak of lightning followed. Suddenly, the fine mist of rain changed into a downpour. After a few minutes, her bare feet were splashing in mud puddles.

What am I going to do?

Headlights slashed through the sheets of falling rain.

Startled, Payton ducked down behind the gray guardrail.

Adriano's Land Cruiser pulled up to her hiding place. "Get in."

Relieved he had not left her stranded, but knowing getting back into the SUV would pull him into the middle of her troubles, she hesitated. "I can't."

"Why not?" he shouted over the rumblings of thunder.

"I can't put you in any more danger."

"I'll take care of myself. You can't walk down a deserted road half-dressed in this storm. If the wrong person comes along, you'll have more on your hands than you can handle."

She glanced down at her soaking-wet nightgown. She began to shiver again. Her feet were battered from jogging across rocks and slivers of glass. The downpour caused her hair to mat against her face. She looked as bad as she felt.

"I'll take you to a hotel," he offered.

She considered her options. Stay hidden behind the guardrail until the storm passed. Walk along the road until she found the motel. Hitchhike a ride to . . . where?

"Hurry up," Adriano prodded, his voice less harsh. "You're soaking wet." He threw the door open.

She climbed over the guardrail, telling herself she'd accept the ride but have him drop her off at the motel and never see him again. She climbed up into the Land Cruiser, and Adriano sped off.

"Thank you," she said. She felt embarrassed, scared, and stupid. She had taken this innocent man hostage with a flashlight and almost gotten him shot, but he had still returned to help her. Any other stranger would have scuffled with her before tossing her out into the street and having her arrested.

"I'm sorry for what I did earlier."

"You said that," he replied stiffly.

"You didn't have to come back . . ." She wanted to ask why he had done such a rash thing but decided not to push her luck.

"I know."

A long moment passed in which she hoped he would forgive her. The last thing she wanted was for anyone else to be hurt because of her.

"Are you hungry?" Adriano hiked his thumb toward the backseat.

"You stopped for food before you came back for me?"

Should she be insulted that he left her in the rain to stop for food?

He grinned, obliterating any annoyance she might have. "I hope you like burgers and fries."

She recalled the half-eaten steak dinner next to her bed at the Adam's Mark Hotel . . . the desperation on the female detective's face . . . the dead policemen . . . She fell back against the seat in a knot of tension. "What am I going to do?"

Adriano raised his fairy-kissed brow.

"What?"

"Aren't you hungry?" He returned his concentration to the road.

"After what I've seen . . ."

He pounced. "What did you see?"

She turned to the window.

Adriano persisted. "You have to keep up your strength. From what I've witnessed tonight, you're going to need it."

He didn't know the half of it. She shivered, an involuntary response to the cold, wet nightgown sticking to her skin.

"You're drenched. You must be freezing." He reached out to adjust the heat setting. "Can you hand me a burger and fries?"

She climbed to her knees and rummaged around in the backseat. "Here you go."

She caught him eyeing the curves of her behind. The sheer fabric of the wet nightgown left nothing to the imagination. She was cold, and her nipples were puckered and dark against the silky material. She plopped down in the seat, smoothing the gown over her thighs and using her hands to cover as much of herself as possible.

Even being in mortal danger didn't shield her from his attractive pull. He demanded her hormones focus all their attention on him. It wasn't only his looks, which were near movie-star perfect. His fearlessly confident, masculine but protective demeanor was the ultimate turn-on for a woman who was tired of hearing the female we-don't-need-a-man-in-our-lives battle cry. He could be leaned on, would demand to be counted on, and he'd fulfill every promise he made. In all her interactions with the big stars frequenting Skye, Adriano Norwood was the first real man she had ever encountered.

Adriano took a large bite out of his hamburger. "Ketchup, please."

She leaned over the seat again.

"Man, oh man."

She snapped around. "What?"

"Nothing."

Had she forgotten to add arrogant, relentless, and exasperating to her descriptive list of his qualities?

She added ketchup to his fries and held them within his reach.

"How about mustard for my burger?" The corner of his mouth lifted in a grin.

"Forget it. No more peep shows."

Adriano ate in silence until he came upon the motel advertised on the highway sign. He pulled his shirt up to cover his head against the rain and ran inside. If a ripped chest, tight abs, and a tantalizing navel could wipe away her troubles, she'd be in heaven. No man had ever affected her this way. She lived in the world of the beautiful people. Movie stars, television personalities, models, and professional athletes made up her social circle. Working with those people tarnished "beauty," and its novelty had eventually worn off. At Skye she could walk right past the hottest adult film star without sparing him a glance. Adriano was impossible to ignore.

It's a hormone thing, she told herself. *Fight-or-flight response gone wild.*

Within minutes, Adriano jogged back to the SUV. "They're full, but the desk clerk says there are a bunch of hotels in the next town."

Payton nodded, uneasiness playing on the arch of her brow. Several hotels later, Adriano announced, "Every hotel in this little town is booked. Travelers driving down to Florida for vacation, and the storm . . . The maid said there's a motel a few miles ahead."

They drove along the back roads of South Carolina with Adriano grilling her for information about what had happened tonight. When she became visibly upset, he backed off. He offered her time to compose herself but was clear answers were expected.

After several miles, they arrived at a one-pump gas station and motel. A sign in the window read ROOMS. Adriano banged on the office door until an old man dressed in white long johns appeared.

Payton waited anxiously in the SUV. She didn't worry about Adriano abandoning her; he'd had his chance to drive away and call the police but hadn't taken it. Somehow her whereabouts had been discovered when only law officials knew where she was being kept. Now she worried about the car with blackened windows finding them again, pulling up behind the SUV and shooting.

Adriano soon reappeared. The sleek lines of his rain-soaked body—twice her size—made Payton question her sanity in recruiting a stranger for help. She'd blindly trusted the *Chicago City*'s reputation when she really didn't know anything about Adriano. He could have pummeled her and tossed her on the side of the road. She wouldn't have been able to fight him off. If she needed clarification about her level of desperation, she'd found it.

She watched as he ran toward the SUV. In another place their meeting could have been more pleasant. Before this happened she had been focused on developing her career, but Adriano would have been a welcome distraction.

He rubbed his hands together in front of the heating vent, and all the sinewy muscles of his arms flexed. "He wants an arm and a leg for the one room he has left. I don't think we have much choice." He looked to her for confirmation.

"I guess not," she mumbled, wanting to be at home in her own bed.

"I'll need the money back."

She turned to the window as she dug into her gown to retrieve it from underneath her breast. Adriano watched, the fairy kiss lifting with sinful interest in her chosen method of securing the cash. She handed him the money. He rubbed his thumb across the bills, his eyes glued to where she had hidden them.

"He's waiting." She nodded toward the impatient-looking man.

In a flash, Adriano handed the man one of the bills and was back inside the car. He whipped the SUV around the building. "The manager says there are no twenty-four-hour stores around here. You'll have to wait until morning to get decent clothes."

She swept her fingers through her wild, wet mane. She crossed her arms over her breasts. Her modesty had quickly disappeared when she stepped out onto the ledge of the Adam's Mark Hotel, but in the confining space of the SUV, it returned with a vengeance.

Adriano read the hand-painted numbers on the motel doors. Only a pick-up truck occupied the parking lot of the one-story, white-brick building. "Here we are. Room 104." He pulled up to the door and cut the engine. "Definitely not the Adam's Mark."

Tiny pieces of hail mixed with the rain pattering across the windshield. "Let me go in first. I'll bring a blanket back." He returned with a black wool blanket and held it open for her. She stepped down into his arms. He wrapped her up tightly, holding her close as they ran for the motel. She liked the feel of his arms: strong and sure. Once inside, he released his hold. She turned and thanked him, stepping away with the blanket but suddenly feeling adrift.

No more than functional, the room would be her shelter from the storm brewing outside. The lingering odor of stale cigarettes filled the tiny room. A double bed, a nightstand with lamp, and a television completed the space. A continuous leak from the faucet had made a wide rust stain in the bathtub. Neatly stacked on the back of the toilet were two sets of towels that looked as rough as sandpaper.

"Definitely not the Adam's Mark," Payton said. "But I'm so tired, I don't care."

They shared a moment of uncertainty. Payton broke the concentrated eye contact by moving to the window. She pushed the dusty curtain aside and peered out into the storm.

Men were after her who would kill her without a second thought. The authorities had to be upset they'd lost their prime witness. Innocent police officers had died tonight in the line of duty, and they wouldn't be happy to learn she'd run to South Carolina.

It was emotionally devastating to try to understand it all. The situation felt surreal, as if she were watching it from outside her body. She couldn't make it through the night alone.

"What happens now?" she asked.

"One option would be to go back to Charlotte and catch my flight to Chicago in the morning. Another would be calling the police and reporting what happened at your place. Or you can tell me what the hell is going on." He moved closer. "Guess which one I'm choosing?"

"The storm is getting worse."

"I know you're scared, but you'll feel better when you tell me what's going on."

She moved to the bed, and he sat next to her, the mattress dipping and tilting her in his direction. "There's only one bed," she pointed out, although she hadn't agreed outright to tell him anything.

"I'll sleep in the chair. Believe me, I've slept in worse places."

She turned, watching him.

"Your feet okay?"

"I'll be fine." She had escaped gunfire and a bad FBI agent. Jagged rocks and chipped glass wouldn't take her down.

Adriano's voice softened with compassion. "Let me look. Slide back on the bed."

She sat with her back against the headboard watching Adriano while he examined the damage to her feet. The curious tone of his skin gave her no clue to his heritage. True, he stood tall, dark, and handsome, but there were undertones in his complexion she couldn't distinguish. His eyes danced while the corner of his mouth hardened in concentration. "You have glass in your feet."

Did the glass come from the ledge, or the side of the road? She didn't know. She hadn't noticed the tenderness of her feet until Adriano placed them across the hard muscles of his thighs and began plucking at the glass. He went into the tiny bathroom and returned with a towel and warm washcloth. He worked intently on removing the glass in silence until he finally asked, "Tell me what this is all about."

"My ex," she began the lie—a necessity to keep him safe. The reporter in him would want every detail, but knowing too much could get him a target painted in the center of his chest. "We had a fight. I ended it. He didn't take it well."

Adriano nodded, his concentration centered on removing a sliver of glass. He squeezed and manipulated her heel until the shard came free. "You broke it off, and he wouldn't accept your decision. His reaction is a bit drastic, don't you think? Ex-husband, or ex-boyfriend?"

"Boyfriend."

"What's his name?"

An easy-to-remember name slipped past her too-relaxed lips. "Tommy."

Adriano moved to the other foot, alternating the warm cloth with the massage of his fingers. "Tommy is crazy in love with you."

Crazy, yes. There was truth in that.

Payton's eyes fluttered. She was exhausted. Adriano made her feel comfortable with his gentle ministrations and softened tone. "Why are you helping me?"

"I have a Land Cruiser with thousands of dollars' worth of repair work needed on it parked outside. Not to mention almost being run off the road, someone shooting at me, and involving myself in an assault against a FBI agent."

He tempered the sarcastic answer with quiet empathy. "I couldn't leave you on the side of the road, not knowing if you were safe. I'll get you to the police in the morning."

"You've done more than enough. I can find my own way."

"And leave me to explain all the damage to the SUV to my editor? The police can meet you at the Adam's Mark and help you get your things. Then you can give them information about your ex so he can take care of the damage to the SUV."

"I'll call the police first thing in the morning." Another lie. She'd be gone by the time he woke up. She would take the keys to the SUV, whatever money was left after paying the hotel bill, and drive and drive.

Adriano pressed the warm cloth against her feet. "I wish we had some gauze and a bandage. It doesn't look too bad, but you still need to keep it clean or it'll get infected." He removed the cloth and kneaded the flesh of her sole. Her bone-tired body quickly succumbed to his rhythm. Her body felt heavy, wet, and cold. She slumped into the stack of pillows.

Adriano glanced up with his dancing eyes. "Your boyfriend must be dangerous. Ramming into the back of us like that. Shooting at you. Getting a buddy at the FBI to kidnap you."

He was fishing for information. Payton conceded she owed him an explanation. He was placing his life in jeopardy to help a complete stranger. But giving him the truth would only put him in more danger. She opted to continue the lie. "That about sums Bobby up."

"Who's Bobby?"

She stiffened. What name had she used?

Adriano's eyes burned into her. "You said your boyfriend's name was Tommy."

"It isn't. It's Bobby. I didn't want to tell you his real name."

"Why not?" He was coming in for the kill, using a tone as soft as silk. "You told me your name—first and last. I could track him down with that information alone. Everything you've said, running away without any clothes, the fear in your eyes . . . This is about more than an angry boyfriend. Why were you at the Adam's Mark Hotel?"

Payton wanted to trust him so badly. She needed help to get out of this situation alive. She was alone and cold and afraid—very afraid. She could tell Adriano the truth. He'd been a big help to her. He had proven he wouldn't abandon her. If the truth was too heavy for him, the worst that could happen would be him running away. The best: he'd help her find a solution to her problem.

"Why were the police and ambulances at the hotel?"

The image of dead bodies assaulted her. The sound of gunfire echoed in her ears.

He placed her feet on the bed. A sign he was about to leave.

"Payton, I'll help you if you're in trouble, but only if you tell me the truth. I've been patient—more than patient, considering everything—but it's time now to tell me everything."

They watched each other for a long moment as Payton wrestled with what to do.

His cell phone jingled. When he left the bed, the mattress shifted, tossing her into reality.

When had he gotten it from the backseat?

His partner had been at the Adam's Mark.

She wouldn't be able to keep the truth from him . . . and when he found out she had lied—he would leave her . . . alone . . . abandoned . . . afraid.

"Adriano." Her voice quivered.

He pressed the phone to his ear and moved across the room. He asked the caller, "What's happening at the hotel?"

He glanced in her direction, and Payton knew she had no more time.

"I'll tell you everything." She scrambled off the bed and ran to him. "Please hang up the phone, and let me tell my side of it."

He stared into her eyes as the male voice on the other end of the phone rambled on. She grabbed the ends of his shirt and clung to him. "Please, Adriano." She buried her face against the muscles of his chest. "Hear me out."

"Are you still there, A?" the man called.

She burrowed deeper into the definition of his chest, holding on for life. His free arm came up to her waist. His muscles loosened, making her sink deeper into his body. His chest felt like silk cloth covering rock. He cradled her into false comfort. Her eyes fluttered for a brief moment before the voice on the cell phone reminded her of her mission.

"Jake, I'll call you back." Adriano disconnected, setting her away from him. He loomed over her, waiting, his patience gone. "Start talking, angel."

Chapter 6

Silk gliding over smooth cotton. Payton's soft curves pressed against his hard body. The give of the mattress when he suspended his body weight above her on his elbows. Pumping deep. "*Adriano,* please." Pumping. The headboard slamming against the wall with every thrust of his pelvis. "*Adriano,* please." Pulling away until the moisture drowning the mushroom tip of his penis dried from the sudden assault of the cool air swirling around them. Inhaling deep the fragrance: the mixed musk of their bodies with the sweet floral fragrance of roses. To the foot of the bed, his knees sinking into the carpet. The rough pads of his fingers grasping her ankles, pulling her silk-covered body across the smooth cotton of the sheets. Eyes closed, tasting. Tasting the surface and beyond. "Adriano, *please.*" Different now, begging for more. "Adriano, *please.*"

Adriano envisioned it all as he stood over Payton while she sat on the bed, gazing up at him, pleading for a chance to tell her side of the story before he made any judgments.

"How much did your partner tell you?" she asked.

"Jake. All he knew."

Payton stared up at him for a long moment. She was deciding what to tell him. Crocodile tears filled the corners of her eyes, but she fought to hold them back. She turned her head and took two quick swipes at her face before looking at him again.

"Don't start with the Bobby-Tom stuff. Tell me the truth." He dropped his arms, lost the angry stance, and released the tension in his voice. "If I wanted to hurt you, I could have when you first jumped in the SUV."

Payton didn't answer.

"If I didn't want to help you, I could've left you on the side of the road."

She parted her lips in contemplation, the words on the tip of her tongue.

"Start by telling me why you don't want me to know what's going on," he gently prodded.

"I don't want you to get hurt."

The truth. Finally.

"I can take care of myself . . . and you too."

He watched her wet her lips with her tongue, immediately drawn back into his fantasy. He had left off with him on his knees at the foot of the bed. The parting of her lips prodded him to swiftly switch their positions. Payton on her knees, her hands delicately cupping him. Her head dipping low, lips parted.

"Do you know Sherman Grazicky?"

The words shattered his fantasy with the force of a rock hurled through a window. All hope that *the* Sherman he was investigating and *this* Sherman, who sent a crooked FBI agent to accost her, weren't the same person was gone.

"I know *of* the sonofabitch."

"He's my boss. I manage his Charlotte nightclub, Skye." Payton stared down at her bare feet.

"What does Sherman Grazicky have to do with what's going on?"

Jake had told Adriano what he knew, but not enough. Police officers were dead. Hotel guests reported hearing gunshots. One man described it as a Wild West gunfight. The informant was too scared to talk. He slipped out of the hotel in the mounting confusion. But before the man slipped away, he told Jake the same thing he'd told the police. There had been a murder, and Grazicky had placed a hit on the key witness against him—a beautiful woman.

"What does Grazicky have to do with all of this?" he asked again.

"I've *seen* things the FBI need me to testify to in order to prosecute him." She wrapped her arms around herself.

His investigative curiosity kicked in. "What things?"

She hesitated, her eyes dropping to the floor. He sat next to her and took her hands in his, encouraging her.

"It all started when I flew to Miami."

"Why'd you go there?"

"Sherman's opening another Skye club. It's under construction, but almost complete. I've been managing the club here, but the Miami location would be a huge promotion. It's in a multimillion-dollar district. Since Sherman lives here, I'd be solely in charge. He sent me there on a scouting mission. Everything went well. I wrote an entire proposal. I was so excited, I thought I'd drop by the club when I returned to Charlotte to tell him how it went and schedule a meeting to present my ideas."

"Go on," he said when she became quiet.

"I knew Sherman would be at the club. He's always at the club. When I got there, one of the security people directed me to the private suites. I should have been suspicious right then. No one enters the private suites without an invitation."

"Why not?"

"It's our little Las Vegas: what goes on in the private suites stays in the private suites. People pay thousands of dollars and wait weeks for access. Once the room is booked, the patron is given a key and a cell phone and no one goes in without an invitation."

"Not even you?"

"Not even me, and I'm the manager. Sherman runs the operation of the suites. Everything is top secret—who comes, who visits, who pays what, when they'll be there—only Sherman knows."

"You never found this suspicious?"

"Honestly, no. The rich and famous can be paranoid. The strict privacy is one reason the club is so popular. More than being suspicious, I was annoyed. I'm the manager, and parts of the club are off-limits to me. It's one of the reasons I wanted to manage the Miami club—Sherman wouldn't be there to limit me."

"But this night the security guard told you to go up to the suite. It had to raise flags."

"Looking back now, yes. Then, no. I was so excited about telling him my ideas. Besides, Skye was closed, so the suites were empty. I figured it was another attempt to impress me."

"By the security guard?"

"Sherman," she answered. "He comes on to me."

Adriano could imagine it, and he didn't like the idea of someone with Grazicky's history trying to blemish Payton. "You went to the suite and what happened?"

"I followed voices to Sherman. When I walked in . . ."

He sandwiched her hands between his, silently encouraging her to go on.

"Adriano." She looked at him, her eyes big and wide with fear. "I heard him tell his bodyguard to kill a man, and then I saw the bodyguard do it."

Holy crap!

Payton had witnessed Sherman Grazicky ordering a murder.

And Grazicky knew she had reported it to the police.

They were dead.

He went stone-still, fighting to keep his face neutral as

Payton watched for his reaction. His mind twisted through a labyrinth of scenarios.

"Understand now why I didn't want to get you involved? Why I didn't tell you?" Payton's voice trembled on the verge of hysteria.

He'd been investigating Grazicky for a year, but never was there any direct evidence of his involvement in any crimes. He had a million questions, but started with the most important one. "Who did he have killed?"

"I don't know."

"What?"

"I can see the man's face as clear as glass, but I'd never met him before, so I don't know who he is."

"The police didn't tell you the victim's name?"

"The body was gone when they arrived at Skye. With so much traffic coming and going, the forensic team didn't find anything to arrest him on. He was picked up for questioning, but with no body, insufficient evidence, and an alibi, he was released."

He'd heard rumblings of Grazicky being arrested on trumped-up charges and having to be released, but he didn't have a source inside the police station who could give him any information. The first he'd learned of a murder was through Jake's informant.

"Grazicky wants you alive—why?" Adriano asked, working out the mystery aloud. "Why come after you if there's no body, no evidence, and no charges pending? The police would rack it up as a crazy female seeing things if he never put a hit out on you." He ran a hand across the angles of his face. "You're running from Grazicky and the FBI?"

"I was placed in protective custody when Sherman found out I was the witness against him."

"It's hard to convict someone of murder without a body and no clue who the dead person is." He left the bed and expended his nervous energy by pacing. "Give me the details about what happened at the Adam's Mark."

"The detective woke me and said hit men were outside. She helped me take the ledge into the next room. I took the stairs and left through the kitchen. I saw the *Chicago City* vehicle—"

"I know the rest." He stopped in front of her. "Except why an FBI agent tried to kidnap you. He could have shot you on the spot. It would have put an end to Grazicky's problems, but he said Grazicky wanted to talk to you. Why?"

She shrugged. "I don't know. Maybe he wants to kill me himself."

Adriano shook his head and resumed his pacing. "No. Grazicky isn't the type of man to get his hands dirty. Jake and I have been investigating him for a year. Special investigators at the authorities haven't been able to prosecute him. It's impossible to directly connect him with anything. He has layers and layers of logistics and people between him and his illegal activities. There's something else he wants from you."

"What?"

"I don't know, but whatever it is, it's going to keep you alive."

Payton bolted from the bed. She grabbed his rain-soaked shirt in her tiny fists. "No one can protect me if I take the stand. Even if he goes to jail, his men will always haunt me."

Her eyes were wild with panic. It stabbed at his chest to see this angel crumbling because of Grazicky. The corrupt FBI agent or Sherman Grazicky—both crooks who would rather kill her than take a chance she knew too much.

"You can't *not* testify," he told her. "What you know will put him away for a long time."

"If it doesn't kill me first."

Payton pressed into him, plastering her body against his. She was shaking, terrified and vulnerable. His hormones flared to life, and at the worst possible time he remembered how long it had been since he shared his bed with a woman.

One of the perks of traveling the country on assignment was the opportunity to experience women of all flavors, but the Grazicky investigation had distracted him, and he hadn't had the opportunity to sample the local southern delights Charlotte offered. Payton clung to him, sweet perfection at his fingertips. Besides her vulnerability right now, Payton wasn't the type of woman he'd be satisfied to spend one night with. He'd need time to pleasure her properly. He stroked her hair once before he moved away on the pretense of taking off his wet shirt. His judgment couldn't become clouded by a pretty face and a slamming body.

"My partner and I are in Charlotte on special assignment to investigate Grazicky. Jake was at the Adam's Mark tonight to meet with an informant who knew about you witnessing the murder."

"I had no idea."

He paced the tight space of the motel room.

Payton blocked his path. "Will you help me? If you can get me clothes and put me on a Greyhound, you'll never see me again."

Reporter mode kicked in. "*You* can break this story wide open. I'll help you, but you have to tell me what you know about Grazicky."

"Just because I worked at his club doesn't mean I was his confidant."

"You've seen the books, which means you have valuable information. Even if you don't know what it is. The IRS put Capone away on tax fraud. You witnessed him ordering a hit and saw his man do it. I want to hear about it before the FBI does."

Payton hesitated. "What will you do with what I tell you?"

"Write the story of the century!"

Jake would keel over when he told him the angel who had kidnapped him was the key to their entire investigation.

"You can give me phone numbers, remember telephone

messages, and tell me the names of the people coming and going at Sherman's estate."

Payton mumbled, "I'm a reporter's dream." Her eyes flickered up and away from his.

He agreed. Payton was a dream—of a different kind. He backed off, afraid he'd alienate her.

"The Charlotte police were supposed to take me to FBI headquarters in the morning."

He started pacing again. "I'll give them a call and tell them about the agent on your living-room floor. It should start an investigation. You'll be safe."

"Do you really believe that?"

"We have to let the police know where you are, and that you're still alive. The Charlotte police department is probably combing the streets for you right now. You're a witness. You can't just walk away. They'll find you, and put *you* in jail."

A shadow crossed Payton's face, and his heart lurched. Her fear was palpable. He couldn't imagine how it would be to have Sherman Grazicky's henchmen trying to kill you.

Payton was in over her head.

"I'll take you directly to FBI headquarters myself. Sherman may be able to buy one agent, but not the entire force."

She watched him with careful eyes, putting her faith—her life—in his hands.

"I'll find a pay phone tonight and tell them about the agent at your place. We'll let the FBI know where you are tomorrow. I'll get you clean clothes, and we'll have breakfast."

"And what do you want in return?"

"You tell me everything you know."

Payton nodded, clearly not eager to relive the trauma.

"Tonight, get some rest."

"I'll try."

He watched as she climbed under the covers, facing the wall, the tattered nightgown hanging from her body as it began to dry.

"Adriano?" She glanced over at him with an innocence that took him by surprise.

"Yeah?"

"Everything'll be okay once I get to the FBI, right?"

"They'll take good care of you tomorrow. I'll take good care of you tonight."

She burrowed down in the bed. Her eyes flashed at him again. "Are you sure?"

"I promise I won't take you to them if I don't think they can help you."

"No, you wouldn't." Payton studied him wearily. "I'm betting my life on it."

Chapter 7

A mite-size succession of sneezes stirred Adriano awake. His eyes opened at a leisurely pace. It took him a minute to focus and remember why he was sleeping on a chair in a cheap motel. A delicate cough turned his attention to the petite lump on the bed above him.

Payton Vaughn would provide him with inside information on Sherman Grazicky, and he'd write the exposé of the century. In his mind's eye, he could see the pose he would have her take for the cover photo. Together with the information he and Jake were gathering, it wouldn't be a stretch to expect to win *Chicago City*'s coveted Reporter of the Year Award. After he had Jake investigate the FBI agent at Payton's house and connected him to Sherman, Adriano might even get a book out of it, and then nothing would stand between him and the *New York Times* bestseller list.

Before Payton turned herself in to the FBI, he'd get his story. He'd never get an interview with her after they took her into custody. The FBI wouldn't botch up again. He couldn't believe the Charlotte police had let a delicate little bird like Payton slip out of their grasp.

Grazicky wasn't someone to play with. The man could frighten women and children, but Adriano didn't scare easily.

He'd keep Payton safe until he got her to FBI headquarters and turned her over to someone in charge—someone immune to Grazicky's money. He'd do everything in his power to make sure Grazicky was off the streets.

Behind the mask of terror Grazicky's organization displayed was a weak and cowardly ruler. How could he put a hit out on an angel like Payton? He had committed crimes and been caught. He had to pay the price. Killing Payton would not make his transgressions go away.

How had Payton ever gotten involved with Grazicky? A vision of her sad, soulful eyes interrupted his thoughts. The evening storm had ended, but not before providing him with a sneak peek of her sensuous body. He'd never forget the way the wet gown clung to the arc of her hips and the curvature of her ripe breasts. The cold rain made her dark nipples stand at attention, teasing him, almost daring him to take her in his arms and tear the sheer fabric away.

In the right place, at the right time, he would have spent the entire evening sampling the sweetness he could pull from her pert nipples. His mind moved with the speed of a locomotive as he imagined the pleasure they could have shared last night. He tried to admonish those thoughts when his manhood became engorged and rigid, reminding himself this was about business—not long-needed pleasure.

Business, he reminded himself. *You'll get the interview, see her safely to the FBI, and go back to Chicago to write the story.*

Hearing Payton sneeze again, Adriano walked over to the bed and handed her a tissue. "Did you catch something?"

She nodded.

"I'll get you some clothes."

She sneezed again. "And cough syrup."

Her innocent eyes pulled with the force of a magnet, and he found himself sitting on the side of the bed.

Payton asked, "When should I call the FBI? They'll say I have to come in—immediately."

"We'll call after breakfast. You won't tell them where you are. You'll just tell them you're all right and I'm bringing you in."

"Where's the office?"

"There's a field office in Charlotte, but I'd bet the agent in your apartment last night works out of that office. It would be safer to get you to the Special Agent in Charge at the Columbia, South Carolina, branch."

"What's wrong?"

"Since the crime was committed in North Carolina, that branch is responsible for handling the case."

"You're worried they'll transfer me back to Charlotte."

It was a possibility. They would need compelling evidence about the rogue agent to convince the Special Agent in Charge not to send her back. He didn't know the results of his anonymous call last night. The agent might have been gone before anyone arrived to investigate his story. It should be simple, but he wasn't fooled into believing bureaucracy and red tape wouldn't complicate the matter.

He watched the uncertainty in her eyes. "Listen, they'll protect you. We'll explain why we came to Columbia instead of Charlotte. Everything is going to work out."

Payton smiled unconvincingly.

To get an unobstructed view of her profile, Adriano pushed a bushel of hair from her face. The rain had made her mane wild, giving her an uninhibited, exotic appearance. They watched each other in silence. He couldn't figure out what she was thinking or what she wanted him to do. He wanted to move into the bed beside her. He'd start with light kisses to her forehead and cheeks. Then he'd take her lips between his and he—

Payton sneezed.

He sprung up from the bed and crossed the room. She was pretty, no doubt, but he knew better than to get involved with a source. It would call the credibility of his article into question.

He stepped into his shoes and grabbed his keys. "I'll get you some clothes. Be back in an hour."

"You're leaving me?"

"I wouldn't leave you." He tried to ease the distress crinkling her brow by lightening his tone. "You owe me a story, remember?"

"Aren't you afraid I'll run away?"

He paused at the door. "You have no clothes, money, or transportation. And you need my help. I'm not afraid you'll leave."

Adriano took the time to remove the logos from the SUV's exterior before he filled the Land Cruiser with gas and asked directions to the nearest town. The damage to the rear bumper would cause the truck to stand out if someone knew what they were looking for, but the *Chicago City* logos were a dead giveaway. A short drive later, he found a small town with a bank, restaurant, gas station, and general store.

The healthy woman behind the counter at the general store watched him suspiciously as he wandered through the women's clothing department. She kept one hand behind the counter—probably on her shotgun—at all times. He quickly remembered he was in the South, not urban Chicago. Here, black men still disappeared in broad daylight. He treaded lightly through the women's department searching for suitable clothes for Payton. A young girl came from the back of the store and asked if he needed help.

"I need clothes for a woman about this big and this tall." He used his hands to measure out Payton's height and width.

Amused, the young girl began to flip through the clothing rack. "What are you looking for?"

"Jeans, T-shirt, jacket. And underwear. Oh yeah, shoes."
The girl nodded.

"Something to do her hair and shower with too."

"Okay, sir," she acknowledged with a southern drawl.

After paying for the motel and buying gas, his cash reserve was dangerously low. Mr. Conners would grumble about the expenses when he saw the credit-card bill. Until Adriano dropped the final draft of the exposé on his desktop.

He moved through the store and found himself a shirt, slacks, and toiletries. He had missed their flight, but he flipped open his cell phone and tried Jake anyway.

Jake sounded panicked. "What's going on? I've been calling you all morning. I need to tell you about Payton Vaughn."

"Relax, man. She told me everything." He cradled several bags of chips in his arms. "She's giving us an exclusive. I'm going to get her to FBI headquarters, and she's going to give me the story." He followed the woman to the counter to pay for his purchases.

"Where are you? I'd like to be there. We've worked long and hard to get this story."

He pulled out his company credit card and handed it to the young woman. "I know, but you keep working on the informant, and I'll get Payton's interview. Anything on the FBI agent who attacked us at her place?"

"I was right there when the police arrived. The man was gone and the place was clean. No signs of a struggle."

"No blood? I hit him pretty good."

"Nothing. If you ask me, the apartment was professionally cleaned, and those same professionals escorted our boy on a very long trip."

Adriano signed the charge slip.

"What exactly did Payton tell you?" Jake wanted to know.

"Thanks," Adriano told the young woman and grabbed his bags. As he loaded the SUV, he recounted Payton's story for Jake and then headed across the street to order breakfast.

"Adriano, for you to brag about knowing women as much as you do, you sure were fooled by this one."

"What do you mean?" He slipped into a booth to wait for his breakfast order.

"My informant told me last night that Payton Vaughn is a whole lot more than a manager to Grazicky."

The static on the phone obstructed Jake's words. "Say again, Jake. My battery's dying." He'd left the charger in his suitcase back at the hotel in Charlotte.

"According to my source, Grazicky is crazy about her. The informant said Grazicky had a man beaten to a pulp because he whistled at her."

"It can't be true." Picturing Grazicky's hands on Payton turned his stomach. "Payton is scared to death of Grazicky." He returned to the counter, paid his bill, and left the restaurant.

"You have to see her, Jake. She's gorgeous. There's no way she's messing around with Grazicky."

"Ask her," Jake said.

"I will. The minute I get back to the motel."

"You left her alone at the motel? *Alone?*" Jake blew into the phone. "She won't be there when you get back."

"She will." He didn't know how, but he was certain she wouldn't break their agreement. She needed him.

Wisely, Jake avoided that argument. "The FBI agent saw you last night, and now he's disappeared."

"I know." His energy was focused on Payton's safety. He welcomed the opportunity to tangle with Grazicky, but he couldn't protect Payton if he was dead.

"Watch your back."

"I will."

"Find out everything Payton knows."

He climbed into the Land Cruiser. "Do you doubt my investigative skills, my brother? I'm usually the one slinging the camera or fighting off the goons to save your butt, but I do remember how it's done."

"This isn't about your wounded ego, Adriano. Grazicky is desperate. You have to stay sharp."

Jake hadn't been there to see the fear in Payton's big brown eyes as they eluded the speeding car chasing them into the night. He hadn't witnessed her grit when she took the crooked FBI agent down. Jake hadn't slept at the foot of the bed with Payton relying on him for security. All night long she muttered, twisting restlessly in her sleep. She tossed left and right, kicking the blanket off the side of the bed. It was all he could do not to climb into bed and take her in his arms.

"Stay focused," Jake warned as if he could read Adriano's private thoughts.

"My battery is dying. I'll call when I know the plan."

Adriano hoped Payton was as innocent as her eyes portrayed. Jake had meant to jolt him back into reality, to keep him from getting wrapped up in a pretty face and perfect body. As Adriano climbed into the SUV and started down the road, he tried to remember the last time he'd been this attracted to a woman.

Working stories with Jake, he spent most of his time with the unsavory elements of society—not much potential for a mate there. When he and Jake cracked a big story and the accolades came, so did the fame-hunting women. With Jake being a faithfully married man, Adriano had more than his share of offers. And he took up quite a few. But the attraction was always fleeting, ending as soon as the woman allowed him penetration of her body. None of those women made him feel hopelessly—and helplessly—under their spell. In the midst of danger, his mind remained focused but never lingered too far from the sexual tension mounting between him and Payton.

He turned off the dirt road when he saw the one-pump gas station. The tires spat gravel as he rounded the building to the small motel. He loved Chicago, but the beautiful weather year-round in the South was a definite perk of his visit.

His trained eye didn't miss noticing the cars parked at the motel. Where there had been only one beat-up pickup truck the night before, there were two new cars; both black with an extra antenna. Unmarked cop cars? Had Payton called the FBI while he was gone? Would they send two cars to pick her up? He estimated Payton to be five-five—five-six at the most—about six inches shorter than himself—and no more than one hundred and twenty pounds. Four cops were not needed to bring her in. And wouldn't they want to be discreet? Especially after the fiasco at the Adam's Mark?

"If they're trying to be inconspicuous, they're doing a terrible job at it," Adriano grumbled.

He drove a wide circle around the formation of cars. He kept his eyes focused straight ahead, trying not to draw any attention. A car was posted near the lot entrance, blocking the pickup truck. The other was boldly parked in front of their motel-room door.

As Adriano passed the cars, he stole a glance inside of each. One man in the first; two men in the car parked in front of the motel-room door. All the men were dressed in black.

This looks like a hit—not a witness recovery, Adriano thought. He panicked when he considered he might be right. Payton could be lying dead inside the motel room. Instantly, his palms began to perspire. He never should have left her behind. With her sneezing and coughing, he had thought it better for her to wait instead of going out wearing only the tattered nightgown.

Stay calm, he told himself.

He maintained a steady speed until he reached the back of the motel, counting the windows until he knew he was at the right room. He coasted up to the back of the building, pulling the SUV up onto the crumbling sidewalk and stopping underneath the window to their room.

He squatted next to the SUV and looked around. With it still being early morning, no one was visiting the gas station, which left the area deserted. None of the hit men had secured the back of the motel. *Amateurs.* Thinking quickly, Adriano jumped up on the hood of the Land Cruiser.

"Payton," he called, looking around to see if he had drawn any attention. He tapped the glass. "Payton. Come to the window." He peered inside, looking down into the rusted tub. "Payton, it's Adriano. Come to the window."

A shadow moved across the window.

He tapped again. "Payton, open the window."

The shadow grew larger and soon the window opened a few inches. From this angle he could only see the rusted tub. "Payton, it's me." He fit his face into the crack of the window.

"What are you doing at the window?"

"Whatever you do, don't open the door."

"What are you talking about?"

He began to work the window open against old paint and rusted gears. "*Someone* is outside in unmarked cars, and I hope for our sakes it's the FBI."

"What are you talking about?" Payton disappeared from the window.

"Payton," he called, working frantically at opening the window. Like the victims in scary B movies, Payton didn't heed his warning. He had lifted the window wide enough to see her silhouette leave the bathroom. "Payton, don't open the door!"

"Who's there?" she shouted.

"Damn." He struggled with the window. "Payton!"

He knew she would be headstrong by the nerve it must have taken to jump into his Land Cruiser. If they got out of this alive, he'd have to explain to her that she needed to follow his orders without question. He didn't have time to negotiate.

He had the window three quarters of the way up when he heard Payton scream. "Payton!"

She reappeared in the bathroom, slamming the door behind her. Her fear-stricken face gave him the strength to shove the window open to its fullest.

"Climb through the window." He stuck his hand inside to aid her.

"I can't fit."

"You have to fit. C'mon."

A crashing noise on the other side of the bathroom door pulled her attention away from his waiting hand.

"Hurry up, Payton."

He extended his arm as far as his body would allow. He would never fit his broad shoulders through the window frame, but Payton's lithe body could squeeze out of the narrow opening.

Payton clasped his hand. He balanced himself on the hood of the SUV while providing leverage for her climb. Her hands grabbed the window ledge, and he pulled her arms as she attempted to jettison herself out of the window. He lost his footing on the rain-slicked hood and fell against the windshield of the SUV. He sprang up as Payton wiggled the top half of her body through the window.

"Adriano," she cried, grabbing wildly at his hands.

He wrapped his arms under hers and pulled as she climbed. They collapsed with a thud on top of the SUV. Sliding down the slippery hood, they landed next to the Land Cruiser in a muddy puddle. He wrapped his arms around her chest, securing her so she fell on top of his body.

"Are you hurt?" Payton asked.

"No. Let's get out of here." He scrambled to the driver's side, knowing it would be only seconds before the men realized Payton had escaped out the window. He slowly whipped the truck into a half circle.

"Hurry up!" Payton yelled. "What are you doing?"

"Stay calm. And get down. I don't want to draw any attention to us."

Chapter 8

Adriano's heart pumped with such force it made his temples pulsate. He kept his eyes on the road, glancing into the rearview every few seconds to measure the distance between the SUV and the first black car. *Was that gunfire?* He remembered hearing the sound before—while being pursued by Grazicky's men. This time there was no doubt someone was shooting at them.

"Get down!" Adriano shouted.

Payton folded herself into a tight ball on the floor of the front seat.

Somewhat familiar with the area from his morning drive, he formulated a plan. A tall cornfield came into sight. He glanced in the rearview again. These men were relentless. He made a hard left, and the SUV rose up on two wheels. He sped through the cornfield, knowing the following cars would not be able to drive through the rough terrain of the field for long. About a mile into the field, he no longer saw either car.

He rolled to a stop. "Payton, are you okay?"

She climbed up from the floor. "You saved my life—again."

"Are you hurt?"

"No," she answered, checking scrapes on her elbows.

He checked the rearview, searching the cornfield. "Did they say who they were?"

"No."

"When they knocked at the door, did they call out FBI?"

"The man kept yelling for me to open up. He didn't say he was from the FBI."

"Grazicky's men. How did they find us? Did you call anyone?" She looked away.

"Who did you call?" His tone was harsher than he'd intended.

"You don't understand. People are dead because of me."

"You think I don't understand? I've almost been killed twice, and I've only known you a day."

"I just wanted to go home." Her voice trembled.

He glanced at her, quickly losing his anger when he saw the tattered nightgown, torn and covered in mud. She was shivering from the cool early morning temperature.

"I'm on your side, but if I'm going to keep you alive, we have to start working together." He placed his mud-covered hand on her knee. "Tell me who you called."

"I called my brother in St. Louis. He'll let me stay with him until this is over."

"Grazicky must have a trace on your brother's phone. You can't go to your brother's. Grazicky's men will be waiting on the doorstep and snatch you before you can kiss your brother hello. He's probably watching everyone you know."

"Is my brother in danger?"

"Grazicky is probably watching him in case you go there." He tried to reassure her, but he couldn't be certain. "He needs your brother alive to take your calls and lure you to his house."

"I have to warn him."

"That's the worst thing you can do. If Grazicky thinks you're close, or that you're going there, he'll have his men waiting. And I don't know what he'll do to your brother while they're waiting for you to show up. If Sherman thinks you might call your brother again for help, he'll want him alive to take the call so he can find out where you are. The best thing is not to contact him until this is over."

Payton shifted toward the window, falling into morbid silence. Tears made a path down her cheeks and dropped onto her shoulder. Coming close to losing her at the motel had scared him. He couldn't imagine how frightened she must be with Grazicky's men relentlessly coming after her. She swiped the tears away, fighting to remain composed. She donned her tough armor before she turned to him and asked, "You're going to keep me alive?"

"I will." He meant it. This was no longer about besting Grazicky. It was about saving Payton from whatever evil things he had planned for her.

"Because you want my story."

A corner of his heart ripped. He was a jerk, and she knew it. His actions were admirable, but his intentions were selfish. He wanted to pull her into his arms and tell her she had him all wrong. But he couldn't, because the truth was he'd only agreed to help her because he needed the story.

"And once you get the story," she asked, her voice trembling, "what will happen to me then?"

He swallowed hard. Seeing his difficulty in answering, she turned away from him again, lapsing into that nerve-wracking silence Adriano had come to hate.

He cleared his throat. "Angel."

She didn't acknowledge him.

"You're right. My helping you was all about getting the story. The second you jumped in the SUV, I started planning my next article."

She turned to him, her expression unreadable.

"I didn't know you then. Twelve hours has made all the difference. I'll make sure you're safe. Story or no story, we're in this together. I won't leave you again."

She watched him, her gaze unwavering. Either she appreciated his honesty or she hated his self-serving motives.

She angled her body toward him. "You'll help me even if I don't give you an exclusive?"

"Keeping you alive is what's important."

"You're in danger now too."

"More reason for us to stay together."

A tremor moved across her shoulders. "I really don't want to be alone."

With her confession, he made a confession of his own. He reached across the center console and dragged her into his arms. Ignoring the mud splatters on her cheeks, he kissed away her tears, wishing he could remove her fear as easily. There was something about her unique mix of vulnerability and resolve that ignited his desire for her. He held her tightly, crushing her curvy frame to his body. He'd wanted to touch her this way since the moment he wrestled her down in the backseat.

He pressed his lips to hers, softly at first, gauging her reaction. He teased her bottom lip, removing the tension and uncertainty. Her entire body relaxed, bringing her curves down on him. The adrenalin pumping through his veins throbbed. He turned his head to obtain the perfect angle and slowly entered her mouth. His kiss told her everything he needed her to know. He wasn't going to leave her. He'd protect her to the end. He admired her. She was beautiful. Even mud-covered and tattered as she was, he wanted her more than he'd ever wanted a woman before.

He apologized with his kiss, assuring he would never again be selfish at her expense. When he was certain she understood him, he pulled away, closely watching her reaction.

"What do we do now?"

His brain was scrambled. He didn't understand the question. His mind buzzed, knowing Grazicky's men were out there searching for them, but his groin argued there was always time for the important things in life.

"We have to get as far away from those men as possible. And then we have to ditch this SUV."

Payton started to say something but thought better of it. She untangled herself from his arms and returned to her seat. She perched on her knees, searching for the two black cars.

He drove carefully through the cornfield until he reached the road. He left the Land Cruiser at the edge of the field and went to check their surroundings. He crouched near a thick stalk of corn, checking both directions.

Payton appeared next to him. "No cars in sight."

"They'll be back." The tension in her shoulders knotted beneath her skin.

"Hey." He caressed her cheek, and she didn't pull away from his mud-covered knuckles. He studied the sharp arch of her eyebrows, the scrumptious curves of her body, the broad flare of her hips and the billow of her breasts . . . and he knew he'd never leave her stranded. "My word means something. I don't make arbitrary promises."

Her big brown eyes swept his face. "Thank you."

What about her made him want to risk his life to protect her?

"I've got a signal!" Payton called to Adriano. He was inside a dilapidated barn changing into the new jeans he'd purchased at the discount store. They'd left the cornfield after finding a one-lane dirt service road that led deep into farmland. They'd stopped to eat and change into the new clothes. Hunger made Payton tear into the breakfast sandwich and hash browns as if they were a gourmet meal of lobster and filet mignon. For the first time in days, with Adriano at her side, she felt secure enough to resume the normal functions of living.

"Adriano," she called again, "I have a signal." The cell phone displayed one bar of battery life. No telling how long the signal would last before the phone died for good.

Adriano appeared, carrying the new button-down shirt in his hand. He'd managed to remove most of the mud from his face and hair, revealing striking features that somehow fit in with their wild surroundings. Every muscle of his abdomen rippled as he approached. Without the benefit of a belt, the new jeans hung low on his hips, dipping in front to give Payton a tantalizing glimpse of the terrain between his navel and his groin. She stole a sweeping look at his package and the long legs carrying him toward her.

"You found a signal?" he asked, taking the phone from her. His fingers brushed hers when he handed her his shirt. Her face heated, and she knew her cheeks would be a hearty pink. She turned away as he dialed his partner.

"Change of plans," Adriano announced. "Can't talk. My battery is low. I need you to meet us." There was a short pause in his conversation before he said, "Yep, the usual. We're on Service Road 182. We'll head north back to the main road."

Payton perched on the bumper of the Land Cruiser, listening to Adriano's conversation.

"Jake will meet us," Adriano said, ending the call.

"You trust him?"

"With my life." He reached out for the shirt. "We've been partners for years."

"Ever been involved in anything like this?"

He hesitated while he stuffed his arms into his shirt. "Never been up against a mobster, no, but we've been under gunfire in Iraq. Jake and I take the stories other reporters find too dangerous to handle."

"Why?"

He raised his fairy-kissed eyebrow in contemplation of an answer. He buttoned the last three buttons of the shirt, leaving enough chest exposed to tease her thoughts away from the danger at hand.

"No one's ever asked you why you do what you do?"

"My mother nags me about changing careers, my father shakes his head, but no one has ever asked why I like doing what I do."

"Why do you put your life on the line just to write a story?"

In her world of glitz and glamour, the most calculated risk she'd ever encountered was if she should have breast-augmentation surgery. Her life was about entertainment, performance, and maintaining a happy façade at any cost. Heroes topped the box-office charts, and saviors signed the next big artist.

"It isn't just writing a story. The stories Jake and I break expose wrongdoing in the world. We make people aware of the things they wish they could ignore. We put it out there in the faces of politicians who are forced to act and answer. Important issues are brought to the forefront, and people with the money and the power to right the situation take notice. I can't change the world alone, but I can recruit those who have the means to."

"Like all the celebrities adopting babies from foreign countries. Or the politicians who are forced to resign when a story about their abuse of power breaks."

"Exactly." He opened the back door of the SUV and began rummaging around. "What do you love about your job?"

"I thought I had the best job in the world, but after I saw that man get shot, I realized what I do is shallow."

"Don't be so hard on yourself. What you do is important too. You provide the illusion needed when life gets too tough to handle. People need release." He slung a camera bag over his shoulder. "How'd you get into the business?"

"I was like most little girls who enjoy dressing up in fancy clothes and wearing their mother's high heels. I always wanted to be glamorous and famous. It drove my parents crazy and put pressure on my older brother to pick up the slack and make a success out of his life. While he was in college, I was working as a waitress in a local bar. I helped the owner with the books, learning all I could about the business. I worked my way up through bars, clubs, and the concert-promotion business. Eventually, someone who knew someone told me about Sherman's club. I met with him, presented my ideas for increasing profits, and he called me the next day with the job. The pay is great, the perks wonderful."

"And you get to dress up in high heels every night."

She searched for condemnation but found none. Instead, desire danced in his eyes. He broke their connection by sliding into the front seat and searching the glove box. He retrieved the flashlight from under the seat and locked up the car. "They'll be looking for the SUV. We'll walk back to the road on the other side of the cornfield. Jake'll pick us up."

She fell into step beside him.

"How long have you worked for Grazicky?"

"A little over a year."

"And you never suspected anything?"

"Suspected what? He's the typical wealthy businessman who probably never received much female attention before he started opening clubs."

"How's that?"

"Flirty, plays the big shot with the celebrities, loves the camera." He looked her up and down. "All over you."

"He's hit on me. I keep it about business."

Adriano didn't look happy about her honesty. "Does his wife know how he acts with you?"

"I've never met her. She rarely comes to Skye. From what I've overheard, she travels and spends money."

"Grazicky has never discussed their relationship with you?"

"No. Why would he?"

"To get into your pants. Tell you how unhappy he is at home, how his wife doesn't understand him the way you do."

His sarcastic attitude made her ask, "Is this part of the interview?"

"Yes."

He'd turned on his reporter switch and she hadn't even noticed. She wanted to ask if his kissing her was a part of the interview too.

After walking a few yards, he started firing the questions again. "We need to find out why Grazicky wants to talk to you. Do you keep his books?"

"He has an accountant."

"Have you ever seen his financial records?"

"I manage the staff, so part of my job is submitting work hours for pay to the accounting team."

"Ever notice any discrepancies in the hours you submit and the final paychecks?"

"I don't see the individual checks, but early on I noticed my final dollar payout didn't equal the accounting department's. I questioned it because my job hinged on making a profit for the club. I couldn't go over the personnel budget and meet my quotas."

"How did they explain it?"

"Sherman pays a bonus to the waitresses who work the suites."

"The infamous suites." He took the camera bag from her shoulder and placed it on his. "Jake and I visited Skye our first night in town."

"Really?"

"I recognized your name, but didn't connect it to Skye until later. You're the person to know if you want things done there."

She couldn't enjoy pride in her work under the circumstances. "What did you think?"

"Nice place. Of course, Jake and I weren't famous enough or rich enough to leave the first level."

"When I open my own club you'll have an all-access pass."

He stopped abruptly, turning to her, and she immediately understood the double entendre associated with her promise. She wanted to ask him about the kiss again, but she'd tried once and he had quickly reminded her of why they were stuck together. He watched her, and she knew he wanted to say something. She found it strangely endearing that a reporter couldn't put his thoughts into words.

"Want to take a break?" he asked. "Your feet must be sore."

"A short break would be good." Her feet were tender, but the sneakers he'd given her and walking through the fields helped to cushion her steps.

Midday, the South Carolina sun was unforgiving and beat down on them with a vengeance. They found a clearing underneath the umbrella of a tree and sat on the ground facing each other. Adriano's perspiration-soaked shirt clung to every indentation of his chest, outlining her every desire. The T she wore gave him unrestricted access to the pert response of her eager breasts. Ignoring his sensuality was impossible. The struggle frustrated her into expending more mental energy, which further focused her attraction on him. She gave up the fight, acknowledging the magnetism between them didn't mean they were going to roll around in the loft of the nearest barn.

"What do you know about Sherman?" she asked.

Adriano removed his camera as he answered. "He's one of the biggest drug dealers in this region, but the authorities have never been able to link him directly with any illegal activity. Jake and I tracked drug shipments to Chicago and found a connection between the imports there with imports in several other major cities. We dug a little deeper and found the shipments originated from three places. After talking to a few informants and tracking money trails, we realized Grazicky's name always came up. We took the information to our editor, and he told us to follow up."

"You could be wrong. Sherman could be an ordinary businessman."

"I could be wrong, but I'm not." He brought the camera up to his face and focused on her.

"What makes you so sure?"

"My instincts are never wrong." He pressed the button and the camera whirled to life.

"This could be interpreted as a personal vendetta. You don't have any real evidence connecting Sherman and the drug business."

"You don't have any real evidence connecting him to the murder, but you know he's responsible."

Chapter 9

Adriano kept a careful watch on every car as it passed. They had been crouched in a ditch on the side of the road for at least thirty minutes waiting for his partner. Silently, he eyed every car, truck, and minivan driving by. He gave her a halfhearted smile. "He'll be here soon."

"Do you think the FBI might have picked him up? It won't take them long to put you in the SUV, and then they'll know about Jake."

"He would have given me a signal when I called him with the mile marker."

"Try him again." She did not want to be stuck in a field when the sun went down.

He pulled the cell phone from his waistband. "I'm afraid that'll have to wait, angel. No signal."

"Why do you keep calling me angel?"

Adriano stopped fumbling with the phone. He watched her, his features becoming dark and introspective.

"Do I remind you of someone you know?"

"You remind me of an angel." He let his gaze linger before checking out another approaching car. "Keep your head down," he said, climbing out of the ditch.

Payton stayed low as she watched Adriano's lofty body

cross the road and disappear inside the car. His silky hair bounced in the ponytail riding his shoulders. The expansive territory between his shoulders rippled underneath his dirty shirt. The haunches of his behind were high and firm, dimpling with every confident step he took.

And he thought she looked like an angel?

At her lowest point, she turned to Adriano to wrap her in his arms. Behind the confident stride and commanding voice, his tenderness and concern made her feel safe. He was sincere in his promise—would not leave her until she was safe. She'd heard him tell his friend the same on the phone. He could have abandoned her several times, but he hadn't. And the sincerity in his voice when he promised he wouldn't told her she could count on him until the end.

Jake tried unsuccessfully to convince Adriano to end the madness. "I still say take her in, A. She'll be safer with them than with you. Getting a story is one thing; getting killed for a story is another."

Adriano glanced to where he knew Payton was waiting. "I won't leave her until I know she's all right. She slipped away from the police at the Adam's Mark, which started all this mess. There's no way I'm trusting them to keep her safe."

"The FBI came to the hotel asking questions about you. It took me an hour to lose 'em."

"It won't be safe for us to meet again."

"It's not safe for you to be mixed up in this. We've done some stories together I still can't believe we had the balls to get involved in, but this is different. You're out there alone with a woman we know nothing about."

"I'm on Grazicky's radar by now. The FBI agent in Payton's apartment has to have figured out who I am by now. And they'll track me back to the paper and to you."

"More reason to pull back until things cool off. We can always pick up the story later."

"If you had been sitting in the SUV when Payton jumped in, would you be so willing to walk away? Or would you want to see the story to the end?"

"Hell, yeah, I'd want to put an end to it. Before my wife found out," he added with a sliver of humor. "You're a reporter— we question everything. Until it's verified by three sources, don't quote it. Aren't you the one who told me that rule? You believe what she's told you so far?"

Adriano never liked the taste of his own words, but his instincts were right about this. "Meet her. Tell me if you think she's conniving enough to make up this entire story."

"I'll meet her, but first I want to know how far things went in the motel last night."

"Nothing happened."

"Because sexing up the source could taint the story. And be seen as unethical by some. What is it about this woman, A? You got a thing for her?"

"I've only known her a few days," he answered cryptically.

"How many days does it take?"

"We would help anyone in this much trouble." *Not to this extent,* his conscience nagged him.

"Not trying to be your mother, A. Trying to watch out for my partner—my best friend."

"I know. It's okay, really. I still have my head on straight." Jake nodded.

Seeing the skepticism on Jake's face and being forced to deal with his guilt over the kiss, Adriano tried to explain. "If you were there . . . if you could see her face—I know you wouldn't have been able to walk away."

"Is this about a pretty face?"

He swiped his hand over his chin. "This woman is in trouble, and I won't abandon her."

"Why do you think taking her to the authorities is

abandoning her? They can protect her better than you can, running around unfamiliar territory in an SUV. A, c'mon. Think about what's best for her. Taking her to the FBI is helping her."

"Grazicky sent that rogue FBI agent to her apartment. I feel it in my gut. If I take her to the police, she'll run, or they won't be able to protect her. No, it's the FBI headquarters only, and we'll only talk to the Special Agent in Charge. I have to do this. Will you help me?"

Jake hesitated before giving in. "Let's meet the woman who has your boxers bunched. Only you, A. Only you."

It was impossible to hear what they were talking about from her place in the ditch, but Payton saw Jake gesture several times in her direction. She crawled on her belly, moving closer to the car. She ducked, pressing her face into the grass when another engine sounded, growing louder as it got closer. An old-model truck passed without incident. When she peeked at the car across the street, Adriano had left the vehicle and was jogging in her direction. He'd been concerned about the passing car too. He jumped down in the bunker with her.

"What's going on?" she asked. "What took so long?"

"Jake had questions."

"About me? He doesn't want to get involved, does he?" Her heart lurched, because if Jake didn't want to help, there was a good chance Adriano would follow his partner's lead.

"Angel." His hand warmed her shoulder. "He's a reporter. He's supposed to ask questions before jumping into a danger-ous situation."

His touch calmed her and set her on fire at the same time. She began to tingle, radiating from her shoulders, across her belly, down her legs to her ankles. The sensation was biting,

intensifying the longer his fingers lingered on her skin. The
tingles prickled and stung, moving from warmth to fire.

"What's wrong?" Adriano asked. "You have the craziest
look on your face."

She scratched at the burning trail of fire moving up her
legs. "My legs are on fire. And my belly. And my—"

"Let me see." He pulled up the leg of her pants. "You're
lying on a mound of fire ants."

She jumped up, scrambling to put distance between herself
and the biting ants. She plucked and swatted her clothing,
fighting the ants off.

"That's the most girly scream I've ever heard," Adriano
said, fighting hard not to laugh as he chased after her.

"What's going on?" Jake was out of the car in a shot, yelling
across the road. "What the hell, A?"

Adriano scooped her into his arms. "Calm down, angel.
You've gotten them all off. It only stings for a minute."

"Check! Check, Adriano." She danced in place, fighting
the urge to run down the road in search of the nearest creek.
The hardest adjustment with relocating, secondary to missing her family, was getting used to the bug situation in the
Carolinas.

Adriano shook out her shirt, moving around her in a complete circle to ensure a thorough job. He moved down each
pants leg, doing the same. "No more ants." He cupped her
cheeks in his palms. "We'll get you a shower and you'll feel
better."

Now she felt plain silly. "Thank you."

"*Hello?*" Jake called. "What the hell are you two doing?"

Adriano took her hand and led her across the street, helping her into the backseat of the car. Jake said a few words
to him over the hood of the car before climbing inside. After
introductions, Adriano told his partner what she'd witnessed.
Jake watched her warily, his keen gaze penetrating, searching
for any evidence of deception.

"You have no idea why Grazicky is opting to kidnap you instead of killing you?" Jake asked. He wasn't confrontational, but he made it clear he wasn't completely convinced by her story.

"None."

"Think hard." He grilled her on the daily operations of Skye and how involved she had been. He quizzed her about her personal involvement with Sherman.

"If I knew why Sherman wants to see me, I'd tell you. Why would I hide it?"

"Back off, Jake," Adriano told his partner.

Jake ignored him. "Grazicky managed the books himself. He never gave you access?"

"Only to the payroll of the workers I supervised."

"Okay. Was there any account, client list, or schedule he let you see? Maybe he was out of town and called and asked you to look up something."

"Did you ever share the management of a client?" Adriano added.

She combed her brain but couldn't remember anything.

"Did you ever go to business meetings together?" Jake asked. "How did he keep tabs on you?"

"He handled the business with the suites. I managed the rest. We'd meet to discuss what I was doing, go over profits and losses."

"You're out there working solo," Adriano said. "If you're both going in different directions, how did you get in touch with him?"

"My calendar."

Jake twisted in his seat, eager to hear more.

"What about your calendar?" Adriano asked.

"My life is mapped out in my planner. I kept a copy of Sherman's calendar too. In case there was an emergency. Sherman lives at Skye, but he spends a lot of time in meetings and doesn't like to be disturbed. I started getting a copy of his schedule from his secretary after he blasted me for walking in on him once. When he found out his secretary had been releasing his calendar, he didn't like it."

"What happened?"

"Nothing major. His face said he was unhappy, but he held his composure. When I went to get his schedule for next month, a lot of the dates had been blacked out."

"Bingo," Jake said. "Where do you keep your planner?"

"My Palm Pilot, but the FBI confiscated it."

"Forensic evidence."

"They promised to get it back to me as soon as they were done."

"You said your life is mapped out in the planner," Adriano said. "What did you do for a replacement?"

"I didn't have to replace it—"

"What?"

"My Palm malfunctioned once, and I spent a week trying to reconstruct my schedule, so I always keep a hard-copy backup. At the end of the day I write everything in a pocket calendar so I'll have a duplicate."

"We have to get that calendar," Adriano said. "Where is it?"

"My apartment."

"You did good, angel."

Jake's eyes popped out of his head, but Adriano didn't see it because he was too busy smiling at her.

She broke eye contact, shifting to Jake.

"I spoke to our editor, Mr. Conners, about this," Jake told her. "He has connections and resources he's willing to use to help, but this adventure is going to cost him a pretty penny. He wants the exclusive story, photos, and—"

"What do you want?"

"Like Adriano, I want to break the story."

Adriano turned toward his partner but didn't argue the point. Despite the kiss they'd shared, this was about business for him. She'd better never forget how danger, adrenalin, and being hurled into a life-threatening situation could throw two people together, heightening their emotions. Once it was over, he'd go back to his life. She'd go back to hers. Business for him, life or death for her.

Jake was still explaining the paper's position. "The paper will probably run a weekly series capitalizing on your story. Publishing companies will want a book. The compensation could help you start over."

"And you two get famous. You left out how you'll benefit."

"It is what it is, but we won't take advantage of you," he retorted.

"Jake, back off." Adriano turned to her. "It's not as callous as it sounds."

"I know." She hesitated, softening her stance. "I want this nightmare over. Reliving it in a memoir doesn't appeal to me. Interviews, photos, writing a book—I'll never be able to put it behind me."

"It's a lot to digest, but we don't have much choice. My help relies on the resources of *Chicago City,* so you'll have to give us the story. Or we can take you to the authorities right now, and you won't have to sell your story to anyone."

She watched him, trying to see past his dancing eyes to the truth. Did he want to be rid of her so easily?

"I'll keep you safe—I've already promised you that—but you'll have to share the intimate details of your life with me."

She couldn't explain the depth of her attachment to Adriano after only one day, but she didn't want to do this without him.

"You need looking after, angel."

She studied him with a deep gaze that refused to let him look away.

He placed a comforting hand on her knee. "Are we going to do this?"

* * *

The plan was simple. Stay alive, retrieve Payton's calendar, and get her to the FBI headquarters in Columbia. Along the way, Adriano would get his story and try to figure out what was so important about Payton's planner. He'd been in worse predicaments with Jake, and he had no doubt he'd get out of this one in one piece. He looked forward to being instrumental in taking down Grazicky and his drug empire. What scared him was his rampantly growing attraction to Payton.

No woman had ever instantly revved his motor and fired him up so quickly. Everything about her was appealing. Mentally battered and physically beaten, she held her head high, keeping up with him every step of the way. Not once had she complained about their walk through the cornfields and farms on her aching feet. Other than the episode with the fire ants, she hadn't groused about anything. She trusted his decisions, depending on him to keep her safe.

Jake drove, with Adriano following the directions provided by Mr. Conners to the house where they would shelter until they could enact the next phase of their plan. Instead of running, they would root themselves on an obscure farm deep in the backwoods of South Carolina—let their chasers come to them, giving them the advantage of being familiar with the territory. Adriano could put safeguards in place. He couldn't do that if they kept running without a sense of direction. In the morning, Jake would return with the essentials they needed, and then they would map out their best route to Columbia. And there was still the matter of retrieving Payton's planner.

Jake drove quietly, not disturbing the contemplative mood inside the car, although Adriano caught him glancing in the rearview mirror at Payton every few miles. Payton's attention remained on the passing scenery. Turning her life over to the care of a man she hardly knew must have wrecked her. From the short time he'd known her, he'd found she was fiercely independent and strong. Her bravery was a front; he knew this from the brief peeks of her vulnerability. She'd hidden her tears when she weakened. Adriano wanted to tell her it was okay to be afraid. She could let her guard down with him. He would be strong when she needed him.

Adriano ended the silence of the drive when Jake pulled up to the huge colonial home hidden from the road by trees and a tobacco field. "How does Mr. Conners know these people?"

"They're distant relatives of his sister-in-law. No one could ever connect them back to him or the paper. He said Tom would treat you like family."

Adriano got out of the car and opened the door for Payton while Jake popped the trunk.

"I'll be back tomorrow. The next day at the latest. If I don't show, know I'm being watched."

"All right." He reached through the window to pound fists with Jake.

"Grab the suitcase," Jake said. "Payton, it's been interesting. Keep your head up."

Adriano grabbed the suitcase from the trunk and rounded the car with Payton.

"One more thing," Jake said, already rolling down the drive, "Mr. Conner told them you're married."

Payton's mouth formed an O at the same time the front door swung open.

Chapter 10

Hiram wiped his nose with the back of his hand. As he aged, his allergies became worse: runny nose, itchy eyes—he wanted to get out of Charlotte as soon as possible. If things had gone as planned, he would be sitting on a beach, missing allergy season, and Grazicky would have Payton locked in one of the rooms of his Charlotte mansion—and would not be hounding his ass. Instead, his plans had been delayed by the police. He marveled over their willingness to die for a stranger. He'd come to the Adam's Mark with firepower two times the deadliness of police issue, but still they fought to keep their witness safe.

For this job Hiram needed the right crew. Grazicky had made it clear his life depended on assembling the perfect mix of ruthlessness and loyalty. As he watched the three people sitting around his hotel room, he was sure he had done it.

"What's the job?" Dan, always impatient, asked. There was a fine tremor to his body that never went away. Hiram suspected it had something to do with the reason Dan kept disappearing into the bathroom, but Dan was good at his work, and who was he to judge the man's recreational activities? His skill at tracking people who did not want to be found was invaluable for this job.

"I need you to find someone." Hiram reached for a tissue and blew his nose.

Dan looked around the room. "What are *they* doing here? I work alone."

"Marvin is here because once you do your job, he'll step in."

Marvin concentrated on the television news and not on what was being said around him. When the time came, he would step in and do what he'd been hired for: eliminate the problem and discard the remains. A direct opposite of nervous Dan, Marvin could sit in front of the television for hours without twitching.

"I guess my skills are needed somewhere in the middle." Kellie hopped up from the bed and ran her hands down the sleek lines of her thighs. Hiram mentally salivated as he watched her red fingertips move across the black leather pants.

"I want you close to me," he answered with a double meaning not lost on anyone in the room. "If I don't get this job done . . . Well, let's just say I need the best. Kellie, your skills are widely varied and highly necessary."

"How much?" Dan asked, a fretful edge to his voice. His fingers trembled as he raked them through his hair.

"Ten thousand apiece. An extra five to whoever delivers her."

"Fifteen thousand dollars? And we don't even have to kill her?" Marvin's attention turned from the television. "Who the hell we after?"

Hiram opened a manila envelope and dropped several photos of Payton onto the bed, spreading them out so everyone had a good look at her.

"What did she do?" Dan asked. "Dump your sorry butt?"

Kellie did not join the others in laughing.

"Don't worry about what she did," Hiram snapped. Truthfully, he wasn't certain himself. Grazicky said she had something on him, but Hiram thought it had more to do with his meal ticket—wife—finding out he had a thing for Payton. "Since when do you have to know that before taking a job?"

Kellie studied the picture, jealousy forming within the squint of her eyes. She wished they had finished the job at the hotel. She reminded Hiram every chance she got that she hated working with this crew.

"What's her name?" Marvin asked, glancing away from the television.

Hiram answered, "Payton Vaughn."

Marvin snatched up one of the photos. "She runs that swanky club—Skye."

"This is a job for Grazicky?" Dan asked excitedly. "No wonder the take is so high."

"Don't ask too many questions," Hiram warned. "Get the job done. I'll handle Grazicky."

Anxious to get started, Dan went to work. "Any idea where she might be?"

"That's what you're here for." Hiram pulled a crumpled piece of paper from his back pocket. "She left in this SUV. Find it, find the driver, and you'll find Payton Vaughn."

Dan and Marvin left the hotel room without another word. Fifteen thousand dollars was good money; finding her first would pay off nicely.

Kellie shoved the photos off the bed, scattering them onto the floor. "Bitch," she said, plopping down on the mattress.

Hiram liked her when she was mad. Sex was better—much better. He lay down next to the hellcat, working his pants open.

"And what happens if we don't get her?" Kellie asked, pulling her shirt over her head.

"Don't worry about it." He tugged at her leather pants.

"Grazicky is dangerous. We have to be ready to get out of here if things go bad."

Hiram worked his way between her legs, grabbing his penis and shoving it home. "We'll finish the job and leave on our own terms. I won't—run—from—Gra—zicky," he said, thrusting into her.

Kellie's nails bit into his back. "You have a plan, baby?"

"Oh—yeah."

Jake worked all night to verify the plans for Adriano and Payton's safe passage to Columbia. He'd obtained an untraceable satellite phone and fake identification. Creating Payton's had been costly. She had no personal belongings, and therefore Jake'd had to stand on the side of the road and take a Polaroid of her. She had no identification, and his contact was growing wary of the strange man from Chicago; he'd charged double the going rate.

Jake found a junk car lot and purchased a beat-up 1983 two-tone Ford Thunderbird. The souped-up engine would give Adriano the power he needed to lose anyone chasing them. The beaten exterior fit in well with the simple, non-flashy ways of the locals. He had to spend another couple hundred dollars to get a title, registration, insurance, and plates from the seller, but he'd done it without leaving a paper trail. After buying the car and phone, the IDs depleted his expense money, and he'd had to contact Mr. Conners for more funds.

Mr. Conners wired cash and increased the limits on Jake's credit cards—enough to finance the rest of this adventure. No doubt, Mr. Conners had grown used to his two star investigative reporters getting into trouble. Jake couldn't remember the last time they'd made deadline. They had been placed on a strict expense budget after Adriano wrecked a vintage Corvette doing their last story. Every story they proposed had to be cleared by the senior editor *and* Mr. Conners himself.

The other reporters envied their clout with Mr. Conners, always asking why the two hadn't been fired long ago. It was simple: they wrote award-winning exposés for the Chicago paper. They made their way up the ranks by agreeing to do stories other reporters shied away from because they were too dangerous. Their methods might be unorthodox, and Mr.

Conners the only one able to control them, but they did their jobs well.

Jake prepared the two suitcases he would deliver to Adriano in the morning. Inside he had clothing for them both, toiletries, and every document they would need to maintain their cover. If they could make it to Columbia safely, they would be out of reach of Grazicky's men. If they could figure out what was so valuable about the information contained in Payton's date book, they could put Grazicky away for a long time. Meanwhile, Jake worried that a new problem would arise. He'd seen the way Adriano had looked at Payton. And he'd seen the way Payton looked at Adriano.

"I hope you both know what you're doing."

"She called."

Cecily smiled over the rim of her martini glass. Finally, Payton Vaughn had done something predictable. Unlike her cheating, very predictable husband, Payton kept amazing Cecily with her craftiness. The botched job at the Adam's Mark Hotel proved Hiram had underestimated Payton—she wouldn't make the same mistake. Where had Payton gotten the guts and tenacity to elude this crackerjack hit team?

This woman intrigued Cecily. Sherman had had other women—she knew this, although she pretended she didn't—but something about Payton held Sherman's interest longer than the others. She'd met Payton during one of her visits to Skye. She was a looker, Cecily couldn't deny that, but there was a sex appeal about her that was more than intriguing. One minute she wanted the girl dead—the threat of her testifying against Sherman and destroying the empire Cecily had built needed to be permanently eliminated. The next minute she wanted Payton in their bed and captive to their every whim. Conquering this woman and sharing her with Sherman was a monumental turn-on. Sherman would be more than thrilled to know how she felt, but he wasn't off the hook, and for now he wouldn't know what she knew.

"Of course she would contact her brother," Cecily said. "He's almost the only family she has."

The big man dressed all in black stood over her like a bad cliché—all killers felt obliged to dress in black and have toxic dispositions.

"She wasn't tough enough or resourceful enough to go into hiding. The hotel escape had to be a fluke. Since you know she called, I suppose the job is done."

"Hiram's people traced the call to a motel in South Carolina, but she was gone when they got there."

"Gone?"

"That's what Hiram says."

"Do you believe him?"

The man answered by tugging at his hat. "They chased a Land Cruiser."

"You can't chase a Land Cruiser if she was gone by the time they reached the motel," Cecily reasoned.

Cecily threw her martini glass the length of the bar. The patrons at the Chicago bar were used to her outbursts, and, other than a few glances, no one acknowledged her explosion of temper. The man standing over her shifted, but his bland expression didn't waver.

"This girl doesn't have the skill to escape a team of professional hit men *twice*. What the hell is the problem here?"

The man's simple explanation: "She had help."

"The help of an incompetent hit team. Hiram is useless."

Hiram was the best hit man in Charlotte, but he was small-time compared to this man. This man, who always dressed in non-descriptive black clothing and said very little, had connections money couldn't buy. Cecily had first witnessed his expertise during her father's introduction to the man. When a Supreme Court judge's presidential nomination had been threatened by a secret past, everyone with knowledge of the judge's strange sexual activities had disappeared overnight. With the judge's nomination came her father's freedom to conduct certain activities unfettered by the police.

Cecily pondered the situation. "Change of plans. *You* bring Payton to *me*."

"Dead or alive?"

"Alive." This girl was so much trouble, why not have a little fun with her before she died? And scare the shit out of Sherman at the same time? What a lovely plan! She could picture his expression when he walked into their bedroom to find Payton tied to the bed. Cecily would make him explain, apologize, and grovel before they used the little bitch.

"Bring Payton to me," Cecily repeated. "And I want her in one beautiful piece."

"Not sure if I can do that."

"Why not?"

"Your husband wants her. Hiram has a whole team going after her. Your husband even paid a government man to snatch her up."

"Then you better get to her first."

The man stood statue still, not acknowledging her order. "Don't tell me you're feeling sentimental toward Payton. Do you really believe you're *friends?* I hired you to do a job. It isn't done yet."

"I've done what our original agreement called for."

"Yes, but let us not forget your intimate involvement in all of this. When Payton testifies, she tells everything she knows, and Sherman goes to jail. Everything will be open to investigation, and if I or my husband go down, everybody goes down. You won't be spared. Understand?"

The man nodded, and she suddenly hated this man's cool demeanor. In all their years of affiliation, she'd never seen him excited. He maintained the same emotionless tone of voice, his facial expressions never betraying his thoughts.

Come to think about it, the only time the man appeared human was when Payton was around.

Cecily had been on hand once to witness one of the man's victims escape from the rope binding him to a chair. In pure terror the man wrestled a hunting knife away from one of the other killers in the room. She was young then, so she hid underneath the staircase in the dark basement, ready to run if the man went crazy and came after her. After all, she'd ordered the hit. It was her first, and her father had insisted she witness it so as "not to take these matters lightly."

This hit man, always dressed in black from head to toe, had stepped up to the man without fear. The victim lunged at him, slicing through the left side of his face. Everyone in the basement panicked, including the soon-to-be-dead man. But the hit man used the opportunity to grab the man, ending his life with one twist of his head. Calmly, he had walked up the stairs and out of the house, leaving a trail of blood behind.

Some hack doctor must have repaired the slice because it left him horribly disfigured, which accounted for his affinity for wide-brim hats. As Cecily watched the ruthless hit man today, she wondered if hiring him might have been overkill.

The man touched the brim of his hat and swiveled around on the heels of his cowboy boots.

Cecily stopped him before he could walk away. "One more thing. I want to know who's driving that Land Cruiser. Within the hour."

She signaled the bartender for another martini. God, she missed her father. He was away, doing business with the Chinese. She knew the nature of the business and understood why she wouldn't hear from him until he returned from his trip in two more weeks, but she hated being separated from him. They talked on the phone every day, and when they were both in town they lunched together every week. He'd taught her everything she knew about the business. As a single parent, he'd loved her enough for four parents.

She lifted her glass in salute to her father. He would be proud of how she was handling the Sherman-Payton situation. And he would kill her husband.

"I've got some information about the driver of the SUV."

"Now we're getting somewhere." Sherman paced the length of the pool, watching for Cecily's appearance. She was due to return to Charlotte today, and he would be ready to play the doting husband when she arrived.

"He's a reporter," Hiram continued sheepishly.

"A reporter!" He'd been foolishly certain the man had been delivering papers out the back of the SUV. "A reporter helped Payton get away from the Adam's Mark? And the motel? Do you have any idea what this means? Reporters are worse than prosecutors. If she tells him what she saw—"

"I understand."

Sherman snatched up a lounger in anger, dropping the phone. He tangled with the chair, tossing it into the pool. Garth appeared, carrying a silver tray with two tropical drinks. Witnessing Sherman's angry explosion, he stopped, frozen, at a distance.

"Give me the phone!" Sherman shouted. He took several deep breaths before snatching the phone from Garth's hand. His voice was tight with anger when he spoke to Hiram. "I don't think you do understand. If a reporter is helping Payton, it's possible she's already told him everything she knows."

"She won't get away the next time, Mr. Grazicky."

"I'm getting close to ending our affiliation," Sherman warned. "If you can't get this done—"

"I'll take care of it."

Sherman gave Hiram an earful of curse words that categorized his annoyance with Hiram's performance thus far. "Did you get anything from the brother?"

"I have someone monitoring his phone. She called. Told

the brother she wanted to see him. I put a man on the house in case she shows up, but I gotta tell you, Mr. Grazicky, I don't think she's heading that way. Why would the reporter take her all the way to St. Louis?"

A question Sherman couldn't answer. "What do we know about this reporter?"

"He has a reputation of being a loose cannon. He's been in touch with his partner, so I put a bug on their phones. I'll find out where they're headed."

"Don't make a mess. I can't stand any more publicity."

"Yes, sir. You'll be happy."

"I want this problem taken care of," Sherman reiterated.

"I understand."

"Bring Payton to me."

"What about the reporters?"

"The reporters are expendable."

Chapter 11

If pretending to be Adriano's wife wasn't enough to make Payton nervous, Tom, an African-American albino, opened the front door of the quaint house nestled between a klatch of trees behind the tobacco fields. She was curiously apprehensive of the white-haired man until he pulled them inside, happily introducing them to his wife, Lila. The couple had promised Mr. Conners help without asking questions, and they'd done just that, insisting she and Adriano eat dinner before cleaning up.

Southern hospitality aside, Payton got the feeling Tom and Lila were lonely on the tobacco plantation and welcomed any company they received. She enjoyed the warm, homey feeling that embraced her while sitting in the living room talking about the life of an African-American albino tobacco farmer living in South Carolina.

It made her miss her brother, Patrick. She couldn't help but worry about him, but Adriano assured her he would be fine as long as she didn't contact him again. Jake promised to keep the situation under surveillance and let her know if anything took place with her brother and his family. She and Patrick had never been as close as they should have been. They loved each other but didn't spend much time together.

Patrick lived in the Midwest; she lived in Charlotte. Other than the occasional commercial greeting card, they hardly communicated. A terrible pang of guilt punctured her chest. She had almost been killed in the Adam's Mark. Did she want to die with their relationship this way? She promised herself she'd visit her brother and his family as soon as this ordeal was over.

A soft tap at the door roused her from solemn thoughts. She tied a towel around her and opened the door to Lila. "Come in."

A smile stretched across her sagging cheeks. "I heard the water stop. I forgot to leave this." Lila placed a silver wire basket filled with perfumes, lotion, and powder on the counter. "You two looked so beat, I figured you'd be turning in early."

"Do you need help with anything downstairs?" She'd offered to help clean the kitchen after dinner, but Lila had promptly and authoritatively shooed her away.

Lila beamed at the offer. "No. Not much to do around here. Tom putts around the house most all day, and I cook. Tom can't stand the sun too long, so field hands take care of the tobacco crop."

"Thank you again for letting us stay."

"I hope you and your husband stop in on us again." She hesitated, her mood becoming solemn. "We don't get many visitors out this way."

Payton offered a smile.

"Good night."

"Good night."

"Almost forgot. Your husband said to draw him a bath."

Draw him a bath? She could just picture Adriano wearing an arrogant grin, telling Lila to pass on the message. She remembered their charade and plastered a complacent smile on her face. She was his dutiful wife today.

"You make a handsome couple," Lila said. "How long you two been married?"

She kept it simple. "We're newlyweds." She hated deceiving these kind people, but it was best they didn't know the truth.

"I told Tom as much. I can tell by the way his eyes light up when you come into the room." Lila dropped a bombshell and then retreated for cover. "Well, I better let you get dressed."

How did Adriano's eyes light up? She had caught him leering at her soaked-through nightgown several times, but that was lust. She felt him fighting the hunger when he kissed her. True attraction, no. Burning lust, yes. Much like the way her eyes drank up every inch of his body when he wasn't looking. But his eyes didn't light up. Did they? She would have noticed that. Wouldn't she? Besides, stressful, life-threatening situations often blew people's emotions out of proportion, and she'd better remember that tonight while pretending to be his newlywed wife.

She'd been apprehensive enough when they came up with the plan, but when she found out she had to pose as Adriano's wife she'd almost called it off. Almost. Posing as Adriano's wife carried its own risks, but common sense told her she couldn't turn away any help. With Adriano being too sexy for his own good, she'd have a hard enough time ignoring the way her heart sped up when he used his tender charm to comfort her.

It had been a brash and dangerous move, but thank goodness she had jumped into his SUV. Commandeering a car had been the only solution with her options so limited. She'd picked the right man to kidnap. He took her safety personally. She shuddered. What might have happened if he hadn't showed up at the motel when he did?

Angel, Adriano had called her when he tackled her in the backseat. *My angel,* he referred to her as that several times in the living room with Lila and Tom. Men had called her by many cutesy names over the years, but she never believed they meant them. Adriano's earnest, dark gaze confirmed his sincerity. She imagined his friends saw him as a tough, no-nonsense investigative reporter who never backed away from danger. The women probably swooned when he showed his sexy, mischievous grin. He was wild and untamable—she'd glimpsed that part of his personality—but his sex appeal made her consider trying her luck.

If she were an angel, Adriano could be an Egyptian god. Tall, well built, with high cheekbones and a heart-shaped mouth, he was a force to reckon with. He possessed the facial features of an African-American, but the cheekbones and long, silky hair confused the picture of his heritage. Serious lines of determination cloaked his expression when he was on a mission, driving like a professional to elude the hit men, but his patience with her hinted at his passionate side. In bed he would be—

Her cheeks heated with a burning blush.

"Stop it," she scolded herself in the mirror. "When this is over, I'll never see Adriano Norwood again." It was silly to let danger trick her into believing there was some sort of growing attraction between them.

Hot water never felt better to Payton. She sank into the bubble bath, shedding her stress over how chaotic her life had become. She languished in the water, scrubbing dried mud, and tending to her battered feet. The steam opened her stuffy nose and soothed her scratchy throat, combating her cold before it became full-blown.

Jake's resourcefulness amazed her. It was clear by his efficiency that he and Adriano had been in tight spots before. Adriano was probably talking with him now on the satellite phone that Jake had provided, planning the next phase of their trip. They needed to get to Columbia as soon as possible, but putting their hands on the duplicate copy of her calendar was equally important. Something on those pages had Sherman worried. He was too scared to kill her—the easy solution to his problem. He needed to see her, to know what she knew—some knowledge even he didn't possess. She pushed thoughts of Sherman and the murder away and sank deeper in the warm tub. She wanted one good night of rest before the adventure that had become her life returned in the morning.

The Murder

"Hey, you're back," Carter said, barely making eye contact as she approached. "How was the trip?" he asked as Payton went up on tiptoe to press a kiss against his cheek. He slapped a card down in the center of the table, playing nonchalant. He adored her, and she cherished his friendship in a town where she knew very few people not associated with her job. Despite his dark exterior, he had a heart of gold.

"The trip was great." She started giving him the highlights, but his cell rang and he was called away on business needing his immediate attention. He didn't elaborate, and she didn't press. She knew certain aspects of the security business were confidential, just as she wouldn't discuss parts of her work with him.

"Sherman around?" Payton asked the lone remaining man at the card table. The other two had called it a night when Carter left.

"Upstairs. Go on up. He asked about you earlier." The man gathered the discarded cards and began to shuffle and reshuffle them.

Payton knew upstairs meant Sherman was hanging out in one of the suites. He often lingered there when Skye was closed and he was in a deeply reflective mood. Whether or not he wanted to be bothered depended on his mood. Tonight must have been a good night with lots of profit because the guard hadn't hesitated to send her up.

She'd seen Sherman get nasty with members of the staff before, but she couldn't honestly say they didn't deserve it. Running an upscale club came with many headaches and often attracted the wrong kind of employees and visitors. Sherman played the hard-ass to her staff, always reminding them she may give them a second chance but he never would. She'd had her own spirited debates with him, but he never crossed the line with her as he sometimes did with the other employees.

The only time she felt uneasy around him was when he hit on her. The first time had occurred in the back of his limo after entertaining clients at a sporting event. The moment they were alone, he made his move. Challenging her to give in to the feelings he'd seen in her eyes—a projection of his own. Never mind he was her boss: he was married. She didn't get involved with older, married men who held her employment future in their hands. She'd let Sherman down as easily as possible, but it didn't keep him from trying again on several other occasions, this time masked as good-natured ribbing. But she'd seen the way he watched her when he didn't think she noticed. And she'd heard the same rumors everyone else had heard about the man lying beaten behind the club because he had looked at her too provocatively.

If she could accomplish her goals, gain the knowledge she needed, and find financial backers, she could start her own clubs with her own quirky rules, she thought as she came upon the first suite. She heard voices, but they weren't coming from this room. She'd thought the guard had told her Sherman was alone upstairs. She moved down the corridor, testing the doors as she passed to find the suites locked tight. The voices grew louder as she approached the distal end of the floor, past the elevator.

When she was only a few feet away from the last suite, she realized there were two voices and they were angry. She turned to leave, but something Sherman said made her stop.

"I will not lose everything I've built because of you."

Lose everything? If Skye went under, so did her dreams.

She moved to the door, standing to the side of the door-jamb. She peered into the room from the crack between the door and the seal. A big, burly bodyguard stood sentry over the late-night meeting. His back was to Payton, but there was something vaguely familiar about him. She was certain she'd seen him working security at Skye before. Sherman stood a few feet away from a man Payton had never seen before. The man was older, well groomed the way only a lot of money can provide. He wore a tailored suit with shiny shoes and held a black evening coat over his arm.

As animated as Sherman became, the man never backed down. He remained hard and locked in his convictions. Payton had never seen anyone who didn't cower when Sherman became this angry. "You've made a mess of things here, and you're not going to cost me one more cent."

"I told you, I'll fix it," Sherman said, and Payton imagined she saw a bead of sweat roll down his temple. There was a quiver in his voice that said he was in trouble and he knew it.

"It's over." The man began to put on his coat. "Everything. This club. The business. You."

"You can't do this, you old sonofabitch!"

The man flinched as if acid had been thrown in his face. He recovered, his voice as calm and smooth as ever. He stepped closer to Sherman, an aggressive act of intimidation. "You maggot. I made you. I'll destroy you. I had hoped to do this the easy way, but if you want to make it hard, bend over and I'll rip your guts out with my bare hands. You're going to learn to never disrespect me. No matter who you are and how important you think you are to me."

Sherman's fists clenched into tight balls, his body shook, but he didn't speak.

The man turned to the bodyguard. "Get the car."

Sherman turned to the bodyguard, his face a sinister mask Payton had never seen. In a split second, when he thought he would lose everything, he changed into the representative of pure evil. "Get the car, but kill him first."

The bodyguard moved for the first time, shedding his statue-still pose to pull a gun from his waistband. Before the man could utter a word, the gun went off and the man slumped to the floor. The bodyguard stepped up to him and fired several more shots—a soft *pop, pop, pop* muffled by the gun's silencer but booming inside Payton's head.

She clamped both hands over her mouth, trapping the bile inside her mouth. She pressed her back against the wall, her mind an explosion of fragmented thoughts.

"Clean this up," Sherman ordered, his breathing heavy, as if he'd just run a marathon.

Her mind was too jumbled to make sense of what she'd just witnessed, but she didn't need to think. She had to react. She kicked off her heels, snatched them up, and ran as quietly as possible down the corridor. She locked her briefcase underneath her arm, not risking it making a sound as it bumped against her side. She ducked into the stairwell next to the elevator and sprinted down the stairs. When she reached the first floor, she stepped back into her shoes, righted her clothing, and opened the door. She was half the distance to the employee entrance when the guard stopped her.

"Leaving?" he asked, as he checked the doors to make sure they were locked.

"Yeah, I'm tired. Sherman wasn't in his office." *No, not in his office. In the suite. With the dead body.* "I'll catch him tomorrow when I have my presentation finished." Surprisingly, her voice sounded normal.

"Good night."

She stepped lively toward the door but stopped before she opened it. She turned to the guard. "You headed out?"

"Soon as I check the bathrooms." The man casually strolled away from her.

"If I were you, I'd clock out before Sherman comes down."

He turned to her and smiled, happy for the heads-up Sherman was in one of his moods. "Thanks."

Payton was so happy that she reached her car safely, she whimpered a cry. She tossed her briefcase across the seat, jumped inside, and activated the locks on the sports car. She fumbled in her purse, her fingers too cold to feel the sensation of her car keys. Finally, she dumped everything onto the seat and fished out the keys. It took minutes before her trembling hands could connect the key with the ignition. The engine roared to life. She glanced up to where she knew there would be one light on, illuminating the suite where a murder had just taken place.

Her mind had truly been scrambled by witnessing the trauma, because instead of flooring the gas pedal and getting the hell away from Skye, she hesitated. *Sherman had just ordered a murder, and she'd seen his bodyguard do it.* She couldn't just drive away. She sat in the darkened parking lot, frozen, not knowing what to do, but she had to see the guard leave the club. Minutes later, he did, whistling all the way to the corner of the parking lot where his beat-up car was parked. He got inside, turned over the engine, and drove away, seemingly without even noticing her.

Knowing he was safe, she could leave. She cracked the window and took several deep breaths, willing herself to get it together enough to drive. In this condition, she'd be wrapped around the first telephone pole she encountered. She didn't know how long she sat there, willing her foot to lift to the pedal, but the back door of Skye swung open again. She shut off the engine, ducking her head behind the steering wheel.

A big, burly man stepped out, looking left to right. Comfortable he was alone, he took long strides across the lot and got inside a big, dark-colored Cadillac. He pulled up to the back entrance of the club, left the motor running, and went back inside. Seconds later he reappeared with a rolled rug over his shoulder. *A body.* He dumped the rug in the trunk, slammed it closed, hopped back inside the Cadillac, and drove off.

Payton leaned over and puked on the floor of her car.

Chapter 12

Wild sloshing noises pushed Adriano to risk intruding on Payton's privacy. Under the circumstances, he had to check on her. His heart pumped a little harder with each step, his imagination going wild at the possibility of Grazicky having found them. Besides, he didn't want to arouse suspicion with Tom or Lila. His defenses on full alert, he slipped quietly into the bathroom to find Payton asleep, her body jerking in response to the nightmare she was having.

He approached the old-fashioned claw-foot tub, and his penis jumped to attention at the sight of Payton's perfect body submerged in a sea of bubbles. He'd never been one for traditional romance, but he was suddenly converted. He imagined himself naked, slipping into the water with her, doing things, assuming positions it should be impossible to achieve in a bathtub. When her lids flipped open and she looked at him with those beautiful brown eyes straight from the movie *Bambi,* his heart leapt out of his chest and landed in the bottom of the tub at her feet.

She gasped, assuming a protective posture, dipping down into the water until only her head and neck were visible.

"I heard noise," he said lamely.

"Nightmare," she answered, relaxing a little.

"Tell me."

"Well," her eyes darted around the room as if measuring the space and calculating her odds for a successful escape.

Her hesitance brought attention to his tightened posture, closed fists, and stiff jaw. His body bowed with sexual tension. There was no way he'd make it through one night of sharing a bedroom with her without acting on his impulses. He consciously fought the strain of his muscles, wished he had some control over his erection, and eased his stance. It was enough for Payton to begin telling her story.

He found a footstool underneath the sink and positioned it behind Payton as she spoke, settling in to comfort her during the rough parts. "Hand me the washcloth," he told her, noticing the bunched muscles in her shoulders.

Engrossed in getting the details right, she mindlessly handed him the wet cloth. He pressed his hand to her shoulder, tilting her forward to better his reach. He wrung the cloth over her shoulders, the warm water sluicing down her back. Her skin was golden, smooth, and tantalizing, and he had the unexpected urge to taste her.

"Where did you go after the man pulled away with the body?"

"Home. I called my brother, but no one answered. I was so scared." She looked at him over her shoulder. "I didn't know what to do."

"Shock would still have most people glued up against the wall."

She seemed to need his forgiveness. She offered him an unconvincing smile, but the knots of her shoulders were softening.

"When I stopped shaking and puking, I went to the police and reported what I saw. They were hesitant about believing me, and when they didn't find a body, *I* became the suspect. For filing a false police report. One of the detectives overheard and came into the interrogation room. As soon as he heard Sherman's name, he jumped on the phone and had the assistant DA there. It was enough to search the club."

"There was no body. What made them believe you?"

"Forensics checked for blood and found traces on the carpet in the suite. There were also specks on the wall and furniture. Someone had tried to clean it away."

"Blood-splatter experts can find the smallest drop of blood in the most hidden places."

She nodded. "That's what the detective said."

"So there was enough blood to raise suspicion and lend credibility to your story. Did the police do DNA testing to identify the murder victim?"

"They had no DNA to match it to."

"Which means whoever Grazicky killed has not been reported missing yet." Adriano filed the information away, more pieces to help solve the puzzle. "I've been thinking about your planner and why having Grazicky's calendar might be significant. Even after he reprimanded his assistant, he let you just walk into the office and write down his calendar?"

"No. Sherman usually scribbles the meetings on paper and gives it to the secretary to put in his calendar. The secretary files the originals because he accused her once of omitting an appointment—it saved her job. She always gave me the discarded originals. I put them in my calendar and then replace them in the secretary's folder."

"Always? It always went this way?"

"Yes. Well, mostly. Lately, I've been really busy with Miami Skye so I've been a little behind in transcribing Sherman's schedule. I have a few months' originals folded inside my backup calendar." She was watching him, reflecting his excitement in her own eyes.

They needed to get their hands on her planner. "Where do you keep this calendar? Exactly."

She told him about the fireproof safe hidden in the floorboard of her coat closet.

His mind whirled, trying to sculpt something out of the small amount of evidence they had.

"Adriano," Payton said, bringing him back to the present.

When his mind returned to the present, he realized the washcloth had been lost and it was his bare hands stroking up and down her spine.

"I'm ready to get out."

His eyes locked on hers, debating if he should climb into the tub with her. Jake was right. He'd fallen for a pretty face and lost every drop of his objectivity.

"Adriano?"

"I don't kiss women often. Too intimate." Why had he just admitted this to Payton? It was his unwritten rule, and not even Jake, his friend and partner, had ever heard about it.

Her eyes roamed his face, unreadable.

"The kiss with you. I meant it." He looked away, severing their connection. He wasn't prepared to handle the level of intimacy he felt with Payton, yet he wanted more. He needed a deeper connection. A bond shared by lovers who are planning for a future of growing old together. He stood and left the room, closing the door behind him.

Adriano felt as if he were falling through pitch-black darkness. His body accelerated against his will, and he felt sure he'd slam into the pavement at any second. Stark fear moved through him as the wind beat against his face. Suddenly the terror disappeared and was replaced by a serene calm that materialized in bursts of pink and blue butterflies, and he accepted his impending death with honor.

If you die, Adriano, who will look after me?

The pavement appeared again. His arms and legs flailed wildly. He couldn't die yet. Payton needed him. His eyes flew open, and he was underwater. *Falling? Drowning?* He jerked upright, sending water over the rim of the tub. He choked and coughed, trying to reorient himself. The small farmhouse bathroom. The tobacco plantation. The old albino, and his doting wife. Black car chases. Payton Vaughn. Beautiful, courageous Payton Vaughn.

He climbed from the tub and drained the water, using a towel from the hamper to clean up his mess. *What was with the dreams? And why did they always involve Payton?* He had never been a man who experienced many dreams—he could recall them all, they were so few—but since meeting Payton, every time he closed his eyes she was there, traipsing through his mind.

If you die, Adriano, who will look after me?

He used the back of his forearm to clear the fog on the mirror. What arrogance had possessed him and made him believe he could save Payton? Why couldn't he do as Jake suggested: get the story, take her to the authorities, and watch the trial on Court TV? Somehow, he'd let a pretty face get him tangled in a mess he might not be able to handle. But it was more than a pretty face, wasn't it?

Growing up Catholic, Adriano had been taught by his parents to pray every night. Above the altar where he kneeled between his brother and sister hung a painting of Jesus in a jeweled chair with two angels at his feet. When he saw Payton's face for the first time, the picture had popped into his head. More than a resemblance to the picture, Payton's aura was pure and good—like that of an angel.

Adriano slipped into his pajamas and pulled the drawstring around the indentation of his waist. He brushed his hair back and secured it with a rubber band. He laughed at his reflection in the mirror. "There is no divine power at work here. If Jake had been on time at the Adam's Mark, I wouldn't have been in the parking lot and some other sucker would have been carjacked by Payton Vaughn."

Don't lose your head over this woman. Keep her safe—as you promised—and then get back to your own business. Useless words. His heart wanted her more than his mind could justify. He knew the consequences, but they didn't matter anymore. Getting Grazicky locked up was important, and his breaking the story would be a big part of it. But he was a man, and Payton was a woman. When the publicity from the story ended, where would their lives be? They would be irrevocably changed, and right now he couldn't imagine returning to Chicago and never seeing her again.

Adriano moved down the hall to the bedroom he would share with Payton. Lila had placed a tray outside the door with two slices of chocolate cake. He vaguely wondered why Payton had not gotten it before lifting the tray and entering their room.

"Why didn't you pick up the tray?"

Payton lay in a small knot on one side of the bed. Lila's gown covered her shoulders but was too short to completely cover her thighs. The nightclothes Jake had bought were purchased with a male state of mind, and although Adriano highly approved, Payton's eyes went wide at the scraps of material. He marveled over the beauty of this woman as he studied the smooth curves of her legs.

She must be exhausted after the past two days, he thought. He'd need her strong and rested for the long days ahead of them. He placed the tray next to the bed, where he noticed an open bottle of cough syrup. She'd caught cold wandering down the highway, half naked in the pouring rain. She didn't move when he unfolded the blankets at the foot of the bed and covered her, careful not to wake her. He couldn't resist the urge to place his hand next to her radiant skin. He softly rested the back of his hand on her cheek but she jerked away when he touched her. He tested the temperature of her forehead.

"Payton?" He gently shook her shoulders. "You're burning up." She shifted, her eyes at half-mast.

His mind raced through a million scenarios. She had pneumonia. She took too much cough syrup. Lila and Tom the albino had harmed her while he slept in the bathtub. Frantic, he climbed onto the bed with her, shaking her until her eyes lazily opened. "Payton, are you all right?"

She moaned, "Yes."

"You're burning up."

Her eyes fluttered closed.

Adriano left the bed, pacing a tight circle in the middle of the tiny room. He was helpless. Could he place his trust in Tom and Lila? He really didn't have a choice, did he? Mr. Conners never would have sent them to the couple if they were anything less than honest and trustworthy . . . but Grazicky had a lot of money and was deadly. The couple had been so nice to them . . .

Remembering their charade, Adriano pulled up the pallet where he had planned to sleep and stuffed it into the closet. He took to the stairs with heavy steps that seemed to shake the foundation of the house.

Tom's head jerked up when he bounded into the living room. "What is it?"

He hesitated only a minute. "There's something wrong with Payton."

Tom and Lila jumped up from their chairs. Lila, lifting the front of her dress as she ran, shot up the stairs. Adriano and then Tom followed. The men stood back as Lila kneeled next to Payton. She called Payton's name, softly, calmly.

"Do something to help her." The plea sounded desperate to his own ears.

Lila's plump hand rested against Payton's forehead. "My God, this child is burning up. Tom, get me the thermometer."

Tom hurried off and quickly returned, shaking down the mercury of the thermometer. Adriano stood helplessly by, waiting for his orders from Lila. She held the glass stick up to the light, shook it again, and then encouraged Payton to open her mouth. She checked her wristwatch several times before determining the themometer was ready to be read. She held it to the light again, frowning at the reading.

"What is it?" Adriano was anxious, on the verge of an explosion. His heart was racing. He could drive strategically, escape hit men and rabid FBI agents. He could shield her body with his, but he didn't know a thing about taking care of someone who was physically ill.

"One hundred and two."

"Should we take her to the hospital?" Tom asked his wife.

"Yes, the hospital," Adriano said, and then remembered their situation. "We can't."

Tom and Lila watched him suspiciously.

"No insurance. Our finances are thin."

"Tom, call the doctor."

"No doctors!" Adriano shouted, stopping Tom. "Payton has a phobia about doctors." He had aided in her escape from the Adam's Mark and helped her outrun paid killers. Now he was in danger of losing her to a militant summer cold. His mind formed a string of "I-should-haves."

The old couple didn't question his bizarre behavior. Evidently, Mr. Conners had explained enough of their situation for them to know if Adriano didn't want to take Payton to the hospital, it was for good reasons.

Lila remained the rational voice. "We could try to bring her fever down. She's sluggish because of the fever."

"And the cough syrup." Adriano grabbed the bottle and held it out for Lila's inspection.

She nodded, not commenting on the medicine. "Tom, turn on the shower in our bathroom. Adriano, help me get your wife into the bathroom. If this doesn't work, we'll *have* to take her to the emergency room."

Swiftly, he scooped Payton's small frame up from the bed and followed Lila into the bathroom. Payton's eyes fluttered, and she mumbled a few words in protest. He sat her on the edge of the tub as Lila directed. Tom left them alone, not venturing far from the other side of the door.

"Get undressed and get in the shower with her," Lila

explained as she turned on the water. "I'm not sure she can stand without your help. We don't want her falling."

Adriano nodded, keeping a steadying hand on Payton as he tugged at his undershirt.

"Tom and I will be right outside. Call if you need me."

"She'll be all right?"

Lila rubbed his back. "We need to get the fever down."

The hypnotic urgency of water beating against tile propelled Adriano into action. He pulled at the drawstring of his pajamas, letting them fall in a pool at his feet. He coaxed Payton to stand and hesitated at the appropriateness of his undressing her before slipping the gown over her head. It was foolish to let modesty interfere when her fever blazed out of control.

"What?" Payton mumbled as he helped her under the spray of tepid water. "What are you doing?"

He held her around the waist from behind, encouraging her to rest her weight against him. "Wake up, Payton," he whispered next to her ear.

If you die, Adriano, who will look after me?

If you die, Payton, whom will I care for?

Payton slowly began to rouse. Groggily she asked, "What are you doing, Adriano?" She whipped her head right and left to avoid the water.

He turned her around to face him, bringing her body close. "You have a fever." He wrapped his arms securely around her waist, holding her upright.

Payton's lashes slowly lifted, and she looked up at him. "I'm so tired." Her arms went around his waist, and she rested her head against his chest.

As the intimate places on her body touched his, Adriano realized for the first time they were *naked . . . together* in the shower. She was totally exposed and vulnerable. Pulling his body away—separating them by inches—would be appropriate, but he couldn't will himself to move. He had wanted to do this since pinning her to the backseat of the SUV. Chemistry was simmering between them, and as they stood nude in the shower, the intimate spray cranked it up to a boil for Adriano. Their bodies fit together better than matching puzzle pieces. The water passing over her breasts, off his abdomen, warmed with his desire. It felt natural—even though he should be ashamed—when he hardened and pressed against Payton's belly.

Lila knocked at the door. "Are you all right in there?"

Adriano cleared the lust from his throat. "We're fine."

Payton stirred in his arms. She looked up at him with a trembling bottom lip. "I'm really cold. Can we get out now?"

Chapter 13

The murder of an FBI agent wasn't news in Chicago, a city crammed with so many newsworthy stories the odds of a reporter getting the front page was rare, but in Charlotte the story was breaking news every fifteen minutes on every television station on the tube. Jake watched the reports, hoping there was a television in the house where Adriano was staying. He was on the phone within minutes of the first report, tapping into the *Chicago City* newspaper's affiliate stations until he found a reporter who could give him off-the-record information.

"Give me an endorsement with your editor, and I'm an open book," Ethan said over the phone.

"Done, and I'll throw in a Chicago-style pizza when you're in town."

"It went down at Bentley's on 27. Know it?"

"No." The only club he and Adriano had visited was Skye, and they had been relegated to the first floor with the other common folk. Even their semicelebrity status as investigative reporters couldn't get them to the second level.

"Swank restaurant Uptown. The official story is the agent was having dinner with his wife when two thugs tried to rob the place. He intervened, was shot, and is now a hero."

"Unofficially?"

"The agent was having dinner with his mistress. When they left the restaurant and were waiting for the valet to pull the car around, two thugs with automatic weapons took him out in a drive-by shooting."

"Do you have a description of the agent?"

The description closely matched the one Adriano had given for the man hiding in Payton's apartment. It took Jake two seconds to put the pieces together. Grazicky's FBI agent had failed in his job and was put down. He couldn't afford to have another witness running around.

"This ring your bell?" Ethan asked.

"Maybe."

"I was working an angle, but my editor shut the story down after Sherman Grazicky made a visit to his office."

"Why would Grazicky want to kill this story?" Jake asked, already knowing the answer but not knowing how much Ethan knew.

"It should've been news at eleven, but like I said, my editor killed the story. The police chased the gunmen. One got away, but the other was shot to death. He was a guard at Skye."

"The police shot him?"

"They're not admitting to it. The officers on the scene say they never fired a shot, but the man was dead inside the car. The bullet was from a police-issue. Ballistics is pending. If they didn't shoot him, who did?"

"Who's the guard?" Jake jotted down the name and description, intending to ask Payton about him later.

Grazicky had to get rid of the FBI agent, and now he was gunned down in a drive-by outside a fancy restaurant. The guard from Skye was probably hired to do the job and then became too much of a liability to keep around. Or the guard knew too much and was dead before the drive-by took place. Either way, Jake smelled a setup.

Grazicky was closing his ranks.

Jake had to get his hands on Payton's planner before Grazicky did.

"If I get a lead, I'll give you a call."

"What about that endorsement?" Ethan asked.

"Anytime. Contact me through the paper." Jake disconnected before he said something to pique the reporter's deeper interest.

He pulled his wallet from his back pocket, flipped it open. A wide smile spread across his face as he stared at the picture of his wife cuddling their little girl. His girls. The loves of his life. After the stint in Baghdad, he'd promised his wife he wouldn't take foolish risks. She worried about him when he was away on a story, all contact severed to maintain his focus and keep his liabilities hidden.

"Baby, if you knew everything Grazicky has done . . . What he's capable of—" He kissed the picture. "You'd want to help Payton put him away."

He grabbed his jacket, a mini-flashlight, and other spyware he'd need, including a sleek metal piece that would make quick work of the locks on Payton's door. He made his way to the lobby, stopping at the front desk.

"Lock these in the hotel safe," he told the manager. He handed the man a small canvas bag with his wallet and other identifying pieces of information. If he were caught, he had several aliases he could assume. He didn't want to lead Grazicky's thugs to his family. Or reveal his connections to the newspaper. Also inside the bag was a letter to his wife, written the day after he was married, telling her how much he loved her . . . in case he ever encountered a mission that took him away from her for good.

Finding Payton's apartment complex proved difficult. His unfamiliarity with Charlotte didn't help, but the apartment was tucked away at the end of a tangle of one-way streets and crossroads with the same name. How could he be on the corner of Peachtree and Peachtree? He was tenacious, determined to get to the planner, so he continued to drive until he found the address.

After parking the car a few buildings away, the first thing Jake did was unscrew the light bulb over her front door. He wasted no time picking the lock. He searched her place in the dark, checking for any intruders. Satisfied he was alone, he began searching for the planner. He started in the obvious place: the makeshift office in the second bedroom. Of course, Payton wasn't the normal club manager, and after an hour of looking he hadn't found the book.

Jake took a different approach, changing his thinking to that of a woman. More precisely, his wife. Where were her little hiding places she thought he knew nothing about? He knew every one and kept a constant vigil on each, maintaining an inventory of the hidden contents. Yes, he'd read every letter from old boyfriends she kept stashed underneath the stairs. She had four hundred and fifteen dollars tucked away in the toilet tank of their daughter's bathroom. He never challenged his wife about this behavior; he knew it stemmed from a tumultuous childhood, and if it made her feel better, he wouldn't disrupt it. But he wouldn't be a victim of surprise in his marriage or his home. Somehow he felt she knew he snooped, but she never confronted him. Despite their dysfunctional behaviors, they loved each other and their marriage was working, so why push it?

"Thanks, baby," Jake whispered as he pulled away the floorboard in the front closet. He removed a fireproof safe, made to keep documents from burning and not theft. Breaking the lock was easier than getting through the front door.

He leafed through the contents of the safe and felt the same passing pang of guilt he felt when checking his wife's hiding places. With the same resolve, he pushed it away. There was a purpose here. He held the mini-flashlight between his lips as he flipped through family pictures, award certificates, and other trinkets. She kept her vehicle registration, insurance papers, and apartment lease here. He constructed a model of her life from these things. It struck him there were no love letters, pictures, or tiny stuffed animals from past lovers. Other than the aging family pictures, Payton appeared to have no personal life. Like Adriano, she'd made her work her life.

There were several appointment books and planners in the safe, dating a year back. No time to read them all—he'd spent too much time searching the apartment. He stuffed as much of the safe's contents inside his jacket as possible. He returned the safe to its hiding place, righted the closet's contents, and made his way out of the apartment.

He noticed the nondescript black car three miles away from Payton's apartment. If he turned off the main road, they would make their move, ambushing him. He had learned drive-bys were a favorite method of attack. He drove until he found the freeway, taking the first entrance. The car followed, maintaining a discreet distance.

A fine sheen of perspiration dotted his brow. He'd just popped up on Grazicky's radar, and the people who irritated Grazicky were ending up dead. If this had been his town, he would know the nearest safe house, informant, or connection to go to for help. He had an emergency route permanently mapped out in Chicago. He knew very few people here.

He thought of his wife and little girl, steeling his resolve. Adriano was in the field, depending on him. Payton was counting on them both. Society needed him most—to rid the streets of trash like Grazicky.

Charlotte Douglas International Airport—the sign provided him with an immediate plan. He followed the signage, falling in line with the airport traffic. He parked the car illegally, but he couldn't chance being caught in the parking garage alone. The black car was several lengths behind, pretending not to watch him. He mixed into the crowd, following the flow to the ticket counter.

"Chicago, one way," he told the ticket representative.

Chapter 14

Payton came awake slowly to a darkened room, her memory returning in tiny slivers. Her life unraveled in quick flashes of detail, culminating in the shower scene with Adriano. She was drowsy, her body a little battered, but all things considered she was feeling okay. She was in bed now, safe and warm, and not alone.

Adriano's front pressed firmly against her front, and his arms encircled her, holding her captive. Payton boldly assessed Adriano's shadowy profile. His attention was focused on the news broadcast's report on what had been christened "The Massacre at the Mark." Why were they sharing a bed? He flipped the television remote over and over in his palm. He was a handsome man—very sexy. She wanted to press her lips to his fairy kiss. His silky hair flowed across the pillow, matching the thick bushes that made up his eyebrows. She wanted to slide one of her fingertips over the bushes, settling an overwhelming desire to touch him.

Why were they lying in bed together? He was supposed to sleep on the pallet. She remembered the shower pelting her naked body. Adriano had held her from behind, devastatingly nude.

Wrapped in his arms now, with him gently massaging

her, her brain became attuned to every move he made—and her body liked it very much. She melted into his muscular chest. He smelled like the rain forest: fresh and woodsy and mysterious. He took her breath away.

"Are you awake?" Adriano lifted his palm to her forehead. The gesture seemed too familiar. During her impersonation of Sleeping Beauty, he had claimed the right to touch her. He propped himself on one elbow, looking down at her. He swept his mane over his shoulder. "Can you hear me, angel?"

"Why are we in bed together?" she asked, keeping her voice low to hide the tremulous effect he had on her.

Adriano's lashes flickered embarrassment. "You scared me. You had a fever," he whispered. "You've been asleep for a day."

"A day?" She questioned the bizarre possibility of it.

"Tom and Lila have been keeping a close eye on you." He shifted, looping an arm over her hip. Tranquility wrapped her in the warm cocoon of his body. His long legs surpassed hers, rippling cords flexing against her thighs.

"Why are you holding me?"

"I couldn't keep my hands off you." His voice mesmerized, and his words mixed with the cool night's breeze to carry her to new altitudes.

"How long have we been this way?"

"Angel," he said, sexual frustration written in every syllable. "It doesn't matter."

His hand came up to grip her shoulder, and he pulled her down onto her back. Shirtless, he was sinful temptation. Roughened around the edges, polished in all the right spots, he had a body meant to be a woman's dessert.

He cupped her cheek. "This is the absolute wrong thing to do." He inched closer, nudging her nose with his.

"Why do it?"

"Do you think I can stop myself?" he answered, his lips brushing her cheek with each word. If possible, he moved closer, the nightgown separating them becoming intrusive.

"You don't have to do this to get my story."

"No. I don't." His thumb stroked her cheek, firmly and with purpose. He moved in, his fairy-kissed brow blurring her vision. He pressed his lips to the corner of her mouth, pulling away quickly. He watched her in the darkness. Nature sounds wafted through the partially opened window, transporting them to a different place. Every stroke of his thumb opened Payton's mind to new possibilities.

Her fingers danced over his silky hair. "You have beautiful hair."

"My mother is half Indian."

"What about your father?"

"My father is African-American. There is also Indian ancestry in his bloodline, but it's too far removed to matter."

She tangled her fingers in the soft tendrils, sliding down to press against the nape of his neck.

"Can you stop yourself?" Adriano asked.

No, she couldn't. The first kiss hadn't been a fluke. His teasing near-miss tonight had only reignited her curiosity.

He dipped his head, and something inside her moved. He stilled one breath away from touching her lips, offering her the chance to stop what was next. Aroused beyond belief, she waited for his kiss. He gazed deeply into her eyes, offering a silent apology for how this would complicate things between them.

He started with a light kiss at the corner of her mouth, but it wasn't enough. She exhaled, her lungs emptying with a brief *whoosh*. She kissed him: soft, firm, and demanding. He kissed the opposite corner of her mouth, and it became hard to breathe. He planned to take his time with this kiss, to show her he'd meant what he said about the intimacy of it. He wet his lips before pressing them to hers. Her mouth opened at the feather-light stroke of his thumb, and he delved deeper at the invitation. He tightened his arms around her, and lifted, bringing her entire body into the kiss.

Her arms went around his neck, and he instantly grew hard. His erection pressed against her belly, insistent and needy. The supreme mastery of his mouth made her forget all her troubles. She unleashed her desire for him, and he reciprocated with the grinding of his hips. She chased his tongue with hers, tasting his passion. He ran his tongue across the enamel of her teeth before crushing their mouths together again. When he tried to pull away, she tightened her grip around his neck, and her fervor coaxed him to linger a moment longer.

Adriano gazed down at her as if in a trance. His fairy-kiss winked at her. While he absorbed her essence, silently gauging her reaction, they remained locked in each other's arms.

He licked his lips, preparing for another kiss.

She tightened her arms around his neck.

His mouth opened over hers in an explosion of pent-up passion. His tongue glided over her lips with carnal hunger. They kissed as if they were rekindling a lost love affair.

If possible, her kiss deepened, bringing with it raw emotions that surprised her. Her entire body responded to him. His hand found her thigh beneath the nightgown, and he wrapped her leg around his middle. She pressed forward, lodging his hardness snugly below her navel. A profound heat simmered at the indentation of her belly—the place of impact between her flesh and the tip of his arousal. The heat consumed her body, washing over her in a rush.

"We're horizontal," Adriano said, leaving her mouth unattended for only a second.

And his erection was the size of the Sears Tower.

"Something nice could happen tonight." His palm cupped her breast, offering a preview.

Against all common sense, she arched into his touch.

"I've been wanting to do this since I pinned you down in the backseat of the SUV." He lifted his leg, ready to climb over her. A flash of light stopped him.

"Oh!" Lila said, her hand covering her eyes. "I didn't mean

to—I wanted to check and see—Oh! I'm sorry." The door closed quietly, the sliver of light disappearing and leaving them in enlightened darkness.

Adriano flopped onto his back, his breathing ragged. "Worse than your mother walking in on you."

She couldn't argue.

His head tilted in her direction.

"We need to establish boundaries."

"Boundaries?" Adriano questioned. "Like one of us has to put a chair behind the door before we get into bed?" He hooked his thumb in the cleavage exposed by the dip of Payton's gown.

"This isn't a good idea."

"What? Acting on what we're feeling?"

"Yes."

"I know what you want me to do to you. I know what *I* want to do to you—*all night long.*"

She folded her arms and gave him her most intimidating glare, but he didn't back down.

"Admit it."

"Sharing a bed isn't a good idea. You admit it."

He lowered his voice to a seductive pitch. "Since the beginning, every time I see you, all I want is to pick you up, throw you on a bed, and lick every inch of your body until you beg me to make love to you."

Payton swallowed—hard.

He sighed, rubbing his eyes. "But this is business. Getting involved puts us in jeopardy. It's not a smart thing to do," he added, clearly trying to convince himself.

Still unable to speak, she nodded, looking away, but not before her eyes flickered with disappointment.

The morning came and went, but Jake never arrived. Adriano helped Tom perform minor repairs to the old barn behind the house while Payton worked in the kitchen with Lila. The scene was a little too *Green Acres* for him, but he would do anything he could to help the couple who were taking them in.

By lunch, his senses were on alert, carefully watching all movement in the tobacco fields. The migrant workers came, did their jobs, and left without ever stopping at the house. With so little contact with others, it was no wonder Tom and Lila were lonely.

"Let's go in for lunch," Tom said, wiping the sweat from his brow with the arm of his shirt.

"Right behind you. I want to finish this patch first."

"All right, but come in soon. The sun's hot." The albino tucked his hat on his head and left the shed.

Being in the barn alone was the safest place on the farm for him right now. He lost all control when he was around Payton. He needed to reset, to remember his purpose and get his mind in check. Impossible words. Jake had always warned him about a time when his emotions would cause him to tumble and fall off the casual-relationship band wagon. This was the worst possible time for it to happen. But he wanted what he wanted, and he didn't know how to ignore it.

"Adriano?"

His body responded immediately to Payton's voice. He walked to the edge of the loft. "Up here."

She looked up at him, her eyes a beacon for his heart. "I'm coming up."

"Careful." He kneeled, offering his hand as she climbed the ladder. He took the huge bowl she carried, setting it beside him. As soon as she came within reach, he lifted her the rest of the way. His camera hung around her neck. He was curious as to why she thought he needed it.

"I brought lunch," she said, smiling with pride.

"And my camera."

"Thought you might want to take pictures."

"Are you offering to give another interview right now?" He

knew she disliked talking about herself when the material was going to be used to open her life to the world's inspection.

"Not necessarily," she answered, leaving him even more curious.

He found a comfortable spot and sat to inspect the contents of the giant bowl.

"What have you been doing all morning?"

"I stacked the hay, and now I'm patching the roof." He removed the sandwiches, potato salad, and a jar of lemonade. "What have you been doing all morning?"

"Cooking." She made a funny face. "Baking."

"How's it working out?"

She shrugged. "I'm not much of a cook."

He unwrapped the sandwich and took a big bite. "Good. Thank you."

"Why do they have a barn?"

"It came with the place."

She smiled.

"The horses are at a boarding stable until the barn's repaired. Two. His son left them behind when he moved across country."

"Do you ride?"

"I belong to the Cheyenne River Sioux tribe," he answered, reminding her of his heritage.

She smiled again, dropping down next to him. "I thought Jake would have come by now."

"Yeah." He took another bite of his sandwich.

"Do you think we should call him on the satellite phone?"

Adriano shook his head. As badly as he wanted to know Jake was safe, calling wouldn't be a good move. "If Jake hasn't come or called, it's for a good reason."

"Do you think he's all right?" she asked, her voice tight.

"He's fine. Jake can handle himself. To contact us would put us in jeopardy and reveal where we are."

"That's all?"

He touched her chin. "That's all. Don't worry. If it were anything else, Mr. Conners would find a way to let me know. Jake and I have done this more times than I can count. He'll come through when we need him. For now we'll lay low and be perfect farmhands."

She smiled unconvincingly.

"What are you thinking?"

"A lot of people have died because of me already."

"Really? Because of you? Or because you were brave enough to come forward and tell what you saw? You know, a lot of people would have run away. Or tried to profit from the information. I see it all the time." He leaned over and kissed her cheek. "Don't doubt you're doing the right thing."

She pulled her knees up to her chest, wrapped her arms around her legs, and rested her chin on her knee. "Think you could spend your life here?"

"On a farm? No. There's a reason I don't live on the reservation. I'm a city boy."

"Where are your parents?"

"My parents live on the reservation with my sister and brother. They enjoy it there." He shook his head. "They're practicing Catholics. Doesn't quite fit in with tribal beliefs, but they make it work."

"Diverse."

"You could call it that, or other things."

"How'd that happen?"

"My grandparents moved off the reservation and attempted to fit in. They became Catholic and raised my mother as one. When my parents were married, they moved to the reservation, but continued to practice."

"What was it like, living on the reservation?"

"It's a self-contained society with schools, healthcare, and employment opportunities. We govern ourselves. We have our own laws and tribal council."

"Would you take me there someday? When this is all over?"

He watched her, wondering how wise it was to plan the future.

Payton dropped back in the hay. "It's quiet here."

"You thinking of giving up the glitz and glamour and becoming the daughter Tom and Lila never had?"

"Is this a reporter's question?"

"Adriano's asking. Not the reporter."

She shook her head. "It's a nice vacation, but I wouldn't want to live here permanently." She became very quiet, the silence swelling between them.

"What?" Adriano asked.

"What happens after I testify against Sherman? When the trial is over, the story has been written, what do I do? It's not like I can go back to my job."

Adriano didn't have a good answer for her. His testosterone offered some very distinct scenarios, but he didn't dare consider continuing their relationship long-term. They were such different people with different career paths. Being together would require one of them to move. He'd made a comfortable home and a good living in Chicago. Moving wasn't on his radar. Relocating would be too much for Payton with all the stress of what she was currently going through. He could never ask it of her. The fact he was even trying to find a solution that would allow them to indulge their attraction spoke volumes. This was unfamiliar territory for a man who kept a supply of available women always ready to rekindle a noncommittal relationship in every big city—and some foreign countries.

"You have the whole world open to you," he offered. He didn't like the despair reflected in her eyes. "What about your brother?"

"He has his career and his family."

"You'll figure it out," he said. The words were meant to comfort, but they sounded shallow even to him. "You're in a bad place."

She sat up. "Thank you."

"For what?"

"Not offering solutions. For just listening and acknowledging how I feel."

He put the half-eaten sandwich aside and moved closer. He simply couldn't resist this woman. Her unique mixture of tough resolve and innocent vulnerability enticed him. Her unassuming beauty made it hard to keep his hands off her. Stroking her, petting her, kissing her consumed his mind the second she entered his space. He leaned in for a kiss, but Payton pressed her palm against his mouth.

"We had this discussion last night."

When Lila, he remembered with a grimace, had interrupted them.

"We're not horizontal, so there's no excuse," she told him.

"Do we need an excuse?"

"People do things in the face of danger they wouldn't ordinarily do."

"Really? How do you know? I've been in the face of danger hundreds of times, and I've never wanted to kiss my primary source before."

"We'll regret it when things go back to normal."

"You're making excuses, angel."

"I'm keeping a level head."

"Since you jumped in the SUV, we've done things your way. It's time to start doing things my way." He wrapped his fingers in her hair, pulling her to him, not stopping until she was underneath him with their bodies pressed tightly together. He angled his head and leaned in to possess her lips, because complete submission was the only thing that would satisfy him. His tongue probed hungrily, releasing the passion he'd been denying himself.

She let him lead her tongue in lavish designs. She was ice in his veins. Kissing Payton opened him up to a level of intimacy he'd never experienced. He wanted to do anything, everything, to keep her with him . . . to have more of her.

He cupped her breasts, enjoying how her head fell back in an open display of satisfaction. He pressed his lips against the sensitive place between her breasts, kissing her slowly while he fought for control. She smelled like sunrises on the beach and was as soft as expensive leather. He gave up so much control for one kiss. Suddenly, overcome with need, he crushed her to him, groping her body with both hands while bathing her face in kisses.

She was so beautiful, silhouetted by the hay where they lay. How could he not want this woman? How had he fought his attraction this long?

"Adriano?" She was breathless beneath him, and it turned him on immensely.

He cupped her cheeks and answered by pressing his lips to hers. His tongue flickered across her top and then bottom lip until he persuaded her to open her mouth and take him inside.

Chapter 15

Sherman Grazicky paced the tight space of the cheap motel room, stopping to observe the raw fear blotching Hiram's face. "You have no idea where Payton is hiding."

"I've looked everywhere."

"The reporter who helped her get away?"

"The newspaper loaned the SUV to Jake Richards. Kellie and Marvin have been taking shifts watching him. He went to Payton's and then jumped on a plane back to Chicago. Alone."

"Did he take anything from her place?"

"Nothing. We have his line tapped, but he hasn't made any calls to Payton."

Sherman pounced on Hiram, grabbing him up by the collar. "I've paid you a lot of money to get this done." He slapped the bigger man, sending an echo throughout the room. He shoved Hiram away, breathing hard. "If the next time I see Payton is in a courtroom, you die."

Hiram stood silent, his jaw rapidly working back and forth.

"I want her. Here. Now."

"I'll find her," Hiram said.

"What about the last hit? I had to step in and clean up another mess for you. You killed an FBI agent in front of a busy restaurant during the dinner hour?"

"It was the perfect setup. Looked like a random drive-by. And we got rid of the security guard at the same time."

Hiram wanted to remind him the security guard had been at Skye the night he'd shot the man and could collaborate Payton's story. Without the man's body, her story was believable because of the blood found on the scene, but there was still some doubt about what had actually happened and her role in it all.

Sherman was so angry his hands were trembling. "You came very highly recommended, but if you don't clean your act up—and fast—your *career* will be over." He strolled to the door, a powerhouse in a stout body. "If I go to jail, I'll kill you, Hiram. From inside prison, I'll hunt you until I finally send someone to put you to a slow, torturous death."

Hiram was the one taking all the risks, chasing Payton through the back roads of South Carolina. All to keep Sherman's neck out of the noose. He should shoot Payton the second he found her, despite Sherman's instructions to keep her alive. That would hurt the old man.

What was that about anyway? Why was Sherman insisting Payton needed to be brought to him alive when she was the only one—other than himself—who could sign his death warrant? And he didn't mean prison . . . If the right people found out what Sherman had done, and who he had ordered killed, Sherman's life would be worth less than his fake birth certificate.

"If we can't find Payton, neither can the FBI," Hiram offered, hoping to defuse the situation before it went too far.

Sherman choked, sputtering his words. "The best you can come up with is if you can't find her, the FBI won't? Are you *insane?* That stupid comment just cost you your life. You couldn't find a dog in a kennel. You're done!"

Before Hiram could pull his piece and put two bullets between Sherman's eyes, his insurance policy sauntered out from the bathroom, a ratty towel tugged around her middle.

"Please. Close your mouth, Sherman," Cecily said, casually

crossing to the bed. She sat on the crumpled sheets where they had just finished playing wicked games, tossing the handcuffs onto the floor without apology.

"Cecily?" Sherman managed.

She took a smoke from her gold cigarette case and made eyes at Hiram to get it lit. He moved across the room, obliging her every whim. Pleasing Cecily would keep him alive if everything went bad.

"What did Payton witness?" Cecily asked, ignoring Sherman's stunned state.

"Cecily," Sherman glanced at him, "what's going on here?"

"Don't ask obvious questions, Sherman." She crossed her legs, clearly in control of the room. "I monitor my investments, and right now you're the most costly thing I own. Now tell me what Payton has on you, and let's find a way to fix it."

Sherman kept a wary eye on Hiram as he stumbled into a seat in the corner of the cheap motel. Hiram waited, keeping his emotions off his face. He waited to see what lie Sherman would tell, because he couldn't tell Cecily the truth. He crossed the room to stand over Cecily, knowing better than to join her uninvited on the bed.

"Don't make me ask again," Cecily said. She didn't possess much patience. She'd grown up a princess, wealthy and getting everything she wanted and more than she ever needed.

"Money-laundering," Sherman said, and Hiram could see the lie forming in his eyes. "Payton got her hands on the books for Miami Skye. She knows where the money is coming from."

Clever, Hiram thought. Cecily knew the funding for the clubs came directly from her father, and her father's money wasn't clean. She'd want to protect her father, and that would mean joining Sherman in his mission to find Payton.

Cecily wasn't stupid. She looked to Hiram and then Sherman, searching for any sign his explanation might be a lie. Hiram would keep Sherman's secret because he was in deep and he wasn't sure he'd be able to get out alive without Cecily.

"It was Hiram's responsibility to keep an eye on Payton. Look where he got me. The meanest prosecutor in Mecklenburg County has eyes on me."

"Hiram isn't best known for his intelligence," Cecily said, running her hand up Hiram's thigh to cup his crotch.

Sherman flinched, but did not speak.

"Tell me the rest," Cecily demanded.

Sherman completed the lie, weaving in a connection between the guard at Skye and the FBI agent's murder. The story fit nicely with the facts, showing Hiram how expert Sherman was at lying.

"The reporter—Jake Richards—knows something," Cecily said. "Beat it out of him."

Hiram smiled down at Cecily. "Crude and to the point."

"Get your people together and do it," Sherman shouted.

Hiram understood the ground was always shifting in his business. He wouldn't be foolish enough to think sleeping with Cecily would save his ass forever. He nodded in Sherman's direction and made a move to the door.

"One slight change of plans," Cecily said, standing and crossing the room to stand in front of Sherman. "Bring her to *me*."

"Cecily, what are you doing?"

"She knows too much. More than me, and I can't have that. I've been neglectful, not keeping a close eye on what you've been doing at the clubs." Cecily circled Sherman, wrapping her arms around him from behind. "Payton's an intriguing creature, with those exotic eyes and perky breasts." She turned her husband to face her, looking him directly in the eyes when she said, "My husband and I want to play with her before she dies."

Jake needed Adriano. Together they could bounce around ideas until they figured out what was obviously hidden in the pages of Payton's planner. Mr. Conners stepped into his office, his dark suit immaculate. "Got something," he announced.

Jake looked up from the pile of calendars, hopeful he'd finally caught a break.

Mr. Conners closed the door before he went on. "Sherman Grazicky is really Simon Grossman."

"What?"

Mr. Conners handed Jake a photo clearly obtained from a police source. In the picture, a younger Sherman held an identification plaque at chest level. "What did he go to jail for?"

"He has a record of petty crimes in his twenties, but then he started hooking up with old ladies and swindling them out of their money. He married the daughter of a woman who inherited a hotel chain. He got her addicted to drugs and then had her sign over most of her money. By the time the family caught on, she was almost penniless."

"So that's how he started in the drug business."

Mr. Conners pushed his fingers through his silver hair, and it snapped back into place as if it hadn't been touched. "Once he went to prison, he latched on to one of the gangs and learned the trade. By the time he was released, he knew all the players he needed to know to get a little business started. He married Cecily, and then his business began to grow."

"He's using her money." He and Adriano had investigated Cecily thoroughly and couldn't find a connection between her husband and his wrongdoings. They'd assumed her traveling kept her in the dark. "Do you think she knows?"

"From what you and Adriano have told me, no. It wouldn't be the first time a wife doesn't know everything her husband is into."

"I've gone through Payton's books a hundred times. I haven't found anything to incriminate Sherman or link him to the drug business."

"Maybe you're looking for the wrong thing. What've

you got?" Mr. Conners took a seat, going over the calendars with Jake.

"What aren't I seeing?" Jake asked aloud and something clicked. "You said Grazicky got involved with the prison gangs?"

"Yes."

Jake leafed through the stack, finding the latest calendar and pulling out the original, written copy of Grazicky's calendar. "That crafty son of a bitch."

"What?"

Jake held the sheet of paper up, dangling it from his fingers. "How do gang members communicate with the outside world while they're in prison? How do they run their business from behind bars?"

"Their clothing?"

"Clothing is more of a way of identifying which gang they belong to." Jake pulled up a file on the screen of his computer. "Look at this. The Charlotte Bobcats' initials C and B can signify the 4 Corner Blasters. Or the jersey can stand for members of the Imperial Gangsters. But those are street gangs. Prison gangs need a way to chatter without the police catching on."

Jake punched up another screen for Mr. Conners to look at. "It's like the tattoos. Gang members use them for identification, especially if they've been in prison."

"What about graffiti?"

"Graffiti is the newspaper of the streets. Gangs use it like we use the Internet. It's more of a warning poster than a formal means of communication. It marks territory and advertises drugs. I'm talking about how gang members communicate with the outside without outsiders knowing. Similar to hand signs."

Mr. Conners's eyes widened as Jake demonstrated. "Sign language?"

"Throwing gang signs."

"You need vacation time."

"I'll teach you what I just said later, after we crack this story. The Bloods and Crips have developed an entire written alphabet." He clicked on a folder that brought the file up for Mr. Conners to see.

"It looks Greek. Somebody actually developed this whole language in order to commit crimes?"

"If only we used our minds for good instead of evil," Jake said.

"These are the terrorists we should be sending our army after," Mr. Conners added with unmasked disgust. He had a nephew in Iraq, and he wanted him home. Outside of the job-imposed impartiality restraints, Mr. Conners was very anti-war, and he participated in many efforts to get the troops home.

"That's all I know about gangs, so you've got me," Mr. Conners said, not quite catching on. "If they're not using one of these methods, how do gangs pass messages in prison?"

"Gangs develop their own language using symbols. The symbols are embedded in pictures or letters to family and friends. Only other gang members know where to look and how to interpret it. This innocent-looking piece of paper probably has hundreds of lines of writing you and I can't see."

"It's a way to hide evidence in plain sight."

"Payton said Grazicky got very upset when he found out she was copying his calendar, so she started taking the original schedule, copying it at home, and then returning it. She never had the chance to return this one."

"You know someone who can read it?"

"Decoding gang communication is an art."

"You threw those signs pretty well."

"Adriano has gang contacts," Jake said, already standing and making his way to Adriano's desk. "Do we know what gangs populate the prison Grazicky was in? Get me that info and I'll have this deciphered."

"We'll have it in five minutes."

"We're about to bust this enterprise wide open."

"And then we can get Adriano back here."

* * *

Sherman locked himself in his office, watching the clock in dreaded anticipation for Cecily's return home. How much did she know? What had Hiram told her? He was in deep crap. He left his seat and paced the room, searching for a way out. He could pack his bags and leave before Cecily returned home . . . but he couldn't leave all he'd built. It would take time to liquidate his assets and transfer his money to his off-shore accounts.

Knowing what he'd done—whom he'd ordered killed—he picked up the phone and made the call to start his contingency plan rolling. He'd been thoroughly educated in prison. He had learned the art of money-laundering in prison, right after he learned everything he needed to know to build a thriving drug trade. Some of his ex-con buddies were his best customers. His money was invested in businesses all over the state, giving him the perfect cover for the income he generated. His accountant understood the intricacies of the global financial markets, depositing large sums of Sherman's cash in countries with bank-secrecy laws. It was possible to anonymously deposit dirty money in another country, where it waited for him to use it. He called his broker and began the liquidation process. With that in place, he analyzed his next move.

Hiram hadn't told Cecily anything. If she knew . . . he would be dead already.

Hiram was sleeping with Cecily. Sherman was sharing his wife with the help.

Sherman noticed the trembling of his hands when he poured himself a drink. He'd been in worse situations than this. Well, maybe not, but he wasn't the average criminal. He possessed the common sense most didn't.

What needed to be done? *Systematically analyze this,* he told himself.

Staying alive was first on the list. Cecily didn't know what he'd done, but Hiram did and he was her bed buddy. He couldn't leave town without his cash. He would wedge himself between Hiram and Cecily, sticking close to her until this was over and he could make his escape. Cecily was as fascinated with Payton as he was. He'd use her newly uncovered sexual deviance to keep her preoccupied with Payton. They'd experimented in their marriage before. When she returned home, he would take her back to those days.

Staying out of prison was priority number two. Hiram thought he'd bought himself some protection by winning Cecily's favor, but Sherman knew better. Cecily could be ruthless. If Hiram failed to retrieve Payton, he'd be dead. Cecily wouldn't give him the endless chances Sherman had given him. That would temporarily hold Hiram in line, but Sherman would keep an eye on him. He'd get people in place to take Hiram out the moment he started looking shaky.

Destroying the evidence against him was paramount to avoiding prison. He would not go back to that hellhole. He had to take Payton out of the picture. She knew too much. Sherman downed his drink, letting the liquid burn his throat as punishment for his stupidity. Annihilating Payton wouldn't do. His illogical hunger for her hadn't been squelched in all that had happened. If anything, he wanted her more, needing to conquer her to save his manhood.

Cecily wanted her.

He wanted her.

Could he use her before he made his getaway? Did he have the time? The temptation was too much to resist. If he said the right thing . . . touched her the right way . . . maybe she'd leave with him. He could force her along. He'd heard about hostages falling in love with their captors. As he waded through the crap of his life, Payton remained the only good thing in it, and to preserve his sanity, he needed her with him.

Chapter 16

Adriano was a decadent indulgence, and, like any dieter, Payton couldn't stop herself from binging. She crossed the yard, heading to the loft where they'd met at midday for lunch the past three days. She watched a shirtless Adriano riding Tom's son's horse toward the barn, the long tendrils of his hair trailing behind him. His hard work had gotten the barn ready for the return of the two animals much sooner than expected. His skin glistened golden with red undertones. He glanced in her direction, doing a double take when he saw her. She saw the flash of his smile across the distance, her body warming at his anticipation.

She climbed into the loft, knowing he would be waiting for her there. He would question her most of the time they were alone, delving for any information she knew about Sherman. But sometimes he asked about her, focusing on her hopes and dreams for the future. She liked those times best, when he was completely centered on her wants and needs. He had the power to make her forget the trauma associated with why they were there, replacing it with honest affection. She allowed herself this time to pack away her guilt and enjoy their time together without regret. It energized her, strengthening her for the fight ahead.

"Let me interview you for a change," she said, pinching off a corner of the fried chicken leg.

"Shoot."

He told her about his family and his upbringing. He demystified the history of his people. He spoke of the hardships still inflicting those remaining on the reservation. He gave her goose bumps when he became heated, outraged at the current political climate.

"You're more diverse than I believed," she complimented him.

"Thought I was a shallow playboy?"

She smiled, not bothering to deny her initial assessment of his personality. "Why did you go along?"

He raised his fairy-kissed eyebrow.

"You knew I didn't have a weapon when I jumped into the SUV. Why did you drive off?"

He watched her for a long time, clearly deciding whether or not to feed her a smart-aleck line. His eyes danced with the truth, always sparkling with hope and promise no matter the situation.

"Well?" she prompted.

"If I hadn't gone along, we wouldn't be here now."

She let it go at that. She didn't question where they were, or what they meant to each other. At that moment he made her feel like the luckiest woman on earth. She had been forced to abandon her life, but could the circumstances be any better? She was tucked away on a quiet farm with a gorgeous, intelligent, dangerously sexy man who never let her forget through subtle touches and quick quips he was attracted to her.

They became the free labor Tom and Lila needed on the financially challenged farm. They grew into the kids the couple wished still resided at home. Their kindness didn't feel forced. They never pried into why the young couple had needed covert shelter. They incorporated them into the family, welcoming them with every action.

Payton and Adriano continued to meet in the loft of the

barn every day, lavishing in their time together but never letting the seriousness of the situation go unrecognized. Almost a week had passed since they'd last spoken to Jake. Adriano was worried. Payton could see it in his eyes every night when they climbed into bed together. He toyed with calling Jake but knew the silence was purposeful and doing anything blindly was too dangerous. Payton tried to comfort him, reminding him of the stories he'd shared with her of their dangerous adventures. He appreciated her efforts, but she felt the tension in his body as he platonically shared their bed, careful not to impose his needs on her.

Days later, Payton went looking for Adriano at lunch as usual, but he wasn't there. Fright immediately gripped her. He would never leave her. Not of his own choice. If Sherman had figured out where they were . . .

She climbed down from the loft, leaving the lunch behind. Adriano had become a staple in her life, and his absence felt obscene. She raced to the house, her thoughts running rampant. She'd seen what Sherman could do. He would force Adriano to tell him where she was hiding, but Adriano wouldn't give in. He had too much honor. He'd die first. The realization propelled her to burst through the back door of the house. She ignored Tom and Lila's surprise when they jumped up from the kitchen table. She didn't answer Tom's call. Instead, she rushed up the stairs, taking two at a time.

"Angel?" Adriano questioned when she rocketed into the room. He was draped across the bed but sat up and moved to the edge when he saw her. He looked ready to jump up and grab her, but the fear on her face stopped him cold. He spoke calmly, as she'd seen him do with the horses when they were in a skittish mood. "What's wrong?"

She stood in the doorway, her chest heaving from the run, anger, and panic. "You weren't in the loft."

"I wanted to try Jake." He indicated the satellite phone. "It's been too long," he explained.

Standing in the middle of the floor, worked up into a froth, she realized how much Adriano had come to mean to her. Not finding him where she expected him to be had sent her over the edge. In all that had happened, she'd never lost her cool, openly exposing her emotions and showing her weakness. At the height of her terror she remained in control until it was safe to let go. Her actions now were shocking, raw and unrestrained. Massive confusion flooded her brain. She couldn't make sense of what she was feeling. She only understood it was too potent to ignore any longer.

Adriano stood and eased up to her. "Why are you so upset?" He was on full alert now, reading her hypersensitivity and misinterpreting it to have something to do with the danger they were in. He stepped up to her, placing his hands on her shoulders. "Something has happened."

"Yes," she said, inhaling deeply to catch her breath.

"Is everything okay?" Tom asked.

Payton didn't turn to face him. Her gaze was locked on Adriano, trying to make short work of figuring out when she'd fallen for him.

"We're fine," Adriano answered. He moved to close the door, assuring Tom there was no problem. "We need a minute."

The door shut with a soft click.

Payton turned to him.

"What's going on?" Adriano asked.

"I don't know."

He calmly extracted the information he needed. "You said something has happened."

"It has."

"Tell me."

She approached him, coming so close she needed to tilt her head back to look up at him. "I thought you were gone."

Understanding moved over his handsome features. There

was something in those dancing eyes that told her he'd
been waiting for her to catch up with him. Everything was on
the surface, bouncing between them with kinetic energy.
Someone had to make a move—step away, or step out. One
of them had to be the voice of reason.

Before Payton could rein in the wild emotions, Adriano
buried his nose in the hollow of her throat and inhaled deeply,
pulling her body into his.

"Not going anywhere without you," he told her.

"What are we doing?"

"I don't know." He used his finger to lift her chin. "But it
feels natural. Right."

"We should stop."

"Too late." He wrapped her in his arms.

She allowed herself a second of his comfort, but fought it.
No matter how sensual or smart or great Adriano was, enough
people had been hurt because of her. She swatted his hands
away. "Stop it."

His eyes narrowed. He didn't like being forbidden. "You
stop it." He captured her wrists with lightning speed, spinning
her until she was pinned between his body and the door.
"Stop pretending like you don't want me. Not after you came
running in here all sexy and frazzled because you thought I
was gone."

She stood immobilized, excited but uneasy about what
would happen next . . . where it would take them.

He dropped to his knees, keeping his eyes on hers every
inch of the way. He tugged the pullover from the hem of her
shorts and buried his nose in her navel. Her limbs went numb,
and a warm shiver moved through the personal parts of her
body. He inhaled deeply, holding his breath for an impossibly
long time.

Payton pictured it all: him on top of her, sinking his member
into her wetness, driving her crazy. He made her want to ex-
periment with dirty things. Her imagination ran wild, willing

him to take her further than she'd ever gone with a man. She could tell by the way he handled her body he could show her things her mind couldn't formulate. He was a sensual, sexual giant compared to her narrow experience. She had obsessed about this moment since their first kiss. He'd turned her into some sort of sexual addict, hooking her on the potency of his physique. All he had to do was enter the same room and her reasoning became distorted, her mind unfocused. Adriano was more dangerous than she'd realized.

Maybe she would dominate him. Push him back on the bed and make him succumb to her needs. She'd be in control, able to take advantage of his body. She'd cater to him through her authoritative acts, and she would liberate his mind in return. He could be her playground. Touching, kissing, pinching the areas she wanted to rule. How much would he let her do before his ruling nature resurfaced and he took charge? She'd never had these thoughts before, been so turned on by a man's body that she wanted to own it, command it, take control of it.

Her knees buckled, and she wasn't sure she could support her own weight. Adriano's possessive stance rushed at her, flushing her with desire. Most women fantasized about firemen or soldiers—Payton's new number-one fantasy involved the Indian kneeling in front of her on the floor. The heat swirling around them made her lightheaded. She squeezed her lids together, shielding her eyes from the bright explosion of his emotions. His tongue flickered against her navel, and she was never happier she had an outie. Her legs gave way, and she began to slip down against the door.

Adriano clutched her waist and pinned her against the wood. "Payton?"

She forced her eyes open, afraid of what she might see but curious about what would be revealed.

He looked up at her, beckoning. "Do you want me?"

"This has gone too far." Her breathy reply would never convince him of the truth buried in her declaration.

"Kissing you isn't enough anymore."

His speedy hands released her hips and grasped her behind. His fingers danced to her zipper, unbuttoning and unzipping until she was too near exposure. He placed his forehead against her belly, and her fingers loosened the fastening at the nape of his neck. She combed his locks free as he shimmied her shorts down her legs. He slipped his fingers into the seam of her panties and pulled the fabric to the side. His nose pressed into the flesh of her mound, turning his head right and left until he penetrated the slick folds of her vagina. Unable to hold back any longer, his head moved aggressively, with animalistic wildness.

His hands led him back up her body. He used his chest to press her against the door. "You do want me. I smell it all over you."

Not being in charge of the situation or her emotions threw Payton off-kilter.

"Your body is responding to my touch. Desire. Heat. I smell it all, and it's good, so stop lying. You want me."

She watched the feral prowess behind his eyes. Like Adriano, she had lost direction over her emotions. Neither had command over what they were feeling or doing. Her body wasn't hers anymore. It was doing its own thing. She had never been wetter in her life, and it was all because of Adriano's thorough handling. Her nipples were sensitive to the point of pain as they strained against his chest, and she liked the pleasure of it.

Adriano's tongue caressed his bottom lip, teasing her, and he said "I want you" before a rainbow of emotions so bright it threatened to burn her corneas exploded outward from his body. She tried to shield her eyes, but he captured her hands. She tried to turn away, but he forced her head back to look at him.

"Let me go."

"Make love to me." There were no shades of doubt, no

questioning of reasoning in his voice. He wanted what he wanted.

Before she could contemplate an answer, he scooped her into his arms and carried her to the bed. In contrast to his touch so far, he laid her down with the gentleness of a lion carrying its cub. He gave her a feather-light kiss, pulling back to gauge her reaction before devouring her mouth.

All rational thought fled for cover. Payton flung her arms around Adriano's neck, pulling him to her. Their tongues fought for dominance. She pawed at his shirt, slipping it, between kisses, over his head. She felt him grow hard against the length of her thigh and decided she wouldn't analyze the situation. She would go with what her body needed. This wild abandon was so unlike her, which was an aphrodisiac in itself. With no consideration of the consequences, she cupped the crotch of his pants, testing the weight and heft of him in her palm. She opened the clasp, lowering the zipper in heated anticipation of what she would find.

Completely naked, Adriano pounced on her with unchecked recklessness. The pullover and black bikini underwear came off with one tug.

"Thank God you never wear a bra." He dove into her chest, his massive hands easily palming her breasts. Using his thumbs to bring her nipples to life, he fed from her until he could taste the sweet cream their children would someday enjoy. He stopped only when a heady aroma floated to him, telling him it was time to enjoy the vanilla dripping between her thighs.

She arched her back while he inhaled her deeply.

"You smell like vanilla when you get hot," he said. His tongue parted her and searched for her core, easily finding the swollen nub.

Her eyes rolled back as he went to work, diligently tasting every drop, pushing and circling the nub that made her shake and groan. "You *taste* like vanilla," he told her, his hot breath washing over her.

She fought with her emotions, trying to separate lust and love: a losing battle even before Adriano gripped her behind and plunged his tongue deep between her hidden folds, searching for the opening to her vagina. After purging her soul, he lapped up the vanilla-cream reward.

Desperately out of control, she pulled Adriano to her, rolling on top of him to take command.

He wrapped his arms around her and flipped her back down on the mattress, despite her protests. "I'm in charge."

His lips planted fierce kisses across the planes of her body, and the heat swelled, drowning her.

"I want you so badly," Adriano said between guttural moans.

She answered him with a kiss.

He flipped her facedown on the bed, wrapped his arm around her waist, and brought her up to her knees. He bound her wrists within the iron grip of his hands.

"I have to take you this way."

She understood. They had been forbidding themselves too long, and now the sexual beast inside him demanded it.

He pushed her thighs apart and used his hand to guide his hard penis into her softness. He rocked with fierce strokes, pushing his torso against her back until they both fell to the bed. Sinful need dictated his movements as he chased his prize.

Payton pled. "Adriano, please."

He pulled away by inches. Nudging her onto her back, his lips quieted her sensual moans. He crawled between her legs slowly, more controlled but with no less prowess. Advancing slowly, he filled her. He placed tiny bites along her collarbone as her fingers combed his flowing hair. She closed her eyes and let his cottony mane dust her face. He nibbled her ear while flexing his hips. She wrapped her legs around his back, but he pried her loose and helped her hook her ankles around his neck. His hips pinioned, pushing his erection deeper.

"I want you so badly," he confessed. "I've wanted you since I wrestled you down in the backseat of the Land Cruiser. Is this what you wanted? Is this why you make me so damn crazy?" He worshiped her breasts and cupped her bottom, driving deep, oblivious to her breathless answer. He rocked and probed until he found the rhythm sure to send her over the edge.

Her cries of satisfaction released his tension, and he didn't try to hold back his own climax. He plunged his hands against the mattress, lifted his torso from the bed, and began a deep thrusting motion. Rocking in the cradle of her legs, he touched every intimately sensitive area of her body. He swung his hair out of his face with the flip of his head. "I want you so badly, angel."

"Now you have me." Her hands started at his scalp and moved down the ripples of his back. He drove into her bottomless cavern, ecstasy pulling him with magnetic force. He threw his head back as he growled from the pleasure.

Chapter 17

"What the hell was that?" Adriano stared up at the ceiling, panting hard, dripping with perspiration. They lay side by side, hand in hand.

"I think you bit me." Payton examined her shoulders and collarbone. "Several times."

His head snapped in her direction. "I've never felt anything like it. The intensity was mind-blowing."

"You were out of control." Her eyes roamed the perfect form of his naked body. "So was I."

His eyes held an unasked question. Trying to find a rational answer to his animalistic behavior, Adriano asked, "Do you think Lila puts something in the food?"

"We haven't eaten since breakfast."

Both listened to the noises of the workers cultivating the farm.

Breaking the tension, Payton jumped up. "I'm going to shower."

He scrambled to the edge of the bed to catch her around the waist. "Wait." He turned her to face him and pulled her between his iron thighs.

"If you tell me you made a mistake, Adriano Norwood, I'm going to kill you."

"Angel, would you let me talk?"

She thought *he* looked angelic with the long, dark tendrils softly framing the masculine lines of his face. She watched as his eyes drank up her body. After a nerve-splitting minute, she demanded, "Talk, Adriano."

"I don't understand what happened here, and I'm not willing to attribute it to the danger we're in making us react crazily."

She heard the mistake speech coming on. If he tried to pretend their tempestuous lovemaking meant nothing, she would crawl under the bed until it was time to return to the authorities. No matter how much she denied it, her heart had been aching for his touch. To deny her the emotions attached to their encounter demeaned what had taken place and reduced it to common, ordinary sex.

He noticed the slight tremble of her bottom lip and continued his attempt to explain the unexplainable. Always composed and the master of his words, he fumbled, searching for the right thing to say. This was awkward after-sex conversation, and she didn't need it. She'd survived too much over the past few weeks to be taken down by the loss of control of her own emotions.

"Being together night and day," she said, "our minds were bound to become preoccupied with sex. Thinking you were missing sparked something in me, and I lost control."

"You're saying it was a mistake." He splayed his fingers at her waist, gripping her hard, as if he were afraid to let go. "You think it shouldn't have happened."

"No, that's not what I'm saying."

"It's what I'm hearing."

"I should go shower," she said, eager to make a quick escape.

"Dammit, Payton." He released her, crossing the room, placing himself between her and the only exit. For a fleeting moment, jumping out the window didn't seem so bad. She wanted to run away from the heady emotions engulfing them. How could something that felt so good be wrong?

"We have to think this through," Adriano said, pacing back and forth. His long strides took him wall to wall in a matter of a few steps.

"Think about what, Adriano? We slept together."

He stopped abruptly, staring at her with a coldness that chilled her to the bone. "It was just sex? This is what you're trying to lay on me?"

"Well," she hesitated, poised for the lie that did not come. "No."

"Either it was sex for you, or it was something more."

"I can't handle this conversation right now."

"We deal with it. Now." He stationed himself in front of the door, a clear indication this conversation was not over. "This is business. I get that. You're my source for the story of the century. I'm your safety net."

Her anger flared. "Don't make me stand here and listen to your self-righteous speech."

"I'm trying to work this out without either of us being humiliated."

"Humiliated?" She lost power over her bottom lip, and it trembled violently.

"That's not what I meant."

"You're a reporter. Your life revolves around choosing the right words to express your opinions. I don't think you mistakenly chose the word. Do you know what's humiliating? How about giving your body to a man you've come to care about and him telling you 'It's only business.'"

"I didn't mean it that way."

"Say what you mean!"

He responded with his own roar of anger. "Stop playing games, and tell me how *you* feel."

She turned her back on him.

"You're the one who hopped out of bed, rushing to get out

of the room. You're the one implying this was a freak sexual encounter. Now you care about me? Which is it, Payton?"

When she didn't answer, he approached. She moved away, but not fast enough to avoid the span of his arms. He roped her and pulled her in.

"Let me go."

He sat down, pulling her onto his lap. "Quiet, angel." He waited until she relaxed against him before he spoke again. "This can't be a mistake."

She looked into the depths of his eyes, and all was lost. She was helpless against giving him the truth. "I was scared out of my mind when you weren't in the loft. More than being afraid Sherman had gotten to you, I was terrified you had left me."

He rewarded her honesty with a kiss.

"What do we do now?" she asked him.

"Let's make love nice and slow."

"I think you bit me."

He laid her gently on the bed, spreading her arms out from her body like angel wings.

"You're not sure?" Mischief sparkled in his eyes. He lifted her leg over his shoulder and bit his way to her sex-soaked mound. "This time I'll do it so there's no question how I feel afterward."

She shivered with every nibble. Liking her response, he pulled the delicate skin between his teeth and placed his mark of passion on her thigh. She writhed from the intense suction in such an intimate place. His expert moves stirred erotic wishes she had never dared fantasize about.

He lifted his head, smiling proudly at the purple-black mark of possession. He slipped his hand beneath her and cupped her plump bottom while he drew a field of butterflies on her right thigh. Each nibble sparked new desires. Each flick of his tongue gave her the right to react more brazenly to the sensation.

He loomed over her. "Any doubt you've been bitten?"

"None."

He kissed her lips, making her hungry for the caress of his tongue. "Can I taste you again?" His hands cupped her breasts while his lips applied suction. He teased her nipples, pulling her nectar from deep within, draining her to depletion.

He smiled down on her.

He licked his lips.

His hand went to hers, and he guided her across the topography of his body. She took him firmly in hand, helping to measure the correct amount of pressure to apply. She stroked him long, slowly, savoring every twitch of his fairy-kissed brow. Her hand gyrated between his thighs. A profound howl escaped the depths of his being. She kissed his chest from her vantage point below. She fondled, bringing him to the full length and hardness she preferred. Adriano returned the favor with the salacious stroke of his fingers between her thighs. She pulled him to her, opening herself to his penetration. Diving in several times, they erupted in an explosion enfolded in butterfly kisses.

At three in the morning, Payton placed a bunch of purple grapes on Adriano's abdomen and fed them to him one by one.

"Did you date in Charlotte or Miami?" This was an area of her life he'd carefully avoided in his questioning. He'd never strayed from the details of Sherman's business. Tonight, after spending the day in bed, he felt emboldened.

"Adriano, are you still trying to *get the story?*" She peeped up at him. "You've gotten everything I have to offer."

"Yes or no?"

"Casually." She fed him another grape.

He folded his arms underneath his head. "I love my work. Jake and me in the midst of danger, hunting for a story, outsmarting other reporters—it gets my blood boiling. I've only recently started photographing our assignments. We couldn't find a photographer who could keep up with us, and I always wanted to learn, so it all came together."

Payton ran her fingers through his hair. "It sounds like you're apologizing for something."

"You won't be able to go back to Skye. What will you do?"

She hated the question. He sounded too at ease in the finality of their association. He'd asked her several times before, and the answer was always the same. "I don't know. I'll have to start over."

He wrapped her in his arms. "This has to be hard for you. I can't imagine giving up my career. Everything I've worked for in the blink of an eye." He kissed the top of her head. "I'll help you think of something. What else do you like to do?"

She buried her face in the crook of his neck. "No more questions tonight, Adriano."

"I didn't mean to upset you, angel."

Thinking of the future was too much to bear. She wanted to wallow in the present. Lie in his arms on the small bed eating fresh fruit off the taut ridges of his stomach until dawn. Dream about the unattainable future she wanted to have with him.

The lump throbbed in her throat. Adriano had become her strength. When he walked away, she would collapse. She questioned if fear of Sherman's retaliation made her feel this way. She knew otherwise. Adriano had looked past her tough exterior and explored the untapped chambers of her heart. Imagining a day without him following her around, snapping pictures with his camera and hammering her with questions about her life, made her whimper in his arms.

He stroked her cheek with the back of his hand. "I'm sorry, angel. If I could have known you before all of this, I would have kept you out of harm's way."

She snuggled closer, trying to lose herself in him.

The certainty of his voice gave way to husky emotion. "Life is so damn unpredictable. Sometimes things happen, and it takes years for us to understand why."

"Us?" she managed around the tightness in her throat.

"Us. Why now? Why in the middle of so much chaos did we meet?"

"The reporter in you is rationalizing. Why can't this be about needs, emotions?"

Opting not to answer, he placed a tender kiss on her forehead. "When this is over, you'll be fine." He tried to lighten the heavy emotion cramping the room. "You were tough enough to kidnap me. You're tough enough to survive anything."

"Can I?"

"Yes."

She burrowed deeper into him so he wouldn't hear her desperation. "Can I survive my heart shattering when I walk away from you?"

Chapter 18

Jake made his way back to Charlotte under the elaborate ruse of investigating the Charlotte school system. Like a lot of systems in the country, there was much turmoil about its running, but it was in a particular mess. The voucher system was set to begin, and local opposition groups were still fighting it in court. A swarm of entry-level reporters had come to town to cover it, but a few national papers were on it too. He slipped into town quietly but wasn't foolish enough to think eyes weren't on him—or soon would be.

Returning was dangerous, but he'd been out of touch with Adriano for too long. If they didn't make contact by the tenth day, Adriano would activate their long-standing contingency plan and go deep underground. The last time this had happened, it had taken Jake over a month to ferret him out of hiding.

Things were coming together on the case, but there was still more to find out. Jake had found a gang member with ties to the gang Grazicky had associated with while in prison. The man was interpreting the combination of symbols and letters now. Jake had hoped for an immediate response, but the gangs frequently changed their code to keep the police confused, and Grazicky's coding was from long ago. It would take a little time to have it deciphered.

Skye was set to reopen soon. Grazicky's lawyers had finally won their case, and the police were being forced to vacate the premises and let him get back to work. Any evidence they hadn't found yet would be lost.

Before making contact with Adriano, Jake moved into a hotel and closely observed his surroundings. He made friends with the kitchen staff and housekeepers but avoided becoming familiar to the front desk. If anyone came asking, he'd be too nondescript for the front house workers to remember. The people working the kitchen always knew who was who in the hotel, and the maids knew who had money to throw around. They also had passkeys to every room, which might come in handy.

After visiting the kitchen via a back hallway, Jake ordered his dinner and left the hotel. He took a quick walk around the theater district of Uptown Charlotte, looking for anything—or anyone—out of place while he waited for his meal to be cooked. He missed his wife and little girl immensely, but Adriano needed him in Charlotte. The vigorous walk did very little to shake the need to hold his wife tight and to make love to her. He headed back to the hotel, anxious to call his family. He'd been very careful when contacting them. He only used pay phones—when he could find an operational one. Otherwise he purchased disposable cells, kept the calls short, and discarded the phone during his evening walk.

"Shoot!"

Jake stopped outside the revolving door of his hotel. A pretty woman wearing a cherry red leather skirt and jacket with a drop-dead figure struggled with a bag of groceries beside her Lexus.

"Shoot." She looked around. Catching his eye, she smiled. "Can you help me? Please?"

Jake melted at her lopsided smile and southern twang. His misplaced lust told him he needed to get home to his wife sooner rather than later. He tucked his hotel room key into his pants pocket and went to help the woman in distress. "Let me take your bag."

"No, I have it. Take my keys." She angled her body so Jake could see the key ring dangling from her fingers. "If you open the back door, I can put these groceries inside."

He aimed the keyless remote at the trunk. "Wouldn't you rather put them in the trunk? This is a gorgeous car. You don't want to chance messing up the leather seats."

"No. The trunk is already full." Her mouth curled up into a radiant, innocent smile. "I have one vice—shopping."

He punched the button, setting off a chirping sound and unlocking the car. He opened the door and turned to relieve the woman of her load. He stooped down to place the groceries on the seat. A big, bulky man wearing a skullcap gripped a gun in his beefy hand. He pressed the barrel to Jake's forehead. "Invite us up to your room."

Blistering pain ricocheted through Jake's skull when he opened his eyes. He blinked, trying desperately to recover his memory. He'd been knocked out plenty of times in the past, and each time it became harder to recover. For the first time in his career, he wondered if he was too old to keep doing this. He turned his head and was greeted with more pain. His vision cleared enough to see he was in a hospital and Mr. Conners was sitting next to his bedside.

Mr. Conners righted the dark brown Dobbs covering his silver hair. Cautiously, he leaned closer. "My God, Jake."

"It looks worse than it is." Jake tried to laugh, but the skin tears near his mouth made him flinch.

"The doctor says you're lucky you got away with only a broken arm. It took twenty stitches to sew up the cuts on your face."

Jake's hand went up, finding evidence of Mr. Conners's claim.

"With all the lumps and bruises, they want to keep you for a while and do more tests. You look like a beaten ripe tomato."

"Don't forget my wounded ego."

Mr. Conners pulled his chair closer.

"Don't take this to my wife," Jake insisted. "No use worrying her. I'll explain everything when I get home."

Mr. Conners nodded. Looking at the jagged scars on Jake's face and the bruises covering the rest of his body, Conners knew his star reporter was lucky to be alive. "It's time to call Adriano in. We almost lost you. I don't want to chance getting Adriano killed."

Adriano. There was something about Adriano he was supposed to remember . . . and it was important.

"How do we call him in?" Mr. Conners asked.

Jake opened his mouth to respond, the answer clinging to the edge of his memory. "I don't know."

Mr. Conners gripped his Dobbs but remained calm. "You remember anything?"

Jake thought before answering. "Coming to Charlotte. Ordering dinner and going for a walk."

"You don't know who did this?" There was alarm in Mr. Conners's voice now. If Jake couldn't identify his attackers, they could get next to him without any warning. "I'm ending this right now. It's time we tell the authorities where Vaughn is hiding. As soon as you remember, I'm going to the police and putting an end to this. I never should have gone along with this crazy scheme anyway. I don't know why I let you boys talk me into half of what I do."

Jake shook his head in protest. "Mr. Conners—"

"I'm calling rank on this, Jake. I want the FBI, CIA, National Guard, and the local police notified. Hell, I want the Boy Scouts present and accounted for. Grazicky is desperate. There's no telling what else he's planned."

"If you're going to play it that way, you have to call the media. The only way to assure their safety is with the media there—camera lights blazing. Grazicky would never try anything on live television."

Mr. Conners considered the idea. He wanted to bring Adriano in safely, and at the same time he didn't want to forfeit his exclusive. Knowing what he did about the case, he couldn't demand that Adriano abandon Payton Vaughn. Adriano would never do it; he was tenacious when it came to getting a story. Grazicky would never chance giving the police more witnesses by trying something in front of news cameras. When Conners thought about it, there really wasn't any other way. "I'll make the phone calls. When you remember how to call Adriano back in."

Jake grabbed his side. He felt like his kidney was ready to burst. "I must look awful, because I feel like crap."

"I hate to push you, Jake, but I need you to remember everything that happened."

"Tell me what you know. Maybe I can piece it together." His eyes fluttered from the pain. "And then I want the biggest pain shot available in this place—doubled."

Mr. Conners was worried about pressing Jake, but he knew Jake wouldn't rest until his partner was out of immediate danger. "A young kid from the kitchen stumbled into it all. You had ordered dinner, but never came back for it. After a while, he brought it up to your room. Before he knocked on the door, he heard noises. He got scared and went for help. Instead of activating the button to call security, the boy was so afraid he accidentally set off the fire alarms. Security started sweeping the floors, getting visitors outside. The sirens and commotion must have been enough to run your attackers off."

"Security found me?"

"Yes. They reported seeing a big guy leave the room with a woman just before they entered. The woman was a real looker. Security described her as a nasty fantasy in red leather."

"Were you able to get my things from the hotel?"

Mr. Conners went to the tiny closet and retrieved Jake's

belongings. "Only what you hadn't unpacked." He pulled up the tray table and placed the suitcase on it.

Jake opened it and began rooting around inside. Nothing jogged his memory. He wished he were at home, cuddled with his wife, allowing her to nurse him back to health. He dug into the secret compartment of the bag, fishing for the photo of his wife and daughter he kept hidden there.

"Where's the satellite phone?" Jake asked, his memory humming to life.

The man had forced Jake at gunpoint back to his hotel room. The sultry woman with him had been the more vicious of the two. After tying him up, she'd beaten him mercilessly when he refused to answer her questions. The big man was forced to pull her away. They believed he was the reporter who helped Payton get away in the SUV. Jake went along, admitting to being at the Adam's Mark and giving Payton a ride to the travel plaza in South Carolina. They kept beating him, until eventually Jake had become delirious with pain and fatigue.

"You remember something," Mr. Conners said, standing next to the bed.

"The pain was unbearable," he offered, ashamed he wasn't as hard as Adriano, able to endure the most treacherous of circumstances. "Adriano takes the risks. I piece the mysteries together."

"What do you remember?"

"I told them about the tobacco farm."

Adriano kicked off his shoes and threw his jacket over the chair. Payton looked up from where she was sitting on the floor, reading one of Lila's home magazines. She had been occupying his mind all day. She offered him a private smile that solidified his purpose. Capturing her with the intensity of his gaze, he opened the first three buttons of his shirt. Seduction was in his eyes, more meaningful emotions in his heart. He grabbed his camera and changed film and lenses before placing it on the bed. With purposeful determination, his strides carried him over to Payton, and he lifted her, settling her down on the bed.

"Lie down."

Enjoying his seductive game, she did as he asked. She watched every beguiling, enticing, magnetic, and inviting movement of his rippled body, soaking in his charm, memorizing it for the long days ahead.

He moved around the bed, posing her. He placed her legs together, arms at her sides. He used a long finger to deepen the dip of her neckline. He fluffed her skirt, accentuating the shapeliness of her legs. He left her this way while he hunted for the one radio station that played without static so far away from the closest tower signal.

Moving to the jazzy tunes, he snapped pictures of Payton sexily draped across the bed. Her eyes remained locked on Adriano, watching as he circled the bed. A playful tune filled the room, and she flashed her smile to the speed of his camera shutter. Only in front of Adriano did she feel uninhibitedly sexy and beautiful. She relaxed into her next pose. Shimmied when the shutter whirled double-time, and bade Adriano to come closer with the arching of her brow.

He discarded his shirt by the time the music slowed, providing the pace at which he would make love to her. Still snapping pictures, he removed one of her shoes and tossed it over his shoulder. The other followed. He pulled away the socks one leg at a time. Never had plain white cotton been sexier.

In a raspy voice, he told her, "Roll over."

His fingers singed her skin as he lowered the zipper of her skirt. The camera continued to whirl. With one hand, he helped her squirm out of her skirt and panties. She felt him moving over her, snapping a series of pictures from head to foot, lingering at her behind.

"Roll over again," Adriano demanded. She complied, and her shirt soon lay in a puddle on the floor.

Shielding her bare breasts with her palms, she asked, "Who will see these pictures?"

"They're for my eyes only," he answered from behind the clicking camera. He removed his pants before climbing onto the bed with her.

He captured every inch of her body on film. He took photos of the soles of her feet, ankles, calves, and knees. He zoomed in on her butterfly-painted thigh, snapping multiple shots. He twisted to shoot the other. He kneeled between her legs as he centered the beauty of her face in the viewing eye.

"You are perfect." He aimed at the silky skin of her shoulder. "Move your hands away."

"No one will see these?"

He focused on her breasts. "Only me. I promise you."

Tentatively, she lowered her hands to her side. He inhaled, as if seeing her naked for the first time. He licked his bottom lip in anticipation and sent the camera into a maddening buzz. He flicked his tongue over one exposed nipple and then the other, quickly snapping pictures as they sprang to life. Moving in tight, he captured the concave of her abdomen and the indentation of her hips. He swirled his tongue around her navel before taking its picture.

She closed her eyes as his demandingly firm, velvety-soft touch parted her thighs. He lowered his head to inhale her scent before taking the first snapshot. The noises of the camera slowed as he concentrated on collecting the perfect remembrance of the place providing him so much satisfaction. He caressed her into full bloom, making her arch from the bed. Whiz. Click. Snap. Churn. His finger swirled, probed, delved, and she writhed in stark pleasure.

Whiz. Click. Snap. Churn. The camera hit the carpet with a thud. His lips were on hers before the sound of the fallen camera resonated through the room.

She pulled him to her by wrapping her legs around his body. She submitted to the entrance of his swollen tip. Her hands wildly roamed his body as she caressed the fairy-kiss over his left eye.

He steadied her for his full entrance by grasping her shoulders. He lowered himself into her, sinking into her all-consuming heat with one thrust. Her fingers combed through his hair, igniting new sensations over his scalp.

"Angel."

"Adriano." Her hands drove down the length of his body, cradling the firm haunches of his backside.

His mission became providing her with a climax unequaled to anything she had ever experienced in her lifetime. "This has been the best assignment of my life." He kissed the hollow of her neck. "I want you to remember this time forever." He nibbled the spot on her shoulder that made her sigh. "You are beyond beautiful." He cupped her breast in his hand and taunted her nipple with his teeth.

"You are everything I've ever wanted in a woman," he whispered in her ear as he rode her into his pleasure zone.

Losing control of the sensations ricocheting through her body, she bucked wildly beneath him. "Adriano—"

He consumed her words with his lips and increased the speed and vigor of his powerful hips until she tensed and called his name. As her body twitched and twisted beneath him, he pulled all his emotion into a concentrated knot below the apex of his heart. His mind raced wildly, becoming lost somewhere between fantasy and reality. His body became tangled in the slow burn of sexual release as he matched the funky rhythm from the radio with the thrust of his manhood.

"Adriano." She whispered his name once more, and he emptied into her, releasing every emotion he didn't dare express in words.

He held her for a long time afterward, not willing to let her go. Finally, he understood Jake's lectures about the benefits of having one special woman in his life. He could picture himself returning home to Payton at the end of the day, using her as inspiration to complete his assignments as fast as possible, anxious to get back to her. He wanted to share the private areas of his life with Payton. She would be fascinated, not judgmental, when he took her home to the reservation to meet his family. She was vibrant and inquisitive, with independent goals; life with her would never be dull.

"Is that a phone ringing?" Payton asked, sitting up.

The tinkling ring caught him by surprise. It didn't sound like the satellite phone's low-pitch jingle, but he knew it was Jake, somehow getting a message to him. He'd been worried about his friend, but he'd known Jake would come through. Still, it didn't stop him from being relieved. He climbed from the bed and fished through the dresser for the satellite phone.

"It's not the satellite phone," Payton said, standing next to him.

Adriano followed the sound, going to the closet and retrieving the suitcase Jake had given them. The ringing became louder. He placed the empty bag on the bed, searching the lining until he found a small phone tucked away behind the fabric.

"Disposable cell," he told Payton, pushing the button to answer the call. "Hello?" he said, remaining cautious until Jake explained the lack of contact.

Mr. Conners's panicked voice came across the line. "Adriano, thank God. Run!"

Chapter 19

Payton jogged alongside Adriano, fighting to keep up with his long strides. Even weighed down with the suitcase and camera bag, he moved swiftly through the field of leafy tobacco plants. The six-foot plants swiped at Payton's face, and the yellow green leaves left gooey deposits on her skin. Dusk was upon them, and the dark southern night was coming quickly. She couldn't see where they were going, but Adriano stood a hair above the tallest plant, his strides determined as he carried them through the maze of plants. She trusted he had a destination in mind.

"Adriano," she puffed, trying to catch her breath, "slow down just a little."

He wrapped his arm around her waist, sweeping her up into his frantic pace. "Can't, angel. We have to put distance between us and the plantation."

"What did Mr. Conners say? Exactly."

"I told you. He said to run."

"How did he sound when he said it?"

He hesitated before answering. He was growing weary of her questions, but he kept his temper. "He sounded worried. Mr. Conners never loses his cool."

She stumbled, going down on one knee. Adriano stopped

a few feet ahead. His back was stiff, and he ran his hand across his face before he turned back for her. "Are you okay?" he asked, helping her up.

"My legs aren't as long as yours." She refused to be a liability. She wouldn't ask him to stop for a short rest, even if her lungs were burning. She had no right to complain, but her legs were still aching from their vigorous lovemaking less than an hour ago. She'd keep jogging to keep up with him, blindly trusting him to get them out of the tobacco fields. She'd ignore the sticky goo from the plants and the bugs swarming around her.

"We have to keep moving, angel," he said almost apologetically.

"I'm ready." She brushed the legs of her jeans. She looked up at him, struggling to make out his facial features in the darkening night.

"Damn!"

"I'll keep up."

"No," he said, pacing a short distance away from her. "No. You're doing fine." He trudged back to her.

"You're mad at yourself?" she asked incredulously. "Why? I'm the one who got you into this."

"I'm protecting you," he corrected her. "It means I have to have a plan, and right now I don't have one, angel. We don't have a car. There's less than a hundred dollars in my pocket. We're walking through this disgusting tobacco field, and it'll be so dark in a few minutes we won't be able to see our hands in front of our faces." He cursed again. "I was distracted," he said, chastising himself but condemning both their actions.

Payton's stomach sank. No matter what happened, she would always consider what they'd shared special. She never wanted to connect it to anything negative. She went to him, placing her hand along his cheek. "But we're alive. And that's only because of what you've done so far. This is a setback. Not the end."

He watched her, wanting to believe she believed her words.

"We were both distracted. Time to get back on track. Do whatever it takes to get to FBI headquarters in Columbia. We're just hours away."

A wide beam of light swept the tobacco field, just missing where they stood. Adriano's quick reflexes allowed him to drop the suitcase and tackle her before the beam crossed them. The air whooshed from her lungs underneath his weight.

"Shh," he said, cupping his palm over her mouth.

When the sound of the car engine faded, Adriano left her, running toward the edge of the field. She called after him, but he didn't answer. He returned minutes later, the perfect planes of his face marred by worry.

"It's a black sedan," he told her. "Couldn't see who was inside." He picked up the suitcase and readjusted the camera bag hanging around his neck.

"Tom and Lila."

"Let's go."

She scrambled to her feet, distracted by what was happening back at the farmhouse. More people hurt because of her. If she'd gone to the police right after she'd left the Adam's Mark, none of this would be happening.

"Jump on." Adriano went down on one knee, indicating she should ride him piggyback.

"I can walk."

"It's faster this way."

She didn't argue, just climbed on his back, hoping the height would give her a view of the house.

Adriano rose, taking off at full speed. She hadn't realized his lean build possessed so much physical strength. He carried her and the suitcase, running through the tobacco field, hardly breathing fast at all. She pressed her cheek to his, absorbing some of his strength to comfort her.

"Tom and Lila will be all right," he told her, never breaking his stride.

* * *

"What's the meaning of this?" Tom pulled his robe tight, tying the belt as he opened the front door. "Why are you banging on my door in the middle of the night?" His grumping was cut short when he saw the huge figure on his doorstep. The porch light cast a ghastly glow across the man's face, illuminating the evil of his intentions.

"What's the matter, Tom?" Lila asked as she came downstairs.

He turned to warn her to go back, but the man's voice stopped him.

"Sorry to bother you folks," he said, straining to sound polite, "but it's sorta an emergency."

"What kind of emergency?" Lila wrapped her arms around Tom's waist, surveying the man behind the partial cover of his shoulder.

"We're looking for our sister." A petite woman dressed in tan leather nudged the big man out of the way. Gorgeous, she was tiny beside the man, but no less lethal.

Lila's grip tightened on Tom's arm, and he knew she sensed a problem too.

"Who's your sister?" Tom asked. "I know most of my workers by name, but some of the new ones—"

"Payton." The woman held up a polished professional picture of Payton.

Tom eyed the photo, his heart warming. She'd never spoken of her troubles, but they were always there—haunting her—reflected in the weariness of her eyes. This picture of her in a more carefree time proved it.

The big man on the porch shifted, his hand disappearing beneath his jacket. The woman stepped in front of him, stopping him from doing whatever he'd planned to do.

"She's here, isn't she?" the woman asked, her voice calm and calculated.

Tom internally debated his options, but there weren't many. If there was any doubt he and Lila were in extreme danger, the bulge beneath the woman's leather jacket cleared it up. Bob Conners had been clear: if anyone comes asking, tell them the truth—don't be a hero. It's the reason Tom and Lila never asked why the kids were hiding out or whom they were running from.

"We're really worried about her," the woman said. "If we could come in and take a look—"

"They're gone," he answered.

The woman's brow eased upward. "Where'd they go?"

"Didn't say. Hightailed it out of here in the middle of the night."

"When?" the woman wanted to know.

Lila answered, "Yesterday after dinner."

The lie came so easily, Tom fought to keep his face straight and devoid of expression.

"Just the same," the man said, "we'd like to come in and look for ourselves."

Payton stood guard as Adriano hot-wired the old truck. Her feet were on fire. She was dirty and tired. Hungry. And very scared. The truck was tucked away behind a house miles down the road from Tom and Lila's farm, which meant the black sedan wasn't too far away. There were lights on inside the house, upstairs, probably a bedroom. Adriano knew the residents. He'd made a stop here with Tom one morning. A husband and wife, three kids, and a dog—typical southern family. They weren't wealthy, as most farmers in the area were just getting by. Taking their truck would cause them hardship. Adriano promised her they would use it to put some distance between them and the tobacco plantation and then leave it for the family to retrieve.

The motor roared to life, and Payton wondered if the truck was in good-enough shape to take them anywhere.

"Let's go, angel!" Adriano shouted, pulling up next to her. He took off before she closed the door, but not before the husband ran out with a shotgun. Adriano pushed her down in the seat, ducking himself as he drove as fast as the rickety truck would go. They were bumping down the road when he started laughing.

"What's funny?" Payton asked as she righted herself.

"I haven't stolen a car since I was sixteen."

She fastened her belt. "And how did that turn out?"

His laughter faded. "Not too good when my father had to pick me up from the local police station."

Payton had fallen asleep, her head propped against the glass, by the time they stopped. Adriano had found a town smaller, if possible, than the last. He parked the truck behind a closed television repair shop and retrieved their suitcase before waking her.

He lifted her down from the truck, holding her closely. "Do you want me to carry you again?"

"Do you want me to carry the suitcase for a while?"

He smiled. "Let's go. There's a motel a few blocks down."

The streets were deserted, lit by a single streetlight stationed in front of the town hall. This town was small but quaint. The buildings were decorated with bright paints and plenty of flowers. The streets were clean, spotless. This was the type of place where time stood still and the realities of murder and the drug trade didn't exist. The news reported stories on the high-school quarterback, not hits on FBI agents.

"Where are we?"

"Sign said Pageland."

The first thing Payton did once they checked into the motel was grab a phone book. Inside the back cover she found a map of South Carolina. While Adriano showered, she measured the miles between Pageland and Columbia.

"What are you doing?" Adriano asked. He emerged from the bathroom with a towel straining to surround his waist. He was shirtless, his torso glistening from the water droplets. His legs materialized from beneath the towel, dark and hair-covered, but Payton knew from experience the hair was soft, like down feathers. He stood over her shoulder, drying his hair.

"Best I can tell—"

"*Best you can tell?* Too much time with Lila. You're turning into a country girl."

The mood turned solemn. "You think they're okay?"

"I'll ask Mr. Conners first chance I get." He sat across from her at the tiny square table.

"We're about two hours away from Columbia. I don't want to hide out anymore. Let's jump on a bus or a train or whatever comes through here and go to Columbia. In the morning."

Adriano scrubbed his hair with the towel.

"What?"

"I'd like to have a contact, someone expecting us, before we go strolling into the FBI office."

"We can't afford to wait any longer."

"I know," he admitted. "Still. I don't like the fact Mr. Conners called instead of Jake. And why not use the satellite phone?" He pointed to where he'd placed it on the bedside table.

"Something has happened."

"How did Grazicky's men find us? Jake and Mr. Conners were the only ones who knew where we were hiding. They must have gotten to Jake."

She reached across the table, placing her hand on his forearm. "Why don't you call him? You pitched the disposable cell, and Sherman can't trace the satellite signal, right?"

Adriano dropped the towel, and his hair fell in dark, tight ringlets around his face. "No. Jake will call when it's safe."

"Columbia in the morning?" she prodded.

His eyes met hers. He was unsure and reluctant, but he knew there was no other way. They were out there alone, their only link to what was going on with Sherman cut off. Their money was dwindling—paying for two bus tickets would be a stretch. Sherman was close—too close. "It's time, Adriano."

He nodded once, standing and leaving her alone at the table.

The silky dark tendrils of Adriano's hair cascaded across Payton's naked belly.

She giggled.

"Keep still," he commanded.

"It tickles."

His tongue moved across her belly, and her insides pulled together tightly in anticipation.

"I want to be on top," she told him.

"No." He tickled the soles of her feet as punishment for asking.

She squirmed, squealing in delight.

"Keep still," he told her.

His mouth moved lower, tasting the crease at the top of her thigh. By infinitesimal measures his tongue came closer, closer . . . Her body moistened, heating in anticipation. She speared her fingers through his hair. Her Indian warrior, determined to possess her body.

His massive hand wrapped around her knee, bending it upward. His fingers tickled down her calf, grasping her foot and placing it on his shoulder. He liked this position, with her open and helpless against whatever fabulously orgasmic things he planned to do.

He spread her wide, his hair obstructing her view as he dipped and drank from her. His tongue connected with the knot of nerves there, and he moaned, shooting bolts of electricity through her. Her back arched off the mattress, her legs flailing wildly. She lost all control when he did this. He knew it, and he liked it. He pushed her, riding her hard until her body convulsed.

Pleased with her response, but not satisfied, he covered her quickly, bracing his weight on the palms of his hands.

"Me," she panted. "On top."

"I'm the operator of this wild ride," he told her, slipping into her wetness easily. He pressed forward, filling her in one stroke.

He tossed his hair back over his shoulder, giving her an unobstructed view of the planes of his face. He looked down at her, connecting with her as he found his rhythm. His eyes danced with serious attraction. The mole above his left brow winked, teasing her to touch it. She lifted her hand, but Adriano caught her wrist, pinning her to the bed.

She wished there were mirrors on the ceiling. She wanted to see his hard haunches flex as he moved in and out of her. She bent her knee, running the sole of her foot down his taut thigh. Gorgeous face, tight body, masterful skills in bed— Adriano was a sex fantasy come true.

It didn't hurt that he'd developed the ability to talk to her with his eyes. He conveyed every emotion he was too macho to speak in the way he watched her. He soaked up her pleasure when she responded to his body.

He was as bad at hiding his sexual anguish as he was good at silently speaking his emotions. He hungered for her, but he was disciplined, fighting the need to take what he needed without regard for what he was obligated to give. One word— one well-placed caress—and Adriano's mind would explode. It was why he never let her be on top. He needed to exercise this control. Not over her, but over himself.

"Come," she whispered to him, and immediately his body shook.

He grunted at the effort to hold on, losing the battle with one word from her. Every climactic wave was punctuated by a thrust of his hips. He cursed himself for coming so soon. He cursed her for making him.

He balanced himself on his knees above her, fighting to catch his breath and regain his senses. She ran her fingertips down the ripples of his abdomen.

"Don't touch me," he said too harshly.

She ignored him, pushing him past his boundaries, making him surrender. She moved down his body, fighting to reach him when he twisted away. She molded her body to his, stroking his thighs, moving in.

"Don't touch me." He shivered. "Too sensitive."

She ignored him still. Her hand slipped between his thighs, finding his package wet and soft but still throbbing. She held him gently, kissing his shoulder before she said, "Good night, Adriano."

Payton rested her head on Adriano's chest in the pitch-black darkness of the motel room. Her arm draped his waist. Exhaustion had claimed him soon after they'd climbed into bed. He hadn't stirred since.

She could hear the occasional car move down the street. She watched the door diligently, praying Sherman's men hadn't followed them to the small town. She wished she could forget where they were. She tried to pretend they were in Hawaii or on a cruise ship enjoying a vacation together, although everything in Adriano's bad-boy body said he wouldn't be so clichéd with his woman. Little things meant more with him, and she was learning she'd had it all wrong when she thought celebrity and a big salary were what she needed to be happy.

She wondered where Sherman was at this very moment. As his house began to crumble, he would become more desperate.

Adriano shifted in his sleep. Joy electrified Payton's heart. How lucky had she been to find him? He stepped out of his life, putting his safety on the line to help her. From the beginning, he assumed the role of her protector and never passed the gauntlet.

I'll have a second chance, Payton told herself. But second—or third—chances wouldn't be as meaningful without Adriano beside her.

She explored his body. The terrain was smooth, the bulge between the mountain of his thighs rocky. She raked her fingertips over the length of his shaft. She stroked him lightly, marveling at his unconscious reaction to her touch. His penis widened and stretched, expanding to its full size. She measured the dimension of him by making a circle with her fingers.

His arm came around her shoulders. "Are you still awake?" he asked sleepily.

She answered by placing a kiss in the middle of his chest.

"Didn't I do my job well enough?"

One by one her fingers wrapped around his manhood. She moved slowly from base to tip and back again.

He moaned.

Her tongue left a wet trail from his chest to his navel while her fingers moved measure by measure from base to tip.

He flipped over on top of her. "Do you think you could wake me up like this every night?"

Before she could answer, his lips were applying a painfully sweet suction to her neck. He kissed her, leaving her body tingling. Without hesitation, one hand went to her breast, his lips to the other.

She stroked his face, dragging the bandana from his hair. The long tendrils covered his face. Her fingers glided through the softness.

His tongue lapped at her nipple. The sensations passing through her body made her writhe and groan. He devoted his time to pampering her breasts. Expertly, he teased and licked. Masterfully, he caressed and applied sensual pain to her nipples. His frequent fondling triggered the engorgement of her breast, and her body was conditioned to drip whenever he entered the same room. She closed her eyes and let her mind swirl around his touches.

"Shh," he warned with a kiss to her lips. "The people next door will hear you. These walls are like paper." His scandalous laughter told her he didn't care if they did.

The instrument Payton had stroked to life pushed between her thighs, demanding entrance. She was lost in his salacious sounds when he penetrated her. He eased inside her ravenous opening as if it were second nature. The sequence he used—rocking, penetration, slowly in, tortuously slow pulling out—made her explode within minutes. Not allowing her to relax, he increased the intensity of his momentum. He claimed ownership of her body, working it at his command until he lost himself in her.

"This feels different tonight," she said.

"Special." Adriano rested his head on her belly.

She tangled her fingers in his hair, pulling him to her until their noses touched. "It's not too late to change our minds."

His lashes batted wildly, trying to process her meaning.

"I don't want to leave you, Adriano. Am I being selfish?"

"Yes." He kissed her lips. "Thank you." His hand ran up and down her leg, his long arms easily reaching as far as the bottom of her foot. "I don't want you to go, but you have to."

"It's the right thing to do."

"I'll take care of you tonight. Tonight, it's okay to be selfish."

Silence engulfed the darkened room. She couldn't feel any worse. She couldn't feel any better. One moment she needed to possess him. The next she admonished herself for even considering backing out now. This was bigger than her desire for Adriano. Sherman was a killer, and she was the only one who could stop him.

"Payton?"

"Yes?"

"I'm glad you carjacked me. I'd rather be here with you in this cheap motel than anywhere else."

"We say good-bye tonight," she told him. She wouldn't be able to look him in his dancing eyes tomorrow and walk away, knowing she'd never see him again. She was likely to turn into a blubbering idiot.

He kissed the cavern of her navel. "We'll say good-bye when we have to. Not a second earlier." He massaged the crease at her hipbone. "I like my life with you in it too much to think about good-byes right now."

Chapter 20

Cecily intended to stick close to home until she understood what Sherman was hiding from her. Her best source of information was her latest bed partner, Hiram. The man was addlebrained, but very—very—well hung and knew exactly how to use his equipment. She enjoyed dominating the big man in bed, dishing out her own special humiliation. Watching him squirm and fearing her more than her husband was the ultimate turn-on.

She climbed into bed naked in yet another cheap, out-of-the-way hotel. She would show her husband that small bit of respect by not traveling in the exclusive circles where she might run into one of their friends, flaunting her affairs. Sherman had not questioned her sleeping with Hiram. He knew better—he understood what side his bread was buttered on.

Marrying Sherman had been the lesser of two evils. Her father insisted she get married, or he would cut her off. And whatever Franco Cimino wanted, he got. He was from good old Sicilian stock. Her gallivanting across the globe had garnered the attention of the wrong people, and he'd made the ultimatum. She wasn't a fool. She knew of Sherman's reputation of hooking up with wealthy widows and naïve heiresses, spending their money until some family member or other threatened to cut off the water. She knew about his prison time too. She married Sherman at a huge wedding, vowing to stick with him for life, and she meant it. He was the perfect husband—terrified of upsetting her, clearly knowing who was in charge. She must admit, over the years she'd grown to love Sherman and his doting ways, but she was her father's child and love could only take him so far.

She struck a match, lighting her cigarette on a long inhalation. She missed her father mercilessly. She would have liked to get his advice about this Payton Vaughn situation, but he was still overseas conducting business. She'd grown accustomed to her father's "business" trips. He'd started taking them shortly after he killed her mother, leaving her behind with the nanny. She always missed him, giving the staff hell while counting every minute until he walked through the door with a package just for her. When she was young, the gifts were always stuffed animals. Now they were jewels.

The best thing about her father was the way he loved her. She'd wandered into the bedroom the night he bashed her mother to death. He stood over the limp, lifeless, bloody body, his breath coming in short bursts. When she whimpered, he rushed to her, becoming the doting father she'd always known. He carried her back to bed that night, sat on the edge of her bed, and they had their first "grown up" talk.

Her daddy told her all about his business, promising to groom her to take over when he was too old to manage it. He explained how her mother didn't love them enough—she'd let another man take her loving—and why he'd had to kill her. Because anyone who didn't love her 100 percent wasn't worthy of breathing. They'd made a pact that evening. No matter what, they'd look out for each other.

If there was a chance he wasn't already, her father became the center of her world. She lived to please him. Spent every moment adoring him. Understood him like no one else did. Their bond was unbreakable.

Cecily took another long drag on the cigarette. Missing her father made her want Hiram more. When they were together, her dominating their scene, she forgot all her troubles. Her cell rang on cue. She checked the number, suppressed her anxiousness, and answered.

"Where are you? I'm waiting."

He cleared his throat. "The reporter gave Payton up. I'm on the way to a tobacco plantation in South Carolina."

"Have you spoken to my husband?"

"Not yet."

"Don't. I didn't like you reporting to Sherman before me when you found the reporter. I'll decide how much Sherman should know."

Jake tried to sound cheerful when he talked to his wife. She wanted him home, and he wanted to be there. When the pain of his bruised ribs became too much to bear, he ended the call. Hobbling to the bathroom of his suite, he swallowed two pain pills and settled on the sofa in front of the computer. With many protests, Mr. Conners agreed to Jake staying in Charlotte to navigate Adriano and Payton's deliverance to safety. He'd moved to an Uptown hotel and brought enough equipment in to set up a headquarters dedicated to bringing Grazicky down and Adriano back to Chicago.

A million times a day Jake toyed with the idea of calling the satellite phone. He didn't know if Adriano would discard it once he found the disposable cell, but it was their only link. Adriano would activate a contingency plan once he felt it was safe to make contact. He knew how to take care of himself, Jake reminded himself. It still didn't keep him from worrying. For now he had to sit tight and wait for the action to play out, doing his part to put Grazicky away. The best way to keep them all safe and end this adventure as quickly as possible was to get the crook behind bars. He knew one thing for sure: when this whole mess ended, he was taking a very long vacation.

Grazicky's men were out there, watching. After what had happened at the Adam's Mark, the private security team in the adjoining room didn't guarantee Jake's safety. The only reason Grazicky wouldn't come after Jake again was if he believed he'd beaten everything useful out of him. Adriano was his friend and his colleague, and Jake respected his opinion. He hoped Adriano would forgive him for revealing his hiding place. The guilt pushed him to work day and night, breaking only for meals and to rest his eyes when the computer screen began to blur. Mr. Conners had shipped him all the files they'd composed on Grazicky, and he spent hours going over them, reconstructing their story from the beginning.

Jake had nodded off at the computer when a knocking at the door disturbed him. He shut down the computer screen and covered the contents of his files. Very gingerly, he shuffled to the door and gazed through the peephole. A uniformed police officer held his badge up.

The officer took a step back when he opened the door, and a short, stout black woman addressed him. "Jake Richards?"

"Can I help you?"

"I'm the new prosecutor assigned to the Grazicky case." She extended her hand. "Lisa Hail. Can I come in?"

Jake accepted her hand and stepped aside. The police officer remained posted outside the door. "What happened to the other prosecutor?"

"Someone scared him off. Threatened his family. Found his kid at a park and put a real scare in her."

"Grazicky."

"Can't prove it."

"So you're taking over."

"I don't scare easy. New York born and bred."

Jake followed her into the living-room area of the suite.

"Mr. Richards, your employer, Mr. Conners, walked into

my office today with a fascinating tale. He claims you're responsible for hiding my star witness. Being the hard-ass I am, I immediately threatened to have him arrested for obstructing justice." She plopped down on the sofa, and the cushions wheezed beneath her weight. "But then Mr. Conners reminded me he holds all the cards."

Jake sat across from her, stalling for time to contemplate what Mr. Conners had done. He had to believe if Conners had gone to see Lisa Hail, there was a very good reason for it. "Mr. Conners came to you?" he questioned.

"Actually, I had him detained at the airport all night until he gave up what he knew." She smiled humorously, checking her watch. "I imagine you'll be getting a call from him within the hour. As soon as my people release him."

Lisa Hail played dirty.

So could he. "You can't afford to extend this investigation any longer. Without Payton Vaughn, and a body, your murder case is circumstantial at best."

"Do you mind if I pour myself a drink of water?" She left her seat before he could answer. "I don't want to aggravate your arm." She stepped into the kitchenette and helped herself to a glass of water.

"How did you get those injuries anyway?" she asked, rejoining him on the sofa.

"Muggers."

"In our fair city of Charlotte? *My* city? No, I don't believe it. Are you trying to insult me? The next thing you'll be telling me is the Mexicans did it. You know everybody blames the Mexicans."

She laughed at a private joke she couldn't wait to share with him. "Or maybe you'll say a woman did it? A woman with superstrength forced you back to your hotel room and attacked a big, strapping guy like yourself, beating the stew out of you." She jabbed her puffy fist into the air. "Tell me everything you know, or I'm going to beat you with a wet noodle." She doubled over in laughter.

Obviously, Mr. Conners had told her too much. He waited for Lisa Hail to get to the point. Already he didn't like her. Her brash mannerisms were enough to render his pain medicine useless.

Lisa stopped laughing so abruptly Jake thought she might be choking on her water. Her face contorted into a snarl. "Let's cut the games, Mr. Richards. Tell me where my star witness is."

"I'm sure Mr. Conners told you I don't know."

"Right before I threatened to lock him up for obstruction of justice and hindering a criminal investigation."

"If I knew where they were, I wouldn't tell you. Your people almost got Payton killed."

"Now, listen—"

"What I will give you is a lead."

Lisa sank into the sofa; the cushions wheezed. "Don't play with me."

Jake moved to his work area and searched through his papers until he found the document he was looking for. "Adriano and I have been investigating Grazicky for a long time. He's tied to the drug trade big-time." He handed her the piece of paper. "Get your forensic accountants to make the connection."

"I don't take orders from you," she huffed, examining the paper. "I know how reporters like you work. You don't make a move without layers upon layers of escape doors. You may not know where your partner is hiding my witness right this second, but you know how to get in touch with him."

"I've given you all the information I'm willing to give right now." He needed to hold back some, because dealing with a person like Hail demanded an insurance policy. He'd given her enough to get started. He and Adriano had used means the police might categorize as illegal to obtain information the authorities wouldn't have access to. If she used it correctly, it would aid in building her case.

"And if I arrest you right now? I did bring an officer with me, you know."

"If you arrest me, I don't tell you anything. I'm a reporter. You can't violate my rights. Even to make your case."

"I'd think you'd want to put Sherman Grazicky away."

"I'm doing everything in my power to make it happen. Now, if you want to combine our efforts, working together—"

"Forget it, Richards. You won't blackmail me."

"Then we'll have to continue working separately. If I find something you can use, I'll get it to you right away."

"I want regular progress reports," Lisa demanded, her cool exterior becoming ruffled.

"Not going to happen."

She took a long drink of water. "The judge could compel you to give up the information."

It became Jake's turn to laugh. "Again, I'm a reporter. I've spent more time in jail than in bed with my wife. When I know Mr. Conners has been released, we can discuss my terms again."

She mumbled something about hating the press.

Chapter 21

The satellite phone rang just before dawn. The sky was shifting from star-speckled black to sunshine-streaked blue. Payton stretched, working her aching muscles. Adriano did everything to the maximum, like a runaway freight train; when he put his mind to something, he didn't do it halfway. Satisfaction lighted her smile. She nudged him with her foot, not wanting to leave the warm bed. He shifted, itching his back closer to her, but didn't fully awake. The incessant ring jogged Payton out of bed. She fumbled with the phone until she figured out how to answer it.

"Hello?" Her voice sounded shamefully like a woman who had been loved all night. She watched Adriano sleep. They were rabbits, but she was ready for more.

"Payton."

The voice on the other end of the phone stunned her. She had mindlessly answered, knowing Jake would be calling and she'd have the privilege—and reward—of telling Adriano his friend was alive and well.

"Listen carefully," Sherman said. "Don't let the reporter know who you're talking to."

Fear aside, she had a million questions for Sherman. How

had he gotten Jake's phone? Why was he being bold enough to call her directly? *Why was he trying to kill her?*

"You should have come to me, Payton," he said. "You know I would do anything for you."

"You killed a man." More questions. Who was the man? Why did he deserve to die?

"It couldn't be avoided, but this whole mess could have been. We would make great partners . . . at work and in other ways."

"You have to pay for what you did. Don't make this my fault. Innocent people—police officers are dead because of you."

"This is bigger than a few cops! This is my life."

"Why did—"

"I don't have time for this, Payton. Come back. Now. To me."

"Are you crazy? You'll kill me."

"If I wanted you dead, you would be. Don't you think my men could have shot you through the window of the SUV? Or busted down the door of that seedy motel and filled you with bullets?"

"Tom and Lila," she breathed.

"The old couple are still alive."

She closed her eyes, thankful for that at least.

"I'm going to need you to come home now, Payton. One of my men will meet you at your apartment and bring you to me."

"No." She couldn't believe he had the audacity to even ask.

"I won't kill you. You know I don't go back on my word."

"Why do you want me then?"

Adriano turned onto his back, but didn't wake up.

"Precisely—I want you."

Payton's crawling skin left no doubt about his meaning. It always came down to sex. No matter how dire the situation, there was always enough time to slip between the sheets. The only thing more powerful was money.

"Get yourself a good lawyer, Sherman," she told him.

He laughed, but it was humorless. "You have three hours."

"Why would you even think I would consider doing this?"

"Because you love your brother, Patrick, and you'd do anything to save him."

Her heart lurched and her stomach tightened. "What?" she barely whispered.

"You I want alive. I could give a damn about Patrick. Three hours, Payton—an even trade: you for Patrick."

She heard her brother shouting in the background, warning her to stay away.

It's real. He has Patrick.

"He has a family," she pleaded.

"Not my concern. It's yours."

"He doesn't have anything to do with this."

"I agree, which is why I'm willing to make a trade." He exhaled loudly, impatiently. "If I didn't care so much for you, he'd be dead the second you returned. I'm going to let him go, but only if you willingly come to me."

Patrick's screams rose above a commotion in the background.

"Okay!"

Adriano moved again.

She lowered her voice. "I'll be there."

"Three hours, Payton. And come alone or the deal is off."

She heard Patrick scream one last time before the line went dead.

The steam from the shower filled the motel room, heating the room to a temperature uncomfortable enough to wake Adriano. Helping Tom around the farm all day, making love to Payton all night, and running from Grazicky's men had sapped him. He'd finally gotten a good night's sleep, and now he was ready to come up with the next step in their plan.

He rolled over, missing Payton next to him in the bed. She wanted to go to Columbia today. He was torn. He needed to know she'd be safe with the FBI, and he wasn't looking forward to ending their time together. He climbed out of bed and slipped into his clothes. While she showered he'd find them some breakfast.

The satellite phone propped on the dresser reminded him of Jake. He was worried. If he could find a pay phone, he'd make a call to the *Chicago City* offices and try to connect with Jake or Mr. Conners. He jotted a note for Payton, leaving it on the television before he left.

Pageland was already buzzing with people going about their day. City boy that he was, he could never get used to starting the day before dawn. It had been one of his motivations for leaving the reservation—not being able to acclimate his internal clock to the work schedule.

He found a pay phone at the town hall. Apparently the Watermelon Festival was approaching, and the town was in a tizzy getting ready for it.

He dialed *Chicago City,* reversing the charges to Jake. Mr. Conners came on the line. He filled Adriano in on everything that had happened over the past few days.

"Grazicky's men connected Jake to Payton. They thought he was the reporter who helped her get away. Long story short: they snatched him from outside his hotel and beat Payton's whereabouts out of him. You get out safely?"

Adriano told him about their hurried escape, omitting their current location. "How bad did they hurt Jake?"

"Broken arm. Bumps and bruises. Nothing bad enough to keep him from working the story. We have a lead." Mr. Conners told him about the secret script written on the paper found in Payton's planner.

"I'll get a disposable cell and call you with the number. As soon as you know what that paper says, call me."

"If I don't end up getting arrested again. That DA in Charlotte is a pit bull."

"Arrested?" As Adriano listened to Mr. Conners filling

him in, he realized how much he was missing while on the run. He chastised himself again for being so distracted by Payton's pretty eyes and tempting body. He had to refocus.

"Payton wants to go to Columbia today. She's tired of running."

"You get the story?" asked Mr. Conners, always an editor first.

"Up to this point." He'd learned so much more about his source than was necessary. He knew her favorite color and the sensitive places on her body where his love bites sent her over the edge.

"Columbia is safe. I checked it out myself. Here's the man you want to see. Got paper?"

Adriano borrowed a pen from a passerby and wrote the information on a corner of a page from the phonebook.

"I want you to call me when you're close. I want to alert my contact before you arrive. Jake suggests we get every reporter in town to meet you."

"It's smart. Grazicky wouldn't try anything in front of a bunch of television cameras."

"Done. The FBI will take Payton into protective custody, and this entire mess will be over. And you can get about writing my story."

"It's the only way," Adriano concluded, not believing it. How could leaving Payton ever be the best thing to do?

"You've done the right things for this woman. You saved her life, and your story will make her richer than she ever would have been working for Grazicky."

It wasn't about getting the story, writing a book, making money, or winning Reporter of the Year anymore. This was about giving up the woman he loved . . . *loved?*

"Gotta go," Adriano said, suddenly feeling melancholy and not much like a hero.

"See you in Columbia."

* * *

Adriano's footfalls hit the cement walk hard as he made his way back to the motel. Was he really considering . . . yes . . . telling Payton he had fallen in love with her somewhere along their journey? He rehearsed what he would say, the inflection of his voice, where he'd have her sit. Nervous anticipation made his mouth go dry. He hadn't been this rattled with a woman since his first sexual encounter. And that's just what it had been all these years—sex. When he was with Payton, the emotions took the physical to a new realm.

After he told Payton he loved her, they'd have to come up with a new plan.

What plan?

Would he leave the *Chicago City* newspaper, move to Charlotte and live the life of the residents there—a neat home, marriage, and two point five kids? Or would he ask Payton to walk away from her life, leaving all she knew to take a chance on a self-professed playboy?

The giddy excitement driving his steps faded, and his pace slowed. He couldn't ask it of Payton. He couldn't ask her to undergo the traumas she'd been through and then leave the familiar to start—what?—with him.

A real man didn't ask the woman he loved to make such sacrifices. It was selfish. He had to consider her feelings.

It was his job to keep her alive, deliver her to the FBI, write her story, and *let her go.* The words made him queasy, but an honorable man would encourage her to regain normalcy in her life. She should reunite with her family. Maybe he could help her get to St. Louis, but then he'd have to walk away, leaving her in the good hands of her people.

By the time Adriano reached the motel, he'd worked through several scenarios, teetering between whisking Payton away forever and ending their association with his pride and honor intact. He knew he would have to do the hardest thing of all—never tell Payton how he felt.

Precipitation wet the lone mirror in the room. The hot

steam from the shower had turned cold. He could hear the water still running in the shower and knew something was terribly wrong.

"Angel," he called, making his way to the bathroom. His heart thumped wildly as he pushed the door open. The water was running, but Payton was nowhere in sight. Confusion made him lightheaded—had she been gone before he left? Where did she go? Why would she just up and leave? He replayed the night before. She was a little bummed out, but not enough to do this.

She couldn't have gone far. Knowing Payton, she probably decided to go to Columbia without him to protect him. She wouldn't want him near Grazicky if she could help it.

Adriano searched the room. She'd left what little they'd acquired behind. No note. She hadn't taken the time to jot him a sentence or two telling him what the hell she thought she was doing and why. Fear warred with anger as Adriano snatched up the satellite phone and ran out the door.

Not thinking clearly, he dialed Jake on the run. When the person on the other end picked up the phone, but remained silent, Adriano remembered his earlier conversation with Mr. Conners. He disconnected. Still running, he dialed Mr. Conners. It took forever for the man to get to the phone. Adriano was back at the town hall before his call was forwarded.

"What's up?" Mr. Conners asked.

"Payton's gone. I need to speak to Jake."

"What's the number?" Mr. Conners correctly deciphered the urgency in Adriano's voice and didn't waste time with stupid questions.

"The satellite phone. Tell him to call now." Adriano disconnected. He jogged down the streets, searching each one for Payton. He bumped into little old ladies and shoved big, burly men as his body reacted without any direction from his mind.

"Hey, boy, slow down." A police officer dressed in traditional blues with a radio belted around his pendulous stomach grabbed him up by the arm.

Adriano's first response was to pull away, ignoring the man.

"Just a minute now," the officer said, tightening his hold. He chewed his cheek. "What's the rush?"

Passersby watched the interaction with interest. The last thing Adriano needed was to call attention to himself. Or worse, get arrested in a small southern town an hour away from the capital where the Confederate flag was flying. He forced himself to regain control.

"Sorry, officer."

The man let him go, still chewing his cheek as he watched Adriano with narrowing eyes.

"My girlfriend left me this morning."

The officer's scrutinizing gaze softened just a bit. This man had lost someone in his past. Adriano played on it.

"I need to find her. Tell her I'm sorry."

"She got family here?" The man was still wary.

"No, we were passing through. Stayed the night at the motel. Had a huge fight. I really need to find her."

The officer watched him, his eyes roaming up and down, probably searching for the bulge of a weapon. Adriano could see him deciding: should he search the out-of-place stranger, run his license for outstanding warrants, or let him go? The man's good nature won out. "Did you check the bus station? A lot of people running away head there."

"Bus station?" Adriano had been in such a state, he hadn't thought to check the most logical place.

The officer gave him directions, a warning to stop running into folks on the sidewalk, and released him. As soon as the officer disappeared inside the general store, Adriano took off for the bus station.

The depot was nothing more than an average-sized room with benches, a vending machine, and two ticket windows. The buses pulled up behind the building for loading and unloading.

Adriano pulled out his wallet and removed his *Chicago City* media identification, fully aware it resembled the credentials policemen carried in their wallets. The Chicago police had been strong-arming the paper to change the ID, but Mr. Conners refused.

He strutted up to the window and pressed the badge against the wire cage. "I need to know if someone bought a ticket," he said with unquestionable authority.

"Are you the police?" the ticket agent asked, his thick southern twang mangling the words.

"You saw my ID," Adriano answered, purposefully being vague. He couldn't afford the big officer from the street arresting him for impersonating an officer.

"You must be state, 'cause you ain't from around here. Ain't no black police here. Where's your badge?"

"I'm investigating a case. I don't have a shield. I'm looking for a beautiful woman, about this tall," he held his hand up as a measuring stick. "She has big brown eyes. Her hair comes to her shoulders. She would have been wearing jeans and T-shirt. She looks like she's very tough, but her eyes give her away . . . show you how vulnerable she truly is."

The ticket agent angled his head in question.

Adriano cleared his throat. "Have you seen a woman fitting this description? Did she buy a ticket from you?"

"Got a picture?"

Thousands of them. In his camera bag. Still undeveloped. "Not at this time."

"Well then, nope."

"Take a second to think."

"Don't have to. Only sold two tickets this morning, and they weren't to this gal you talkin' about." He pointed across the room. "To the woman and her baby."

Out of options, Adriano cursed. Then he remembered, "She might have bought the ticket last night."

"Cletus ran the ticket counter last night."

"Where's the bus schedule from last night?"

The man shuffled through some papers and produced a schedule. Adriano turned away, examining the listing. In such a small town, there wasn't the bus traffic like in Chicago. Only three buses had gone out yesterday—all before they'd arrived in Pageland.

"There's a bus going to Columbia this morning," Adriano said. "Do you have any passengers scheduled to get on?"

Thank God the bus station's transactions were computerized. The man punched the keyboard, and the data flashed on the screen. "Looks like five people bought tickets. The bus is scheduled to leave in"—he glanced at the clock above his head—"twenty-five minutes."

Adriano turned, checking out each person in the station. The woman with her baby, an old man, and a teenage couple. Payton was nowhere in sight. He went over to the teenage couple and described Payton; they hadn't seen her. He persuaded the girl to check the restroom for him.

"Nobody in there, mister," she announced when she returned.

Adriano felt like he was riding an out-of-control rollercoaster. He'd admitted to himself he'd fallen in love with a woman for the first time in his life, only to discover her gone—probably forever. He couldn't even begin to know how to come to terms with Payton's absence. He dropped down on the bench next to the teenage couple, fighting to regain his rational mind.

"Hey, mister," the young man said, "if you're looking for your girl, ask Romeo." The boy was watching him, offering compassion over his plight through the inflection of his words.

"Good idea," the girl said.

"Who's Romeo?"

The girl nodded, indicating he should look out on the platform where the buses loaded. The boy answered. "Romeo is a pimp from Columbia. He comes down every couple of days to recruit girls. He knows everything about every woman in town."

"Payton wouldn't get involved with a pimp," Adriano admonished.

The boy threw his hands up. "Just trying to help. I didn't say she was one of his girls."

"Sorry," Adriano apologized. Actually, the boy had a good idea. He thanked the young couple and went to seek out Romeo.

"You police?" Romeo asked when Adriano approached. The two girls standing with him scattered. "Those were my cousins. I'm looking out for them until they get on the bus. Besides, I already paid my taxes this month—and donated to the police benevolent fund with four girls, which is two over what our agreement calls for."

"Relax, I'm not the police."

"I saw you flash your badge at the ticket counter." Romeo was dressed in casual dark blue silk slacks and shirt. On his feet were three-thousand-dollar blue gators. He was young, but his work had been hard on him, leaving him with a variety of scars across his upper chest. Both his biceps were tattooed with what Adriano knew to be prison art. While they talked, he lit a thin cigar and placed it between a perfect, gleaming white set of teeth. He had the pimpin' attitude down to a T—calm and in control, smooth, and sharply observant of his surroundings. Their entire conversation, his eyes were roaming over Adriano's shoulder, watching, on the lookout for his next victim.

"I'm not a policeman," Adriano repeated, pulling out the badge he'd shown the ticket agent. "I'm investigating a story, and my source slipped out on me. I hear you're the one to ask where she might be."

Romeo chewed his cigar while he studied the badge. "What's it worth to you?"

Knowing he was tapped out of money, he found something else to offer. "Look, man, I don't have the clout a lot of reporters have. My budget for this story is gone. Spent it on the source that ran away. I got to get this story done, or it's my ass."

Romeo watched him, seriously scrutinizing his story. "You're a horrible liar, Mr. Reporter. Again, what's it worth to you?"

Not having much time to play with, Adriano dropped all pretense. "I'm a reporter for the *Chicago City* newspaper. You're too slick to be from around here—and I'm including Columbia. You get in trouble in Chicago, you give me a call." He handed the man his card. "I'll owe you one."

Romeo read over the card, glancing up at Adriano. Adriano held his gaze. One sign of weakness and Romeo would try to take everything he could and leave without giving any information in return.

After a long moment, Adriano said, "I don't have much time."

Romeo tucked the card inside his shirt pocket. "What's this source look like?"

Adriano described Payton, not liking the way Romeo's interest piqued. "Have you seen her?"

"Might know the woman you're talking about. She didn't look like she fit into this small hick town, so I offered her my services. Thought she could use a nice meal and a hot bed for the night."

Adriano's fists clenched. If Romeo had touched Payton, he would be dead within the hour.

"Chill. She didn't take me up on my offer."

"Where did she go?"

"Last I saw her, she was waiting for the bus to come through." He angled his body. "The police stepped through, and she got squirrelly. Ducked behind the Dumpster. I haven't seen her come out."

Chapter 22

"Angel." Adriano kneeled down next to Payton in her obscure hiding place shielded by the Dumpster.

She'd seen him talking to Romeo and knew the pimp would give her up, but she had nowhere else to run. She would have to face Adriano and make him believe their association was over.

He reached out and stroked her cheek. "Why did you leave?"

She wanted to tell him everything, melt in his arms and hope he could make everything all right. But she couldn't. She'd asked enough from him. He'd gotten his story. Their relationship was inconsequential since they both knew it would have to end eventually. The only thing of importance right now was saving Patrick. Sherman had given her a three-hour deadline, which had been impossible to keep without finding her way back to the main highway and hitchhiking back to Charlotte. After placing a pleading phone call to him, he'd allowed her an extension, but the clock was running again.

"Come here." Adriano stood, helping her up. He walked her to the bench farthest from Romeo and his growing entourage. "Tell me why you left."

"You've kept up your end of the deal. I can go into Columbia alone. You should get back to your life. Start writing your story."

"You think I'm so shallow I'd just dump you off in Pageland and tell you to go the rest of the way by yourself?" He sounded offended. "We talked about this last night."

"We did. Adriano, it's time to say good-bye. We let things get complicated between us. It's best if we end it cleanly."

His anger flared. "And it's cleaner to walk out in the middle of the night, without even a note? I didn't know what happened to you."

"Now you know I'm fine." She swallowed hard, suppressing her true feelings. "Go back to Chicago, Adriano."

"We're done?"

She nodded.

He pushed up from the bench and crossed the dirt parking lot. He paced for a few strides before returning to stand over her. "You left the shower running to throw me off."

He was too astute for his own good. Payton didn't bother to try to explain.

"You didn't want me to know you were gone. Why?"

"I didn't want this scene."

His neck snapped back as if she'd slapped him. "You wanted to walk away from me without the drama?"

No. She never wanted to leave him. Never. "Yes."

"This meant nothing to you."

She exhaled, hating herself for lying but knowing there was no other way. It would be hard enough to get Adriano to leave. If he knew how she felt about him, he'd insist on getting involved in saving Patrick.

"Payton." His voice cracked like a whip. "This meant nothing?"

"It was what it was, Adriano. Now it's over."

"Bull. You're lying."

She turned away.

"Everything you said, everything you did, is a lie? You don't feel anything for me?"

She couldn't look at him. The truth would be reflected in her eyes.

"You're going to let me walk away believing that?"

She pressed her lids together, trapping the tears. Couldn't he see the truth? "This is hard for me too."

"It doesn't have to be—"

"Which is why we have to end this now. Before I try to concentrate on being a witness."

"You want me to go?" His words were so softly spoken she almost didn't understand.

She faced him. "Yes," she answered, and a piece of her heart ripped away.

Adriano watched her, and for the first time since she'd met him, his dancing eyes clouded in sadness. He stood rooted in front of her, waiting for her to take the words back, but she couldn't. Sherman had been clear: come alone if she wanted Patrick to live.

"You just tore my heart out," Adriano said before he turned and walked away.

Adriano was at the motel packing up when the satellite phone rang.

"What's up?" Jake asked. "Mr. Conners said you broke your cover to get a message to me."

Adriano tried to regain his composure, to sound matter-of-fact. "It's over. I'm coming home."

"What do you mean 'it's over'? How can it be over when we haven't cracked this investigation wide open? We still need to—"

"Jake," Adriano broke in, "it's over. Payton's gone. She's on the way to Columbia—without me—where she'll tell the FBI what she knows, they'll arrest Grazicky, and life will go back to normal." He slammed the suitcase closed.

"What happened?"

"Nothing happened."

"A, I know you. What's up?"

Adriano started packing his camera and was suddenly overwhelmed. He had snapped hundreds of pictures of Payton. How would he handle it? Looking at images of her, but not being able to touch her? He dropped down on the bed next to the suitcase.

"A, you there?"

"I'm in love with her."

"You're in love with Payton Vaughn?" Jake asked incredulously.

He answered with a simple "Yes."

"What did you do? What happened between you two?"

"Everything and nothing. Too much and not enough."

Jake pondered his answer.

"I don't know, Jake." He moved to the window of the motel room. "One minute we were complete strangers, the next I'm closer to Payton than I've been to any woman in my life. All in a matter of"—he counted the days on his fingers—"nineteen days."

"This is bad."

"You don't know how bad. About the time the insanity took over, little voices inside my head were telling me we could actually make it work. One of us could move to be with the other."

"Insanity is right. A, man, you have to break it off with her."

He leaned his lofty body against the wall and folded his arms over his chest. "You're right. I know you're right. It's just . . ."

"I mean, where do you think this can go? The DA and FBI will question her and hide her away until she testifies. When this is all over, she'll have to go back to her life. And you'll have to go back to yours. Being emotionally attached is going to make it hard for both of you."

He dipped his head, studying the carpet pattern. "Don't have to worry about that happening. Obviously, this is one-sided, because Payton's at the bus station right now, waiting to go to Columbia alone. Here I am about to die, thinking the FBI would take Payton into custody and I'd never see her again, when she up and runs out in the middle of the night to get away from me." He admonished himself for the self-pity. "Testifying and putting Grazicky away is more important than us having a relationship."

"You don't sound convinced."

"Yeah, well. How soon can you book me a flight?"

"A?" Jake said after a short pause. "I don't know Payton as well as you do, but I think you're missing something here."

Jake was the analytical one, but Adriano knew he had let his emotions cloud his judgment and derail him from his job.

Jake went on. "The day I met Payton, she was scared. She tried to put on a good front, but she was afraid. She always kept you within sight and didn't let you move too far away. If she was this dependent on you after one day, I can't see her being less attracted after you get involved."

Adriano propelled himself away from the wall with the heel of his shoe. He remembered their conversation last night before they'd made love. Separating in Columbia had bothered her. "Why would she tell me she wanted me to go?"

"Why would you *leave* her? After everything you've gone through, knowing Grazicky is on her trail, why would you leave her before she got to Columbia?"

"I wasn't thinking. She said what we were doing didn't mean anything."

"And you were hurt, so you were ready to hop a plane back to Chicago without knowing if she made it to Columbia."

Adriano cursed himself. Again, he'd let his emotions steer him in the wrong direction.

"Don't beat yourself up," Jake said. "You'll learn how to play this game soon enough. You're a rookie at being in love. The question is, why would Payton freely go. To try to make it to Columbia by herself?"

"She'd do it to protect me."

"From what?"

"Grazicky and his men."

"Unless Grazicky was in your motel room last night, it doesn't make sense."

Jake's words made the light go on for Adriano. When he'd woken up, the satellite phone had been on the dresser, not on the bedside table, where he'd left it the night before. "I have to stop Payton," Adriano announced, already running for the door.

"Go get her, A. You have to make this right. Everything."

Payton moved inside and sat on one of the hard benches inside the bus station. She checked the clock again—she still had another hour before the bus to Charlotte was scheduled to arrive. She was scared, starved, and heartbroken. She'd never forget the crushed look on Adriano's face when she'd been forced to turn him away. Of everything she'd been through, it would leave the greatest scar on her conscience.

Romeo had moved inside also, throwing her hopeful glances when he thought she wasn't looking. He'd been charming with his offer to "run his business ventures," but she knew better. She'd been involved with one "harmlessly" flirty boss, and it had wrecked her life.

She was watching Romeo work his magic on his "employees," her mind drifting to Patrick and what could be happening to him right then when Adriano walked through the entrance. The camera bag hung around his neck, and he gripped the suitcase handle while wearing an expression of fierce determination. His rugged, handsome face was polished with brazen cockiness, but she knew the real man underneath. He was more sensitive than he was smug. The black T-shirt stretched across his chest had seen better days, but he wore it like a high-fashion suit. He'd pulled his long, silky hair into a fastener at his neck, but the wily tendrils still managed to cascade to his wide shoulders. His lips were pressed together, accentuating his strong cheekbones. She couldn't see the fairy kiss above his left eyebrow at this distance, but she knew it was there, waiting to tempt her. Even furious, Adriano spelled S-E-X.

She couldn't handle another scene with him. She would not be able to keep lying to him. The intensity of his piercing eyes would wear her down, and she'd confess every feeling she was hiding. She tried to angle her body away from him, but his determined strides hypnotized her. It made her shiver to think all that untamed energy was focused on her. The patrons scattered in the bus station felt it too. Conversations stopped—even the baby stopped crying. Everyone came to a standstill, all eyes trained on the man making his way across the room to her.

He stopped in front of her, setting the suitcase at his feet before he spoke. He was too much man—tall, handsome, adventurous, loyal. He crowded her space, scrambling her brain and making it impossible to think clearly. His first words melted all her defenses.

"I didn't want to give you my heart, but you took it anyway."

A warm feeling traveled over her body.

"I don't want to think about you every minute of the day, but I do."

His words knocked out a chink of her armor, but it wasn't enough for him, and he kept going.

"When I lay down, I want to sleep—not dream about you—but it happens every night."

She had to stop him before she did something crazy. "Adriano—"

There was no deterring Adriano when his adrenalin kicked in and his goal was in sight. He plowed right over her, steamrolling to his destination. "I want to be everything to you."

And there it was: the declaration she was too cowardly to

make. The one she was too strong to make. She had learned a lot from him while they were together, mainly how to stay focused on obtaining the prize. In this case the prize was her brother's life.

"You want me to be able to walk away," he said.

Yes. She needed him to walk away because she was finding it too hard to do.

"Sorry, angel, I can't."

"This is bigger than us."

"Nothing is bigger than what I feel for you. Believe me. I'm standing here, trying to get you to admit you feel something for me. *I'm* the man who insists on all my relationships being casual, but I'm trying to talk you into staying with me until we see it through, when you're sitting there like you don't care. *I'm* the man who makes women cry when I walk away. Women don't break me down. But I'm still standing here, trying to convince you."

The only thing she wanted to do was jump in his arms.

"I can't let you make me feel this . . . hopeless when I know it's not true, angel. I've laid everything out here. Now it's up to you. Do you feel anything for me?"

Her heart raced. She wanted to tell him . . . badly . . . but she couldn't. Because of Patrick, but also because what she'd said earlier was true. They would have to end it sooner or later, and there was no good in letting it go any further between them. It would only make the inevitable harder.

"Regardless of your answer," Adriano said, "I'm still getting you to Columbia safely. I promised I would, and I will. No matter what goes on between us."

"You can't." The panic was renewed.

"I will. I keep my word."

"I'm not going to Columbia," she confessed.

He raised his fairy-kissed brow. "Where are you going?"

She didn't answer, but let her eyes drop to the ticket she was clutching in her hand.

Adriano snatched the ticket away before she even saw him flinch. "Charlotte? Why are you going back to Charlotte?"

"Adriano, let it alone. I know you promised, and I'm letting you out of our deal."

"My word is important to me. Even you can't make me go back on it."

"What are you going to do? Drag me to Columbia so you can feel good about keeping your promise? Things have changed," she added, knowing she'd slipped and said too much.

Adriano was all over it, morphing into the investigative reporter she'd first met. "What's changed?" He sat next to her. "I know something happened last night. What? Did Grazicky's men get to you somehow?"

No, not me. Patrick.

"I won't let you do this alone. What happened between last night and this morning?"

"Adriano," she pleaded, "you need to walk away now. If you really feel something for me like you said, you'll do what I'm asking."

"What you're asking is stupid. I've gone along with your schemes, and they never work out. You were the one who wanted to go back to your apartment where the rogue FBI agent was waiting." He shook his head. "No. We do things my way."

She was positioned between two men who were dangerous in their own ways. The tears welled up in her eyes. She wouldn't be able to ditch Adriano. He'd never leave without a good explanation, and the truth would cause him to become more determined to come along.

"You don't want to tell me what's going on? I'll follow you onto the bus. And when we get to Charlotte, I'll follow every step you take. I'll call Jake in to help me tail you. You're not getting out of my sight until I know you're safe with the FBI."

"You can't." Her voice took on the annoying quivering sound it made before she started crying. She hated women who cried.

"Watch me."

She thought of Patrick, dead because of her, and the first tear fell. Once it plopped onto her hand she couldn't stop the flood that came next. All these weeks she'd been able to contain her tears, but Adriano's insistence in helping her—his courageous unselfishness—pushed her over the edge.

"Angel?" He wrapped her in his arms. "What the hell is going on?"

"You can't follow me. You'll get Patrick killed."

"Patrick? Your brother?"

"Sherman has him. If I don't turn myself over to him, he's going to kill Patrick."

Chapter 23

Sherman had to keep Cecily from finding out about Patrick or she'd do something dumb and get them both thrown into jail. Recently learning about his wife's deviant sexual appetites, he was still a little behind the curve. She was any husband's dream: rich, good-enough looking, hardly ever in town, with an outrageous affinity to the sexually bizarre—but she wasn't Payton Vaughn. He had succeeded in roping Cecily in. Payton was still elusive.

Hiram entered his office, head hung low. The man worried Sherman would snap, punishing him for sleeping with Cecily. Not now. Not yet. He was a welcome diversion, keeping Cecily too busy to know what Sherman was up to.

Sherman stood at the window, looking down onto the sparkling pool. "She's coming on the Greyhound."

"When?"

Sherman whipped around. "Do I have to do every aspect of your job? Maybe if you got your head out from between my wife's legs you could see what's going on."

Hiram shrank back, remaining quiet.

"Pick her up and bring her to me." Sherman turned back around. "You know where I'll be."

"What about the brother?"

"Stop bothering me," Sherman spat.

Hiram scooted out of the room, his tail between his legs. Sherman loved dogging the bigger man, proving who was in charge.

After locking the door, he returned to his desk. He unlocked the middle drawer of his credenza and pulled out an envelope with everything he needed to get out of the country. He fished out the tiny key, replaced the envelope, and called the butler responsible for keeping the house staff in line.

"Have the car brought around," Sherman said. He hung up before the bothersome man could ask any questions. The butler never let Sherman forget he came with Cecily. He donned his suit jacket and headed for the car. He wanted everything in place when Payton arrived, which meant he had to get his hands on his cash. He'd allow Cecily to join him with Payton—but not the first time. The first time he wanted her to himself. Prove to the high and mighty wench he could have anyone he wanted—including her. Once Cecily got her hands on Payton, Payton would beg him to take her away with him. And he'd be ready. Ready to take the girl and the cash and walk into the sunset.

"You did good," Cecily said, stroking the welts on Hiram's back. This session had left her breathless. She sat on the edge of the bed in the dilapidated motel and lit a cigarette. "You can get up now."

Hiram rose to his feet but didn't leave the spot.

"You do what my husband asks, but the second you pick Payton up from the bus station, call me. I'll give Sherman some alone-time with the bitch, and then I'll arrive on the scene."

Hiram nodded. He looked particularly anxious to get away.

"Are you telling me everything, Hiram?"

"Everything."

She eyed him suspiciously. She didn't trust him any more than she trusted Sherman. "You can leave."

Hiram scurried off to the bathroom, grabbing his clothes from the floor. She waited for him to dress and leave before she placed a phone call.

"I'll need you soon," she said.

The man with the jagged facial scar on the other end of the line didn't need more of an explanation. "Where and when?"

"Yo, Jake?"

"Who is this?" Jake held the phone to his ear with his good shoulder.

"Class, a friend of Adriano's. You wanted one of my boys to read something."

Jake shoved some files out of the way, reaching for a pencil. In all his hours buried in paperwork, searching for a key piece of evidence, he'd forgotten about the gang interpreting the sheet of paper found in Payton's planner.

"Go ahead."

"It's an appointment. It says, 'Meet Franco Cimino after closing.'"

Jake jotted it down and read it back, assuring himself he'd gotten it correct. He read his note, knowing he'd heard the name before.

"Hey, tell A it took a lot to find an OG who could read this. He owes me one."

"Got it."

Class disconnected. He'd be stricken to know he'd just volunteered information that might bring down the drug trade—a business deeply entwined with gang life.

Jake tossed the phone aside and, using his good hand, started plucking away at the keyboard. He'd thought about breaking the cast off several times. It hindered him from getting his work done. Typing one-handed severely slowed down the process. He had scanned the Grazicky files for hours, never finding a link between Grazicky and Franco Cimino. His eyes started to tear, and a terrible headache set in. He stepped away from the computer screen to order lunch and grab an aspirin.

"Let's think about this for a minute, Jake," he said to himself. He downed the aspirin and swallowed a gulp of water.

"You've heard the name before, which means it has to be in one of these files somewhere. If it isn't in Grazicky's file, where could it be?"

He walked to the window and watched the foot traffic below. "What kind of name is Cimino?" Immediately, he thought it had a gangster ring to it. He returned to the computer, fired up the Web and entered Cimino in a genealogy page.

"Sicilian? Well, this investigation officially hit another brick wall. No one involved is Sicilian." His words trailed off. His back went straight. He cursed the cast and frantically searched the paper files sitting on the floor next to his workstation. "Holy sh—"

He searched for where he'd thrown the phone earlier. Finding it, he punched in Mr. Conners's number. "Go through the archives. Send me a picture of Grazicky's in-laws."

Ethan never really believed Jake, the reporter from the *Chicago City* paper, would ever take his calls, let alone bring him in on an existing case. Jake was being secretive about the whole investigation, asking Ethan to meet at Jake's hotel and bring along any family history he could dig up on Sherman Grazicky. Ethan wasn't stupid. He wanted out of the tiny newsroom, and Chicago would be a good place to grow his career. He made an excuse to his editor about following a new lead, gathered the information Jake wanted, and headed over to the hotel.

"*Chicago City* really knows how to treat its people," Ethan said, stepping inside the expansive suite.

"It took a long time to get here," Jake said, offering his good hand.

Ethan lifted his briefcase. "I brought everything I could find on Grazicky and his wife." He took a seat on the sofa. "I also brought what I could find on the dead FBI agent." He balanced the briefcase on his knees before he opened it and removed a videotape. "Got stock footage on Skye too."

Jake took the tape and slipped it into the VCR. "Good looking out."

"You want to tell me what this is all about now?"

Jake took a seat across from him, remote in hand. "My partner and I get the byline at *Chicago City,* but there'll be a bunch of reporters wanting exclusive television interviews."

Ethan's mouth literally watered. He knew from the first phone call Jake was on to something big. "You offering?"

"If this is what I think it is, I'm going to need help to bring Grazicky down. You up for that?"

Grazicky was responsible for many crimes in the city, including the new influx of drug activity, but no one had the balls to take his empire down—including the authorities, whom Ethan believed were mostly on his payroll. This would be more than getting a big story or jump-starting his career. He'd be partially responsible for helping to clean up the streets. He didn't have a family of his own, but he had nephews who had been approached by drug dealers.

"Where do I sign on?"

After Payton told Adriano everything, she felt much better. From the first moment she'd met him, he'd had the power to subdue her fears with a gentle caress or well-timed word. His hostile reaction to Sherman and what he'd done to blackmail her set Adriano on edge. He wanted to destroy Sherman for his crimes—the drugs, the murder, kidnapping Patrick—but mostly for upsetting her. It was a good feeling to know he cared so much about her.

She'd allowed herself a minute to be embraced by Adriano. She'd had a moment of weakness when her tears got the best of her. With him holding her, she found new strength, and now she was ready to get her brother back.

"You're seriously suggesting we ask Romeo for a ride to Charlotte?" Adriano questioned.

"Do you have a better idea? I have to get back before Sherman does something to Patrick. You're insisting on finding an alternate plan—"

"Other than giving you to Grazicky, yes."

"Sherman's expecting me on the bus. Going by car will give us extra time to find a way to save Patrick."

Adriano eyed the pimp, noticing Romeo's gaze never strayed too far away from Payton. She had that affect on men, and Adriano was coming to hate it.

"If I agree to this, you have to do something for me," he said.

"Now?"

"You didn't answer my question, angel," he said, setting Payton away from him.

"What question?"

"How do you feel about me? Us?"

"That's two questions."

He watched Romeo. "It'll take two answers to get me in the car with him."

Payton looked in Romeo's direction, but Adriano caught her chin and brought her back to him. "Was this only about sex because you were lonely and scared?"

Her eyes roamed his face.

He held his breath, anxious to know her answer. He'd never been this knotted over a woman before. He finally understood what Jake meant when he'd said Adriano would know when the right woman came along. He didn't want to think about what life would be like without seeing her every morning. They hadn't been separated since they'd met, and he didn't want to let her go now.

Payton reached out and stroked his hair. "I do care for you, Adriano."

He smiled, and he knew it would be a big, goofy smile if he could see it himself. It didn't seem to bother Payton. She dropped her head, hiding her own smile.

Getting her to admit her feelings was the easy part. After they got Patrick back and put Grazicky in prison, they'd work on the hard part—finding a way to be together.

Romeo had about two-thousand conditions before he would agree to drive them to Charlotte. It wasn't until Payton stepped up and asked that he agreed. Adriano pulled her close to his side, keeping a protective arm around her at all times. She climbed into the backseat, and he joined her, sitting the suitcase in the front seat with Romeo.

"What kind of phone is that?" Romeo asked when the satellite phone jumped to life. "This is some serious spy shit."

Adriano ignored the man and answered the call.

"A, we got Grazicky by the balls."

"Payton's here." He leaned over, holding the phone between them.

"The note on the sheet of paper inside Payton's calendar was an appointment Grazicky scheduled with Franco Cimino. Payton know the name?"

She shook her head no.

"She doesn't know him, Jake."

"The appointment is for the same night Payton witnessed the murder. I'm betting he's the dead guy."

Adriano watched Payton, gauging her reaction. "Who is he?"

"This is the sweet part. Franco Cimino is Cecily's father."

"Sherman killed his wife's father?" Understanding lit Payton's face. "It would explain why he'd want his appointments kept confidential. If he was into something with his father-in-law and didn't want his wife to know."

Adriano spoke. "Everything we've investigated never flagged anything on Grazicky's wife."

"I tapped into a source at the television news station. Seems Cecily's father is—was—the granddaddy of illegal crimes. Think Grazicky might have been moving in on his territory? Overstepping his boundaries as a son-in-law?"

"It would fit his MO," Adriano said. "Everything we know about this guy screams he's an opportunist."

"There's more," Jake said. "Now that we know who we're looking for, I'm on the way to the coroner's office with dental records in hand."

Payton squeezed Adriano's hand.

"Grazicky has Payton's brother."

Jake cursed.

"If she doesn't go to him, he's threatened to kill Patrick."

Jake cursed again. "What's the plan?"

"We're on the way back. Grazicky is expecting her in a couple of hours by Greyhound. We're getting a ride and can be there in . . ."

"Thirty minutes," Romeo supplied.

"No doubt Grazicky's men are watching me," Jake said.

Adriano contemplated the situation for a long moment. "How long will it take you to find out something from the coroner?"

"Who knows? I can be there in minutes. It might take days for him to match dental records with a John Doe—if the body is even in the morgue."

"Mr. Conners said something about calling in the media. We'll meet you at the bus station and pretend to get off the Greyhound when it arrives. With the cameras, Grazicky wouldn't be stupid enough to try anything."

"What about my brother?" Payton asked.

* * *

It was a phone call Payton was thrilled to make. She gripped the satellite phone, waiting for Sherman to pick up.

"You'd better be at the bus station," Sherman said when he came on the line.

"I will be soon."

"Are you calling from the bus?"

"Yes, there's been a change in plans," Payton said.

"There are no changes—not if you want to see your brother alive again."

"How long do you think you'll live when Cecily finds out you had her father shot?"

Nothing but silence answered her question.

"I want my brother to meet me at the bus station. Alone. Or every piece of evidence I have will go directly to Cecily."

Chapter 24

Sherman Grazicky watched the spectacle on television. Reporters and cameramen covered the biggest story to hit Charlotte since that ballplayer had his girlfriend killed for getting pregnant. Sherman pulled his chair up to the large television screen, his eyes scanning the crowd. Brilliant bursts of light from the reporters' cameras popped off like a field full of lightning bugs. Everyone was shouting out questions at the same time, trying to get the scoop from anyone in authority. The police were out in full force, and a nosy crowd was being contained behind yellow police tape. They weren't visible, but Sherman knew the FBI would be mixed in the crowd, trying to blend in with the regular assholes.

Finally, Payton stepped into camera range.

"Payton," he breathed, not remembering she was this beautiful. Her tenacious demand to release her brother had only sparked Sherman's interest in her. She was as tough as she was beautiful, and he couldn't wait to tame her. He drank her up, savoring this time to have her to himself. His erection swelled as he imagined the things he would to do to her—the things he and Cecily would do.

As he watched Payton on the screen, he wondered if she was too classy to handle the blood and gore of what his work sometimes forced him to do. He never let his women see his moments of ruthlessness, but Payton had gotten by him and witnessed his greatest crime of all. She'd proved her moxie well enough—turning against him, eluding Hiram and his hit men, challenging him over Patrick. She was the real thing. He was planning on keeping her around for the long haul, so she needed to accept the real Sherman Grazicky. The sooner, the better. There was a lot to be done before he could leave the country.

Sherman had plenty of loose ends to tie up before he stepped onto that chartered plane waiting at the private airfield. Payton had to be convinced—or blackmailed—into leaving with him. He didn't care which way it went down, as long as it happened. Hiram and his men needed to be paid. And Cecily would have to be disposed of . . . discreetly . . . after he'd gotten all the money from her he'd ever need. His people were working frantically, transferring funds, liquidating assets, verifying deeds and titles. If all went well, Sherman would end up with the girl and more than thirty-seven million dollars.

On the television, Payton hugged her brother. The reunion was sickening, but it would prove valuable when bargaining with Payton later—demonstrate how willing Sherman was to give her anything she asked for . . . as long as she gave him what he wanted, when he wanted it. There was a serious man standing next to her, not letting her out of his sight. Sherman figured it to be the reporter—Adriano Norwood. That was one man Sherman couldn't wait to dispose of.

That rattlesnake of an ADA, Lisa Hail, moved into the picture and said something to Payton. The happy-reunion smile faded. He'd expected this. His attorney had warned him the police and/or FBI would be snatching her up first thing.

Sherman continued to scan the crowd with the aid of picture-in-picture and panning cameramen. Yes, his people were in place. Unnoticed by the crowd, but they were there doing what he paid good money for.

"Careful, careful," he said to the television. "Bring her to me. Bring her to me."

"What did Mr. Conners tell the media to get this crowd?" Payton asked. The camera flashes started the minute she and Adriano stepped into the bus terminal, and the police converged on her at once. With the prestige of the movie stars and millionaires who hung out at Skye, this would cause a scandal all the way to Hollywood.

"He has his methods," Adriano answered, taking a protective grip on her hand.

It had been carefully orchestrated, but it was still disconcerting to have all this attention focused on her. Adriano stayed at her side, shadowing her as she searched out Patrick.

"Payton! Payton!" Her brother rushed to the front of the yellow police tape.

"Patrick?" She broke free of Adriano's hand and ran to the tape, embracing him. "Did they hurt you?" She hugged him tightly, not realizing how much she'd missed him until he was there with her. She would never allow distance to come between her and her family again.

"Nothing I can't handle. What about you?" He craned his neck to look her over.

"I'm fine."

"How did this happen? How did you get involved with these kinds of men?"

"We'll tell you everything later," Adriano interjected. "Payton's not safe here."

"Who is this man?" Patrick asked, and Payton could tell by his expression he'd taken an instant dislike to Adriano.

"He's watching over me," Payton answered.

A squat black woman broke through the police line. "Ms.

Vaughn, I'm Assistant District Attorney Lisa Hail. We really don't have time for a family reunion. We need to get you out of this crowd."

Two policemen approached, grasping each of her arms as they moved her along the yellow police tape.

"I love you," Patrick called as she was swept away.

"I love you too," she answered. "Adriano?"

He'd been swallowed by the massive crowd. She tried to find him, but the officers kept nudging her along.

"Adriano?" She didn't want it to happen this way. Adriano should be at her side until this had been resolved—until they had decided how to handle their relationship. She didn't want to be separated from him now. This was not how they'd planned it.

A cheering section called out her name as they passed. She recognized several of the employees from Skye. She shrugged off the policemen and shared hugs with her friends, using the time to search for Adriano.

"Ms. Vaughn," Lisa Hail huffed, "I really must insist you let the police do their jobs. Do you want to be killed here? We have to get moving."

The policemen grasped her arms and propelled her through the bus terminal.

"Wait," Payton protested. "Wait for Adriano. Where's Adriano?"

"Mr. Norwood is not my concern," Lisa informed her.

Payton tried to turn and retrace her steps, but the policemen would not let her. Panic-laden anxiety made her stomach roil. She felt trapped, caged in the hands of the officers in the middle of the crushing crowd without Adriano.

"Adriano?" she called over her shoulder. "Adriano?"

She couldn't find him in the swarming crowd. Where had he disappeared to so quickly? He had been holding her hand. She couldn't see her brother. She felt lost, scared. Where were Adriano and Patrick? The two people she most trusted in the world.

The police pulled her along until they ducked through an employee exit.

"Watch your head, Ms. Vaughn." One of the policemen placed his palm atop her head as he pushed her inside an unmarked car with bulletproof glass.

The police shoved Adriano back and away from Payton. He watched helplessly as she was whisked away from him. His first inclination had been to push past the policemen and possessively shield Payton's body with his.

Then Jake stepped up, pulling him in for a hug with his good arm. "Good to see you alive, partner."

"What truck ran you down?" Adriano tried to joke as he took in the bumps and bruises.

Jake slapped him on the back. "This went better than we planned."

Adriano glanced back, looking for Payton. "Where are the police taking her?"

"The ADA took Payton and Patrick into protective custody."

"We trust her?"

"Hail? Yes. She's a pain, but she's honest. Has a good record for putting mobsters away. And she doesn't scare easily."

Jake told him about the events leading up to the mob scene, but Adriano continued to search for Payton, feeling bereft without her near.

"This is Ethan." Jake introduced the man standing a few feet back. "He's with the local television station."

"Jake told me how you helped." Adriano offered his hand. "Thanks for everything."

Ethan nodded, shaking Adriano's hand. "We need to get you out of this crowd too."

He looked back once more. Payton was nowhere in sight.

Jake placed a hand on his shoulder. "This is how it has to be, A."

"I know." *Let her go—end it quickly. Don't linger on good-byes—it would only cause more pain. There was no way it would have worked between them. Too much distance between them. Too many bad memories associated with their relationship for Payton.*

Above the noise, Adriano swore he heard Payton call for him. "Payton?"

Seeing the distress the separation caused his friend, Jake said, "Let's get back to the hotel."

He nodded and followed Jake, but he missed Payton already.

Payton refused to answer any more of Lisa Hail's questions. "I want to talk to Patrick, and I want Adriano here. This is not what I agreed to. Where is the FBI?"

"You don't make demands. I'm in charge of this show, Ms. Vaughn."

"I'm not answering any more of your questions until I see Patrick and Adriano."

"No phone calls. No visitors," Lisa instructed the police officers who were assigned to protect Payton.

"I'm a prisoner here," Payton protested.

"If you choose to feel that way, there's nothing I can do about it. I have a job to do, and I plan to get it done without any more casualties."

Payton fell silent when she remembered the police officers at the Adam's Mark who gave their lives to protect hers.

"And one more thing, Ms. Vaughn. I don't know how you managed to elude the police when you ran from the Adam's Mark, but don't try anything funny. You *are not* to leave this hotel room except to go to the courthouse or the police station. In the morning, after you've rested, we'll go over what will happen the next few days. For now, sit tight. The officers will get you whatever you need."

"It's not supposed to be this way. I didn't do anything wrong. I'm here to be a witness, not a prisoner."

Lisa grasped her chunky hips. "And just how do you think it's supposed to go? Officers are dead. A man has been killed. The most important witness to all of this ran off on a romantic interlude in the middle of the investigation. How exactly do you think you deserve to be treated?" Lisa didn't wait for a reply. "You will be treated with dignity and respect. You will *not* be catered to like you're a queen. You're not at Skye anymore, *Dorothy.*"

"I want to see your superior."

"These are my rules, and you'll be living by them for a good while."

Payton searched the policemen's faces for support. They remained blank and detached. Obviously, they agreed with Hail or didn't have the clout to disagree with her. Trapped, Payton marched off to her private bedroom and flung herself across the bed in tears. She hated women who cried! Everything had turned out so wrong. Ambition had planted the seeds to a garden of weeds that quickly grew out of her control. Confused, she wondered where her life would go from here. And how she was expected to survive without Adriano's dancing eyes watching over her.

Her sobs turned to hiccups before she drifted off to sleep.

"Ms. Vaughn?"

She bolted upright, finding a plainclothes officer standing next to her bed.

"There's a phone call."

She watched the man, not knowing whom to trust. Sherman had FBI agents under his control. Who was to say this wasn't a trick?

"ADA Hail will have my badge if she hears about this," the officer said, "but Ethan did me a big favor in the past. Saved my career."

She didn't know who Ethan was, and she didn't care. Only Adriano would have the connections to call in a favor big enough to make a police officer risk his job. She scrambled across the bed and snatched the phone off the receiver. The officer left her bedroom, closing the door behind him.

"Hello? Payton? It's Adriano. How are you?"

"Adriano!" she exclaimed.

"I'm here, angel. Are you okay?"

"I'm fine, but Hail won't let me use the phone or have visitors. Why won't she let me see you? Is Patrick all right? Where is the FBI?"

"Patrick is staying here in the hotel with me and Jake. Mr. Conners called the FBI in Columbia, and they're fighting it out with the office here about who will have jurisdiction over you. Mr. Conners makes a lot of friends in Washington through the paper—he'll get it straightened out when he gets here."

"How will I see you again?"

"It's not unusual for the police to sequester you until they get their statement. They don't want us to have the opportunity to fabricate a lie."

"If we wanted to do that, we would have done it before we came back."

"Cooperate with Hail, and it'll be over soon."

"Any luck identifying the body?"

"Not yet, but Jake gave the coroner and Hail everything he had, and they're checking it out. Grazicky is pissed we got one over on him. And he's desperate because you know about Cimino. Watch your back, angel."

"I will, but I need you here. When will I see you again?" A long pause made her repeat the question.

"Angel, I'll be in the courtroom every day. You'll see me there."

"The courtroom?" The trial could be months if not years away. "I want you here with me now. I'm scared," she admitted.

Another long pause.

Adriano's voice wavered. "I know, angel, but I can't be there with you."

"But you will when Hail says it's all right?"

He didn't answer.

"Adriano, you aren't trying to end it."

"Angel, you live in Charlotte. I live in Chicago."

"You made me admit how I felt about you. Now you want to back out? Why? Did Jake say something to you? Patrick?"

"This is bigger than us—you told me that. Putting Grazicky away has to be the priority. You're the source of our investigation."

He'd turned into the reporter again. "You have to get the story." Payton tapped the phone against her forehead while she tried to compose herself.

"I promised to get you to safety."

"How can I be okay without you? You're making no sense at all."

There was sadness in his voice. "I have to go. The sooner we find the body, the quicker it'll all be over."

"Adriano?"

"Yes, angel?"

"I lied to you. When you asked me how I felt about you."

"You don't have to do this."

"I love you."

A long pause.

"I love you, Adriano Norwood. I do."

"I love you too, angel."

Chapter 25

"Are you talking to my little sister?" Patrick boldly entered Adriano's bedroom in the suite. "I found the audio tapes. I listened to your interview."

Adriano eyed him carefully, not able to get a good read on his mood.

"I don't need you to defend my little sister anymore. I'm here. I would have been here in the beginning if she had let me know what was going on. Payton pretends to be tough, but she's a sweet person. She never would have worked for Grazicky if she knew he was a criminal."

"I know," Adriano answered, still remaining careful.

"But that's not what you two were talking about on the tape."

Adriano knew he owed Payton's brother an explanation. Patrick loved his sister, even if distance had caused them to become estranged. He'd left his wife and kids behind to jump on a plane to support her and ended up Grazicky's hostage. He had the bruises to prove it.

Patrick went on. "Let me refresh your memory, since you seem to have forgotten what was said . . . just like you forgot to turn off the tape. You were talking about things men and women talk about when they're in a relationship. Not interview material about a drug lord and killer."

"Payton and I have become close. I don't deny it."

"The tape was running when you—while you were having sex with my sister. From what I just listened to, it sounds like you took advantage of Payton because of what she was going through."

Jake entered the room, circling like Patrick was a wild animal. "What's going on?"

"Your partner took advantage of my sister."

"Adriano cares about Payton," Jake said, defending him.

Adriano held up a hand, indicating Jake should stay out of it. Patrick approached him. "Is that true?"

"I love her."

"You got her story, and then you slept with her, but not once did you warn her about how dangerous Sherman Grazicky is."

"I've been with her every time he sent his men after us. She knows he's dangerous."

"I've been with *him*. I've looked into Sherman's eyes. He's not going away until he gets his hands on Payton. Instead of protecting her, you left her out there alone, not knowing what's coming."

Adriano's only defense: "I love her."

"Love her?" Patrick glanced at Jake. "What's that supposed to mean? Are you planning a future with her?"

Adriano felt as if he were standing in front of his father trying to justify getting caught with one of the elder's daughters.

Patrick shoved his fists into his pants pockets. He spoke calmly, but his face twisted with restrained resentment. "You fix this, because if Grazicky touches Payton, I'm coming after you when I finish with him."

Payton was awakened by harsh voices on the other side of her bedroom door. Remembering the last time she was awakened this way, she jumped from bed, ready to run at the sound of the first gunshot. There was a scuffle. She could hear the officers trying to subdue someone.

"Angel!"

"Adriano?" She raced to the door, swinging it open to find Adriano being held between two officers. "Let him go," she shouted.

One of the officers looked around.

Lisa Hail moved between them, separating Payton from Adriano. "You were told not to come here," she said to Adriano.

"Why can't he come here? I've given you my statement."

"I want to see Payton," Adriano said, pulling away from the officers. His hair had come undone in the struggle and partially obstructed her view of his face.

"Let's get something straight, Norwood." Lisa pressed her finger in Adriano's chest. "Ms. Vaughn is the witness I need. You didn't see anything valuable. You have nothing to offer to this case."

"Leave him alone," Payton said, stepping around the wide woman and shoving her finger away from Adriano's chest. "I've done what you've asked. Adriano stays."

Lisa turned on her. "You think this is a game? You think you and your reporter are going to build a little love nest here? I have a case to put together."

"We've been doing your job for a long time now," Adriano said. "Go find your own evidence. How hard can it be? The man is a major drug dealer and has killed at least one person."

Lisa's face puckered, but she didn't argue the truth. She spoke to the officers. "If he steps out of line, arrest him." She huffed out of the hotel room, and the officers went back to their posts.

"Angel." He crushed her in his arms, pressing his lips to hers before she could take a breath. He kissed her for a long time, gently stroking her back, reluctant to release her.

She led him into her bedroom, where they'd have privacy.

"What are you doing here?"

He sat on the bed, dragging her into his lap. "I missed you."

"How's Patrick?"

"Going stir-crazy at the hotel. Lisa took his statement, but he never saw the men who grabbed him. Never even heard Grazicky's name mentioned until he was released at the bus station. Jake and Ethan are driving county by county to the medical examiners' offices with Franco Cimino's dental records. Patrick is going with them. Did you speak to your parents?"

"Last night." She crushed his broad cheekbones between her palms. "I've missed you so much."

"Me too, angel." He kissed her again, angling her for better access to her body.

"What's going to happen now?" Payton asked. "Hail won't tell me too many details about the case."

"Her case is still weak. She has a witness to a hit ordered by Grazicky, but no body and no motive. She's working the case harder than the last ADA. She'll find what she needs. Jake and I will stay on top of it." He kissed the tip of her nose. "You just stay safe."

"How long is this going to go on? I watch Court TV. Sometimes these criminals don't go to trial for years."

"Angel, the authorities might not be able to keep you safe after a trial. Even when they put Grazicky away . . . he has connections." He sounded sad. "Has anyone mentioned the witness-protection program?"

"You mean like the one gangsters go in to start a new life? I'm not going into any program. No, no way." Mild panic set in. "I've heard about that in the movies. You have to change your name and your appearance." Full-blown panic took over. "You can't have any contact with your family or friends ever again." She gasped. "That means you, Adriano. I'd never be able to see you or talk to you again."

"You can't go on the run forever."

"I won't cut contact with my brother. If I've learned anything from this, it's to value my family. And I won't leave you."

"I would rather be without you, knowing you were alive, than to jeopardize your safety."

"This conversation is over, Adriano. I'm not leaving my family, my friends, or you. Right now I want you to tell me how much you love me, and how much I should love you."

Adriano gathered his thoughts before continuing. "How would this work between us, Payton?"

"I don't know. Since I've met you, you've been telling me you want to be in charge. Here's your chance. Find a way. If you love me, Adriano, find a way to have me."

"Do you think I don't want to be with you?" he asked, his voice edgy. "I love you."

"You don't love me if you let me go." Her voice wavered, making it impossible to hide her emotions.

"I love you more than I have ever loved anyone in my life." He dropped his head to her chest. "What kind of man would I be if I didn't put your happiness above what I want?"

"I won't be happy without you, Adriano." She lifted his face to look at her. "Don't you understand? We're not over."

Adriano's eyes searched her face, desperate to find an answer. "I came here to do the right thing. I know I should let you go. You have to rebuild your life. I know all this, but I love you, angel, and I don't want to give you up."

"Don't."

"I love you, and it's real. It has nothing to do with being thrown into a dangerous situation together and my adrenalin getting the best of me. *I love you.* I always will."

He opened the buttons of her blouse, slipped it off her shoulders, and tossed it in a nearby chair. He admiringly cupped her breasts.

She honored him with a sparkling smile.

"You have the most amazing breasts I've ever seen." He nuzzled her breasts, bringing her to giggles.

"Don't make me laugh. I'm mad at you for being willing to give up on us."

"I never wanted to give up on us. I wanted to do the honorable thing by you."

"Leaving me?"

"Not disrupting your life. Being together is going to take major adjustments on both of our parts. I didn't feel I had the right to ask it of you, considering everything you've gone through."

"Losing you would be worse than anything I've experienced so far."

His fingers moved to unbutton her slacks. "This is our life. I want you to be happy."

Getting lost in the depth of his soulful eyes, she used her thumbs to stroke the fairy-kiss over his bushy left brow.

"If there's anything you need to be happy, I'll do it. I promise," he told her.

Her fingers moved through his silky hair.

"Got me?" He lifted her chin. "I offered you an out, and you didn't take it. You won't have the opportunity again."

"Got it." She locked her hands behind his neck.

Love filled the room with an emotional haze that warmed their naked bodies. His fingers moved sensuously over the concavities of her body, and her skin sizzled in the trail left behind.

"I love you," they both declared, staring into each other's souls.

She pushed him over onto his back and straddled him. She traced the fairy-kiss before moving to the hardness of his nipples. His erection pressed urgently against her behind. His breathing deepened. She smiled at his intense response to her. Her response was just as intense to him, and she began to guide him into her.

He flipped her to the mattress and quickly covered her body with his.

"Why won't you ever let me be on top?" she asked.

"You have to know your place."

"I do. With you."

"Correct answer."

He moistened his lips, and she pulled him down for a kiss that would end the argument in her favor.

"I want to be on top."

He fell back on the bed, taking her with him. "Why do you insist on being on top?"

She removed the silky strands from his face. "Don't I deserve to be?"

"I can't argue."

She watched him.

"What is it?"

She answered with a giggle. "I've changed my mind."

He flipped her to the mattress.

"Make love to me, Adriano."

"Only if you make love back."

In the middle of the night, Payton lay very still, afraid to open her eyes and find Adriano gone. Finally she drew the courage to pry her lids apart.

Adriano smiled down at her. "I want to show you something." He clicked on the bedside lamp before taking her hand and leading her out of bed. He walked her to the other side of the room. She followed, her eyes locked on his bare torso and its intricate network of sinew and muscle. His hair cascaded down his back in dark waves, begging to be touched. Even after making love to him dozens of times, her stomach flip-flopped every time she looked at him naked.

"Look," he told her, directing her eyes to the floor.

Her eyes grew wide. "What did you do?" She fell to her knees at the end of a blanket made from the photos he'd snapped of her while they were hiding.

"I had extra time on my hands while I waited for you to

recover." A cocky smile lit his face. In that moment she
knew everything would be all right. She didn't know how
they would work out their relationship; she only knew Adriano was as committed to it as she was.

"It's a hard time to remember." Her hands went to her chest.
"But it's a great time to remember too."

He kneeled behind her, wrapping his arms around her
naked waist. "Don't get misty. Look over there." He pointed
to the far corner.

A gasp of delighted recognition. "The night you made love
to me with your camera."

"I'm thinking we can put this blanket to good use." He
turned her around inside the tight circle of his arms, bringing
them face-to-face. "I could make love to you on it."

"I can go you one better."

"Why do you insist on being in charge?" he teased.

"Why don't you let me make love to you with the camera
this time?"

On a blanket of photos, Adriano hovered over Payton's
body, tracing the silhouette of her nakedness while she slept.
He pressed his palm against her stomach. He wanted to be
with this woman forever, giving her his child. The thought
was so uncharacteristic of his nature, it made him sit back
on his heels. Payton made him want to do unspeakable things.
It scared him how she controlled him with a tight rein on the
strings of his heart. So many men had told him the time
would come when a woman knocked him for a loop, but he
never believed it. Not until Payton barged into his life.

He lay down next to her, watching her breathe evenly in
and out. He had been doing it for hours, trying to remember
every contour of her body, every angle of her face. Being
away from her for one night had been unbearable. How would
he do it for weeks or months at a time? The urgency to find a

solution overcame him. He didn't know how he would do it, but he knew he would never go back to Chicago without her.

"Adriano, I'm cold."

He lifted her from the photo blanket, and she wrapped her arms around his neck and yawned. He was driven to take care of all her needs. No matter how small. He placed her carefully on the bed, covering her with a blanket. She had fallen asleep again by the time he climbed into bed with her.

Chapter 26

Jake opened the door to the suite, and Lisa Hail barged in. "What the—"

"Is Norwood here?"

"I don't know." Jake, Ethan, and Patrick had just gotten back from driving end to end of North Carolina, visiting every coroner's office in every county, leaving Cimino's dental records for possible identification of any John Does.

"Norwood, get out here!" Hail flung the bedroom doors of the suite open in search of Adriano. "Now, Norwood!"

Jake followed her, wearing only his boxers. "You can't bust in here demanding to see Adriano like this. What's the problem?"

Lisa flipped around on her heels, making her trench coat balloon around her short, stubby body. She poked her finger in his chest. "Don't mess with me!"

Ethan woke up from where he'd fallen asleep on the sofa.

Patrick appeared in the living-room area, tying his robe. "What's going on? Has something happened to my sister?"

Adriano joined them in the living room. "What is it? Has something happened to Payton? Your men are supposed to be looking after her. If you can't—"

Lisa trudged up to him. "Listen to me good. All of you. I don't know who you think you are, but you will not interfere with my case. I've already had to compromise with the stud here"—she hiked her thumb in Jake's direction—"who was beat near to death by a woman."

"A woman?" Ethan asked, amused.

Lisa continued her tirade. "The FBI is on my back. Grazicky's men are still out there somewhere—watching and waiting for their chance to make a move. Which brings me to you. Loverboy." She pointed at Adriano.

"Did something happen?" he asked, but Jake, Ethan, and Patrick watched her histrionics in silence.

"Someone followed you to the hotel where I'm keeping Payton and all your buddies set up camp outside. They're hungry for a story, but I don't have one to give them because *you keep interfering in my case!*" She whirled on Jake again. "Don't think I don't know about your road trip." She turned in a complete circle, looking at all the men in turn. "Because of your antics, I had to move Ms. Vaughn again."

"You moved her?" Adriano asked, already alarmed about not knowing where she was. "Moved her where?"

"That you'll never know," Lisa answered. She let the realization settle in before she went on. "I know you all care about Vaughn, but can't you see what you're doing is more harmful than helpful? Did you consider what would happen to her if I had to cancel her as a witness? Grazicky would never say forget it and let her walk away, and I wouldn't be able to protect her any longer."

"Can I see her?" Patrick asked.

"No!"

"I want to talk to my sister."

"None of you will have any contact with her until I think it's safe. Keep it up, and you'll all go to jail," Lisa hissed.

Patrick objected. "But—"

"Let me be clear, gentlemen. One more stunt and I'll have all of you arrested and tossed in jail." Lisa stomped out the door, slamming it behind her.

Patrick lunged at Adriano, and they hit the floor together. Jake and Ethan fought to separate them, pulling them apart and holding them at arm's length.

"Remember," Jake shouted, "you both want the same thing—Payton safe."

"You're putting my sister in danger," Patrick shouted. "You'll get her killed."

Jake cut off Adriano's reply. "Adriano wouldn't do anything to hurt Payton. He sacrificed everything to help her when she was a complete stranger to him. What do you think he'd do for her now that he's fallen in love with her?"

Patrick stopped pressing into Jake's outstretched arm.

"Can you two stop fighting and concentrate on helping Payton?" Ethan asked.

Adriano and Patrick let their fighting stances slowly fade.

"All right, shake on it." Jake took a step back. "We need to work together on this."

Adriano offered an apology. "I've only wanted to help her from the first. I won't let anything happen to your sister. I love her."

Patrick stared at Adriano, resenting his sincerity. It would have been more satisfying to tear him apart with his bare hands. "Where do you think they took my sister?"

"I can make some phone calls." Jake went to the bedside table and lifted the phone receiver.

"No need." Adriano blew out a long breath.

Jake, Ethan, and Patrick all turned to him, waiting.

"If I know Payton like I know I do, she's on the way here."

"This is your last day, your last chance," Sherman told Hiram, but Hiram already knew.

Payton was back in Charlotte, heavily under guard. The police hadn't taken chances hiding her this time. Not after the Adam's Mark incident and the drive-by shooting of the FBI agent. They'd get her story, keep digging until finally they dug up some obscure piece of evidence on Sherman. And then they'd all be dead.

"You have twenty-four hours," Sherman said. "And then you're dead."

Hiram turned to leave. There was nothing left to say. The only reason he wasn't dead over the Patrick screwup was the press. Sherman knew his eagerness to get the girl had caused him to make a mistake. Against Hiram's advice, they'd let her brother go. It was like Payton had something on the old man.

"Don't bother going to my wife. She can't save you."

Hiram left the house, his mind swirling. He placed a call to Kellie the second he drove away from the sprawling mansion.

"You got eyes on the girl?"

"They moved her," Kellie answered. "Blocked all the streets in a three-mile radius to do it."

Hiram cursed. "We have to do this. *Today*."

She read his meaning clearly.

"We finish this today. Get the girl to the old man, and then go. Don't bother to pack."

"Where should I meet you?"

"Back at the hotel. Call all the guys."

He disconnected, dialing Cecily immediately. She was lethal, but smart. She'd tell him the best way to get to Payton. Despite her ruthlessness, he knew she had a soft spot for him. He hadn't performed like her little sex monkey for months for nothing. This was his insurance, and he was cashing it in.

From sunup to sundown, Payton answered questions about Sherman Grazicky, the murder she'd witnessed, and her adventure with Adriano. The FBI investigator joined the party, firing question after question. When he stopped for a sip of water, Lisa Hail and her team started.

Adriano had compromised her safety, Lisa said, so Payton

had been moved from her hotel before breakfast and taken to a safe house. The three-bedroom brick ranch sat clandestinely in the center of a middle-class Charlotte neighborhood. She knew as the police drove her in the back of the unmarked car what she had to do if she ever wanted to see Adriano again. That's why she committed to memory every detail of their route.

At nine o'clock, her day ended and her plan started.

She showered and dressed in her pajamas. She smiled and joked with the police officers playing cards in the living room, serving them snacks and drinks, offering to clean up their mess. She hung up their coats, taking the cash from the wallet of one of the overly amorous officers and hiding the crumpled bills in the pocket of her robe. Mission accomplished, she turned in for the night.

The night-shift officers soon came on duty. It astounded her that these trained professionals worked the graveyard shift every night but couldn't keep their eyes open after midnight.

She dressed in jeans and a pullover sweater and retrieved the knife she'd stolen from the kitchen from under her mattress. It took a little work to chip away the old paint around the window, but then it opened effortlessly. She slipped over the windowsill and out into the night.

Anxiety tied her stomach in knots. She climbed over several fences. She moved briskly past the unmarked police cars keeping surveillance on the safe house. The officers watched the nondescript woman walking on the opposite side of the street but were satisfied she posed no danger and let her pass unmolested.

Her memory wasn't as good as she believed, and she got lost roaming through the neighboring streets. She started to question her sanity. She couldn't blame her behavior on fear this time. The force pulling her to escape protective custody and run to Adriano could only be attributed to the magic powers of love.

She knew Adriano meant what he'd told her: he would find a way for them to be together. But he couldn't keep his promise if he didn't know where she was. They shared more than a sexual attraction. Their future was uncertain, but it existed. Not even Lisa Hail would keep them apart. Payton was tired of being her prisoner.

Traffic noise ahead made Payton hurry. At the end of the block was a main thoroughfare. She ran to the pay phone outside a convenience store and dialed a taxi service.

Adriano sat in the wingback chair facing the door of the hotel lobby. His head bobbed, eyes ebbing with every shallow breath. Exhaustion claimed more of his body as the seconds ticked by. He had tried to get some rest after Lisa Hail blew out of their suite, but failed. His mind churned with thoughts of Payton and wouldn't allow him to sleep. Headstrong and afraid, she wouldn't consider her own safety. She wanted to be near him, and she would get there—no matter what she had to do to accomplish it. If Lisa had been more cooperative and given him Payton's whereabouts, he could have tried to talk sense into her. But Lisa was clear and unyielding—no contact of any kind between them until her investigation was over. So Adriano sat exhausted in the lobby of his hotel waiting, playing out every minute of his time with Payton, asking when she stopped being a source and became the love of his life.

Jake grasped Adriano's shoulder. "Maybe she's not coming, A."

He rubbed his sandpapery lids with two balled fists. "She's coming, all right."

"Ethan's still on the phone trying to find out where they moved her to. I made a ton of calls. We'll track her down soon. Why don't you get some sleep? I'll keep watch for her."

He checked the time. "I could take a shower and change, but I can't sleep until I know she's all right. If Lisa would stop being such a—if she would tell me where she's keeping Payton, I could go to her and make sure she knows how I feel about her."

"You haven't told her?" Jake asked.

"I did, but . . . there are things to work out. How are we going to be together, Jake? Do I give up everything I've worked for at *Chicago City* now that it's this close? Or do I ask her to leave her home to follow me to Chicago?"

"Why don't you just ask her what she wants? It's not so far off she might want to be swept off her feet and come to Chicago with you. Women get off on that kind of stuff."

Payton wasn't an ordinary woman.

He stood and stretched the angry kinks knotting his shoulders. "I'll be back in thirty minutes."

"From everything you've told me, Payton is tough mentally and physically. She'll come out of this on top."

He gave a cautious nod of agreement before leaving Jake. He went to the bank of newspaper machines near the gift shop. The inset of one newspaper still headlined a picture of Payton being led away from the bus station by the police. He searched for coins and purchased a paper from the box. Standing at the elevators, he scanned the articles. He read the titles; each announced the return of the star witness against Sherman Grazicky—charges pending for his "alleged" crimes.

Screams rang out, piercing his concentration. He dropped the paper and ran back to the lobby.

Mass confusion. Jake wasn't sitting in the wingback chair where he'd left him. Hotel guests scrambled to get out of the way. A bellman struggled with a big, burly man. A loud pop resembling gunfire rang out, and the crowd screamed collectively. Adriano rushed against the current of people seeking cover and spotted Jake wrestling through the crowd toward the entrance. Adriano followed, reaching the turnstile of doors just in time to see Payton shoved into the back of a white cargo van.

* * *

Seeing Jake sitting across the lobby, Payton sighed with relief. She'd made it to Adriano. She hurried in his direction.

A large man stepped into her path. "Payton, what are you doing here?"

She clutched her chest. "Carter. You startled me. I didn't get a chance at the bus station to thank you personally for coming out to support me. It meant a lot." She glanced in Jake's direction. A waitress had him engaged in conversation.

"I wanted to be there," Carter said.

"I really appreciate it." Her gaze wandered in Jake's direction. Adriano would be somewhere nearby.

A man of few words, Carter had come to be a substitute big brother to Payton at Skye. His self-confidence lacked because of a deforming scar on the left side of his face. When she took the job at the club, she befriended him immediately, and he happily reciprocated.

Carter glanced over her shoulder. "I read you were in police custody."

"You know how the papers exaggerate." Payton forced herself to answer nonchalantly. She wanted to catch Jake and find Adriano before someone recognized her face from the news coverage, but Carter was a friend.

The waitress moved away from Jake.

"Listen, Carter, I have to go."

He grabbed her elbow, stopping her. "I'm afraid I can't let you."

"What?" An instant adrenaline rush told her she was in trouble.

"I need to take you with me."

"Where?"

"Mrs. Grazicky wants to talk to you."

"What?" Shocked, she tried to pull away from Carter.

"You're taking me to Sherman? Do you know what he'll do to me? He wants to kill me."

"*Mrs.* Grazicky wants to see you. Let's do this without making too much of a scene."

She'd never met Mrs. Grazicky personally. What could she want? After everything she had done to elude him, Payton wouldn't go to Sherman or his wife willingly. Patrick was safe. He had nothing to blackmail her with.

Payton screamed obscenities to draw the attention of the hotel guests. In the scuffle, she met Jake's eyes. The lobby became a maze of confusion with people running and screaming about they didn't know what. Jake was swallowed up in the people running for cover.

She continued to struggle, trying to buy enough time for Jake to reach her. She didn't know what he would do with a busted arm, but she didn't have many options. She fought Carter with all her strength but was no match for his raw brawn. Carter tossed her over his shoulder and carried her away.

"I have an anniversary gift for you, sweetheart," Cecily said, swishing up to her husband on a cloud of perfume. She was superbly dressed as usual, in blue silk pajamas, even if it was only to go to bed with him. It was one of the things that made Sherman fall in love with her: she always did her best to look good for him and to please him. He imagined he wasn't the best lover, because he'd had so little practice before her, but she never complained, submitting to his late-night gyrations with a hearty smile and thrust of her hips. Although he'd been angry to find her in the motel with Hiram, it had also turned him on to imagine watching her doing wicked things with another man.

"Our anniversary isn't for another month, and I've put you through so much this year, I'm just happy you haven't left me."

"I've never shared my childhood with you, Sherman, but there are things . . . There are things I wish I'd never seen, but we can't change who we are. We can pretend to be different things to different people, but in the end, we are true to our nature."

"What are you saying?" Sherman had discarded his newspaper, and every bit of his attention was focused on his wife.

"I'm saying I know all about your *activities* at Skye. I know you sell drugs and women in Chicago. I know about the special auditions the waitresses have to pass before they can work at the club."

"How?" he asked dumbly, contemplating who could be the spy. If Hiram had told her about the murder, he'd filet the man himself before grinding him up for fertilizer.

"It doesn't matter. What matters is I can't judge you because I've never told you where my family's money comes from."

Sherman listened with mixed fascination and horror as Cecily told him about her childhood. He pretended not to have found out this information from a jailhouse snitch many years ago. She gave him the graphic details of how she'd witnessed her father killing her mother. He knew about that too. The jailhouse snitch had disposed of the body. She explained how easy it had been for her father to launder money obtained from white slavery to build a legitimate nest egg suitable to pass down to a first daughter.

"Does it make you love me any less?" Cecily asked, a flicker of worry in her eyes.

"Your father sounds like a perfect monster." He knew from experience he was a crafty monster, too attuned to Sherman's business for his own good. "How did he raise such a perfect daughter . . . perfect for me?"

After sharing a sloppy kiss filled with the remnants of old passion, Cecily returned to the matter at hand.

"What do you have there?" Sherman asked, taking the cell phone out of her hands.

She leaned into him, pressing the right combination of

buttons until a vivid picture appeared on the small screen. He looked at his wife, full of questions. His mind raced. This was wonderful. This was terrible.

"My man found her."

Sherman turned to the screen again, wishing— only for a fleeting moment—he was alone to stare at the picture of Payton tied to a chair in a sparse room. Blindfolded, she was trussed up, apprehensively waiting for what she knew would come. The sight made his groin stir.

"Where is she?" he asked.

Cecily smiled. "I'll take you, but first we should talk about what we want to do to her before we kill her."

Chapter 27

Full of surprises, Cecily had her man Carter take Payton to Sherman's second home in the upscale University neighborhood. Sherman wondered exactly how many of his secrets Cecily knew but never revealed. Sherman kept the home mostly for a place to take his current mistress, so it was the perfect place to stash Payton. The neighbors wouldn't look twice at a strange woman coming or going.

Hiram and his ragamuffin crew left the bedroom after moving Payton to the bed. Sherman was torn. He entered the room eagerly awaiting Cecily's appearance but wanting a moment alone with Payton. Her hands were crudely tied behind her back, and a black sack covered her head. Her body trembled, but she was quiet. Her feet were flat on the floor, and she sat ramrod straight, her bosom heaving with every intake of breath.

In this captive position, she was deliciously enticing, and the things Cecily had planned would only make her more irresistible. He removed the black sack, and her eyes grew wide with fear. He held a finger up to his lips, signaling she should be quiet. With one yank, he removed the gray utility tape from her mouth.

"Beautiful Payton Vaughn. You've caused me a lot of trouble.

Not to mention the amount of money I had to pay these goons to find you." He grimaced. "I want the evidence."

"Sherman, I don't have it. I—"

He held his finger to his lips again. "Don't demean the honesty of our relationship by lying or, worse yet, making promises you have no intention of keeping."

"It was a trick to get Patrick back. I never had anything. We just figured it out."

He watched her, wanting it to be the truth. "It's the only way you'll get out of this alive."

"I don't have anything. I swear."

"The reporter?" It was a rhetorical question. No doubt the reporter had the evidence, itching to print it on the front page of the newspaper. "This complicates things. Now I have to get the reporter to give it up before I kill him."

"Kill him? You can't."

Sherman waved away her plea. "You'll forget about him soon enough. Once we're far away from this place." He stroked her face. "No more about him."

"What are you going to do with me?"

"More like, what are *we* going to do *to* you?"

"We?"

"My wife and I." He sat next to her, brushing her thigh with the back of his hand. He nodded toward a table on the other side of the room with an arrangement of various sex toys. "If you could have accepted what I offered you from the beginning, this wouldn't be happening. Instead you chose to turn on me. I don't tolerate disloyalty well."

"I saw you ordering that big man in the other room to murder someone. Your father-in-law."

"Quiet!"

"How could I accept murder?"

"Highly regrettable. I take full responsibility. It wasn't planned. The man threatened to call in his markers because he found out about the drug business. He's the king of white slavery, but he wants to restrict my business ventures. He told me drugs would bring too much heat. He was only worried about himself. If he would have called in the loans, my businesses would have gone bankrupt."

"And your wife is fine with this?"

"Don't you get it? Cecily would have packed her bags and run home to daddy if she knew we'd had a disagreement. She's truly daddy's little girl. Without her money and my businesses, I would be broke. I won't go back to living that way."

"So you had him killed."

Sherman couldn't stop touching her. "Careful. We don't want Cecily to know. She has plans for you, and quite frankly, I'm excited about seeing my wife do another woman. We wouldn't want to ruin the party." His eyes wandered to the closed door. "Cecily will know soon enough. You've made such a stink, it's only a matter of time. That's why we have to do what we're going to do, and then you and I have to get out of the country."

"I'm not leaving the country!"

He smiled. Payton would do what he told her to do. Or he'd put her on the plane unconscious.

"Your wife is in on this? She doesn't mind you sleeping with another woman?"

"Most of what we'll do tonight is her idea. She's very eager to meet you. I'm just lucky to have the pleasure of an understanding wife who is more than happy to let me get my shot at you first."

Alerted by a rustling outside the window, Sherman walked across the room and peeked out the vertical blinds. The street was dark. All the residents of the quaint neighborhood were tucking in the children and settling back in their easy chairs for a little television. No one had the faintest clue what was going on in their neighbor's home.

A brushing sound caught his attention. He scanned the darkness but saw nothing. His nerves were on edge. He had to finish this, get out of the house with Payton, make it to the plane, and get out of the country without Cecily catching on. It would be tricky, but he'd get it done.

"If you keep me here until after the trial, I can't testify," Payton offered.

"True, but who knows how long that tenacious ADA will keep this going? I can't keep you here for months." He had to get out of town. Tonight.

"If I don't give the ADA any information, there won't be enough evidence to convict you."

"Do you think I believe you haven't told her everything already? You're going to walk away and forget the murder? You should have done that from the start." He shook his head. "Unfortunately, I seem to be Charlotte's public-enemy number one. The prosecutor would dig up other charges." He sighed heavily. "And now we have the issue of your kidnapping." The hole his crimes had dug was too deep. Getting rid of Hiram would help, but there were other matters.

Payton asked again, "What are you going to do with me?"

He watched the desperation make her facial features sharper, more beautiful. He enjoyed this word game. It evoked crude fear in her. The anticipation of her fate was making her forehead wet with perspiration. Taking her would be better than conquering a virgin. Power over a beautiful woman was the best aphrodisiac of all.

"My stress level is through the roof." He kicked off his shoes. "Can you think of any way the two of us might be able to take care of it?"

Confusion and then recognition knitted Payton's trembling bottom lip.

He continued his torment. "At fifty-three I probably seem like an old man to you. Well, I'm not. What are you? Twenty-something? I have needs and desires—just like the reporter you ran off with. I can only imagine what he did to you."

"Adriano took care of me."

He grunted. "The first time I walked into Skye and saw you standing behind the bar, I wanted you. For months I tried to get your attention." He began to unbutton his dress shirt. "The only thing you ever wanted to talk about was business."

"Sherman—"

"A woman is most beautiful when she's scared. Her fear brings out the best in a man."

Rambling, Payton pleaded with him. "We have to work this out. I don't care about testifying. That's why I ran away."

"You might have had a chance of convincing me of that if the police hadn't whipped you out of the bus station into protective custody." He let his shirt drop to the floor at his feet. "There may be a way you can get back in my good graces."

"What?"

"You don't care about testifying against me?"

"No," she answered readily. He almost believed her.

"Then agree to go away with me."

Her bottom lip dropped.

"It would be so much nicer if you came voluntarily."

"Go where?"

"I'll tell you once we're on the plane."

She remained quiet, but her eyes darted wildly.

"I'll give you some time to think about it. We have all night. Have you ever slept with a white man?"

"I've never been with any man I didn't care for—black or white." A cross between disgust and panic twisted her mouth. "You're talking about raping me."

He laughed loudly. "Amateur psychiatry. I love it." He cupped her chin. "My dear, I'll take you any way I can." He shoved her back on the bed.

She batted her eyes wildly, refusing to let the tear clinging to her lash fall.

He struggled to remove her sweater. Frustrated, he pushed her onto her stomach and freed the knot binding her wrists. He dug his knee into her back to keep her in place.

"Don't even think of trying anything. Hiram and Carter are in the house. If I call out they'll come, and when they come they'll shoot first."

"Call Hail!" Adriano shouted to Jake as he went after Payton.

He ran to the first of the taxis lining the driveway of the hotel. Ripping the driver's door open, he grabbed the man and pulled him from the vehicle. No time for polite explanations. He was losing sight of the white cargo van. As he pulled away from the curb, Jake jumped in the front seat.

"Stop!"

He slowed enough for Jake, with his broken arm, to get inside.

Ethan wrenched open the back door and jumped in. "What the hell's going on?"

"I told you to call Hail," Adriano said to Jake, weaving into traffic to follow the van.

"I'll call her from here. Just drive." Jake pulled his cell phone from the clip on his waist.

"Is this about Payton?" Ethan asked, trying to get up to speed.

"They took her," Adriano answered, his concentration on the road. Frantic, he cut, crisscrossed, and dodged through the traffic. He never lost sight of the van.

"We've got him," Ethan announced.

"What are you talking about?" Adriano asked while Jake made the call to Lisa Hail.

"We must have driven through some dead spots, and when we got back to the hotel, I dropped off to sleep."

"What?" Adriano asked impatiently. He didn't have time for long explanations. Payton was in the back of the cargo van speeding down the highway, getting away from him.

"We've got a match on the dental records. Franco Cimino. Cause of death: multiple gunshot wounds."

Finally, concrete evidence to support Payton's claim. Tangible proof to be used to put Grazicky away.

"Did you get that?" Jake asked the person on the other end of the line.

"I faxed the information to Hail before I came downstairs to tell you," Ethan said.

Adriano watched the van dangerously swerve in front of a car as it changed lanes. He had to keep Payton alive in order to testify . . . in order to tell her he'd realized he'd give up everything, including his job, to be with her.

"Back off," Jake said. "Let them think they've lost you, but keep them in sight."

It was a good idea. If they kept driving the way they were, they'd flip the van. He dipped between two cars. "I'll kill Grazicky."

Jake spoke into the cell, giving the police their coordinates. "Where the hell are they taking her? Out of Charlotte?"

Adriano got on the expressway, keeping a safe distance, and continued to follow the van. An eternity later, they exited.

"We're in the University area of the city," Ethan offered. "Very upscale."

"Don't lose them," Jake coached while giving the police directions over his cell.

The white van pulled into the unlit driveway of a pastel pink house. Lights were on inside. Quiet stillness engulfed the neighborhood. Manicured lawns with bikes strewn about. SUVs and family vans lined the driveways. In the distance a dog barked.

Adriano recognized the two black sedans parked in the driveway from the cheap motel in South Carolina. He remembered the horror on Payton's face as he pulled her through the bathroom window and could only imagine how she was suffering now.

"Who lives here?" Adriano asked.

"Probably one of Grazicky's mistresses. He has houses for

them all over town." Ethan had been keeping his own file on Grazicky, hoping it would be his big story to break, propelling him out of small-town television news to a more commercial market. He had the pretty-boy good looks for it, but did he have the stomach for investigative reporting? Adriano couldn't allow him to become a liability. The only one he planned on saving tonight was Payton. Adriano knew Jake was capable even one-handed. Ethan looked too polished to want to get into the mix.

"Drive to the next block," Jake said, ignoring the policeman's order to stay put until they arrived. "The police say they're no more than three minutes away."

Three minutes was an eternity. "Payton could be dead in three minutes." He parked the taxi on the next block up from the house. "I'm going in."

"I'm with you," Ethan said, getting out of the car.

Carter braced his elbow on the mantle above the fireplace. His eyes were glued on the hallway, down which Sherman had Payton hemmed up in a bedroom. His ears were open to the conversation Hiram and his merry-losers were having. Cecily was somewhere in the house, preparing for her big entrance but allowing her husband enough time to get started.

Hiram sat with his elbows on his knees, head in his hands. Beside him, Kellie was trying to persuade him to leave. "When they come out of the bedroom," she whispered, "they'll have the big monkey over there kill us."

She was right, of course.

"Look what Carter did to Dan—sliced his ear completely off. We have to leave now."

"We haven't been paid," Hiram reminded her.

Marvin pulled his attention away from the TV. "Nobody's going anywhere until I kill the woman and collect my fee—plus the bonus money."

Hiram threw Kellie a warning look. If Marvin could hear her whispers, so could Carter looming by the fireplace.

Kellie turned on Marvin. "The way Sherman's in there fawning over the little witch, he's not going to let you kill her. Now shut up!"

Marvin began to heat up. "Did the plan change? No. Hiram, you need to keep your woman in line before she blows this for us."

Kellie pummeled Marvin with colored words.

Hiram jumped up from the couch. "Everybody shut up!"

"Yeah, everybody shut up." Carter stepped into the middle of the incompetent mix of killers. "Marvin, go outside and keep watch. Hiram, take Kellie out to the van until it's time to go."

Hiram moved as if he would challenge Carter, but Kellie grabbed his arm, relieved to be leaving the house alive. "Let's go."

With the living room quiet, Carter could think. He stood at the end of the hallway and listened for noise from the bedroom. He could only imagine what Sherman was doing to Payton. Guilt threatened to propel him down the hall into the bedroom. Payton had been the only one at Skye to treat him decently. She hadn't batted an eye at his deformity. The more time he spent at Skye spying for Cecily, the more he had grown to like Payton. The scar on his left cheek throbbed angrily. The look of betrayal on her face tonight almost made him back out of his deal with Cecily, but he knew her and he knew her father—he wouldn't have lived past midnight. Besides, Cecily had enough dirt on him to put him on death row.

A shrill scream rang out from the bedroom. He started down the hall but stopped suddenly, quickly remembering his last stint in prison. Sherman and Cecily wouldn't really hurt Payton. They'd get it on with her and be satisfied. Sherman would never go through with having her executed.

What are you saying? You kill people for a living. You know the score.

"Death row," he mumbled.

It's too bad Payton's a friend, but it's how things are. She was in the wrong place at the wrong time. Her bad luck.

He sat on the sofa and turned up the volume of the television, trying to drown out Payton's screams. He would finish this job, dispose of the bodies, and get the hell out of town. He'd never do business with Cecily Grazicky again.

Chapter 28

"I recognize her," Jake told Adriano. "She's the one who set me up."

A man and a woman hustled out the front door of the pink pastel house. Adriano gave Jake a sideways glance, questioning the petite woman's ability to "grab" him.

"She's the one who broke your arm?" Ethan asked.

They crouched behind a parked car across the street, watching as the couple climbed into the white cargo van in the driveway. The red taillights came on, but the van didn't move. A huge man came out next and stationed himself at the left perimeter of the house.

"I have a bad feeling about this," Jake said. Police sirens sounded in the distance. "How far away do you think they are?"

"Close," Adriano answered, "but we can't wait."

What would be Grazicky's motivation for keeping Payton alive once he heard the sirens?

Ethan spoke. "I don't like this. What are they waiting for in the van?" He shared a look with Adriano. "How many do you think there are?"

"At least one more. I don't see the big guy who hauled Payton out of the hotel."

Time was limited. The arrival of the police would cause the

hit men to panic. If Payton were still alive—"I'm going in," Adriano announced.

"The police are almost here," Jake said. "These people are armed."

"I'm with you," Ethan announced.

"Do you know how to handle yourself?" Adriano wanted to know.

"I do all right." The corner of Ethan's mouth slanted upward.

"You stay here and wait for the police," Adriano told Jake.

Jake shook his head. "You think I can't handle myself because of this?" He lifted the cast on his broken arm.

"Yeah, something like that."

A police car turned onto the street. The officers left the flashing lights on, and a red and yellow warning illuminated the dark neighborhood. The van peeled out of the driveway at top speed. The police car pursued. The man standing guard outside the house had jumped in the van before it left and another man had come out of the house and ran to the street to see what was happening.

"I hope there are more cars coming," Jake commented.

"With smarter drivers," Ethan added.

Instead of going inside to warn the others, the thug disappeared behind the house. They were scrambling. They would run. They would take care of any loose ends.

Adriano pointed left, at his own chest, and then right. Ethan nodded his understanding.

In a flash, Ethan disappeared behind the house. He caught the thug off guard. The man turned around, and Ethan's fist connected with his jaw. The man whirled, reaching inside his jacket, but Adriano was there to deliver another blow. The gun clattered to the ground, and Ethan kicked it away. Adriano pummeled the man with a succession of blows, working out all his fears on the man's face. The thug countered with a right, and then a left. Ethan approached from behind, and Adriano stalked from the front. The man took a fighter's stance, ready for one last round. Adriano kicked him solidly in the center of his chest. The man did a Fred Sanford impersonation, clutched his chest, and fell to the ground.

Jake was there, hustling for the gun. He held it on the thug. "Don't move!"

"How do we get inside?" Ethan asked, barely breathing hard. Adriano had misjudged the pretty boy.

"The front door." He nudged the writhing man with his foot. "How many are inside?"

The man mumbled incoherently, still clutching his chest. His breaths came in short puffs.

"Let's do this," Adriano said.

"Let's." Ethan's mouth slanted upward again, and Adriano knew the expression for what it was: the thrill of the fight. He'd done many foolish things with that same look on his face. Suddenly he felt old and weary of the game.

"Go!" Adriano took off to the front of the house.

Cecily's hand came down hard across Payton's face. "Can't we remove the gag? I want to hear her scream."

Sherman pressed his lips to Cecily's mouth, quieting her. "The neighbors will hear," he told her, hoping it would be enough. The first opportunity Payton had to talk, she'd tell what she knew about Cecily's father. If Sherman wanted his plan to come off, Cecily couldn't find out about her father's death until after he'd gone.

Payton watched them, intent on not crying. She held her screams, batting away the tears threatening to fall. Her stubborn refusal to give Cecily what she wanted—a quivering, crying weakling she could dominate—only fueled Cecily's creative mind. Cecily pounced on the bed, locking Payton's arms between her thighs.

Cecily had dressed the part for Payton's seduction. A black leather skirt and corset matched her stiletto boots. The material was tight; every curve of her body was outlined against the leather. She'd always wanted to try this game, and now she had the chance. Her eagerness thrilled Sherman. He almost wished they could keep Payton and do this again.

Horny beyond belief, Sherman fumbled with his belt buckle. "You might enjoy this," Sherman said.

"I think she does," Cecily laughed.

"This will be the last time you have a man." The belt fell to the floor, and he started on his pants.

Cecily cackled, and he started on the pants again. Completely nude, he approached the bed. Payton tried to wiggle free of Cecily's hold, so the woman struggled to handcuff her in the leather cuffs dangling from the bedposts. Too erect to wait any longer, Sherman converged on Payton, groping her breasts. She fought, heightening Cecily's pleasure.

"I want to hear her beg," Cecily said, ripping the tape away from Payton's mouth.

Sherman lunged at her, trying to cover her mouth before she could speak.

"He killed your father!" Payton screamed, struggling to catch her breath. "I saw him order the hit."

The room went still. The crazy, cackling fun Cecily had been enjoying died with Payton's words. She extricated herself from Payton's body and left the bed.

"Liar!" Cecily shouted. "My father is away on business."

"Call him."

"Don't listen to her," Sherman said, pressing the tape back to Payton's mouth.

"Why would she accuse you of killing Daddy?"

Sherman could see Cecily working it out in her head. She wouldn't discount Payton's claim easily.

"She'd say anything to stop what's going to happen to her." He moved slowly toward his wife. "She's dead, and she knows it. She's trying to come between us."

"You said I could leave the country with you," Payton said.

He swung around to find she'd worked the used tape away from her mouth. "Shut up! Shut up or I'll have you killed now."

"What is she talking about, Sherman?" Cecily wanted to know, backing away from him.

"Don't let her do this, honey. Let's finish what we started." He reached for her hand, but she angled away from him.

"Your father didn't want your husband's drug business calling attention to his business," Payton yelled. "He threatened to call in his loans."

"How does she know so much?" Cecily asked.

Sherman could see it in her eyes. She believed Payton. She was waiting for one piece of indisputable evidence before she condemned him.

"She's a manager at Skye. She must have been spying on me for the FBI."

Cecily shook her head. "No. There's something else going on here."

Sherman stormed to the bed, ready to silence Payton permanently.

"Don't touch her!" Cecily shouted.

Sherman turned to his wife. "She's lying, Cecily."

"We'll see." She moved around Sherman to stand closer to Payton. "Describe the man you saw my husband have killed."

Payton recited every detail of the meeting she had witnessed. Sherman felt as if he were watching the deadliest moment of his life replayed on the movie screen. She described the scene perfectly, not leaving out one minute detail.

Cecily turned slowly. "You killed my *father?*" Her eyes were cloaked in an emotion he'd never seen her express. "For money? Do you know how much I'm worth? You could have had everything you wanted, if you would have just asked."

"I don't want to come begging to my wife for everything I need!"

"Now I'm not good enough for you, you stupid ex-convict? *You killed my father!*"

"You believe her? Over me?"

Cecily moved to the bed and began loosening Payton's restraints. "Go. Get me the proof. Carter will go with you."

"Wait!"

Payton's first instinct told her to fight, but Adriano had taught her many lessons while they were on the run. She had one shot. She had to take it at the right moment to make it count. She relaxed her fight against the cuffs, allowing Cecily to release her.

Sherman stood paralyzed, his mind racing for an alternate plan. If Payton returned with evidence of Franco's death, he'd be killed. As it was, Cecily doubted his word and was sending Payton to prove her claims.

"If you're lying," Cecily told Payton, "I will kill you myself."

"I'm not lying." Payton moved stiffly off the bed.

As she crossed the room, Sherman saw everything he'd worked for fading away. If he made it out of this alive, he'd be poor or, worse, imprisoned again. Desperation made him react recklessly. He jumped across the room and yanked out the bedside drawer, scrambling inside until he found the gun he kept hidden there.

Cecily turned to see what had captured Payton's attention.

Knowing Sherman would kill her as easily as he was going to shoot his wife, Payton rushed him, executing a hard chop to his windpipe with the heel of her hand. He lurched, grabbing his throat and dropping the gun. The blow hadn't been forceful enough to render him unconscious, but it did make him stagger and gasp for air. He went down on his knees, choking and trying to breathe.

Cecily didn't hesitate. She whipped a knife from the waistband of her skirt. The long silver blade sparkled in the lighting. Payton's last coherent thought was to question how Cecily had fit the gaudy thing inside her tightly restrictive clothing. She realized Cecily's original intent had been to use it to cut her throat after they were done playing with her. She became woozy and her knees gave out just as Cecily grabbed a fistful of Sherman's hair, yanked his head back, and slashed his throat from behind.

Blood arced across the room, spraying across Payton's tank top. She screamed, pressing her palms to her mouth. She felt queasy, dizzy, confused. The room wavered, swimming before her eyes.

"*You killed my father!*" was Cecily's battle cry as she plunged the knife between Sherman's shoulder blades.

With an anguished grunt, Cecily doubled over on the floor next to Sherman. She cried out in a high-pitched wail that would bring the hit men to see what was going on. Payton knew she had to get out before they arrived. They'd kill her first and sort out the details of what happened later. She crawled across the room, making a wide circle around the pool of Sherman's blood.

The bedroom door swung open, and Adriano burst inside. Grabbing Payton under the arms, he pulled her across the room, out of Cecily's reach. She hustled into his arms, pulling him down on the pink carpet with her.

Cecily came back to herself, shouting between sobs. "Carter! Get in here!" When he didn't answer, she used the edge of the bed to climb up from the floor. Her steps unsteady, she moved past them, unaware they were there. She moved into the hallway, screaming for Carter to kill everyone in the house.

"Are you okay, angel?" Adriano held her tight, examining her torn, bloody clothing while eyeing Sherman's dead body.

"Cecily," Payton said, grabbing onto him. "We have to get out of here."

His keen reporter's eye spotted the table lined with sex toys and the bed with the cuffs still dangling from the posts. "What did they do to you?"

Payton gripped his neck, not willing to let him leave her side. "They didn't hurt me. Look at your face!" She bounced to her knees and gingerly cupped his face in her palms, examining the scrapes and welts.

Jake appeared, positioning himself next to Sherman's naked and bloody body. He turned the man's head to check for a pulse, finding the slash across his neck. "What the hell?"

The room swelled with policemen and FBI agents. They buzzed around the house, searching for the others involved. After everyone was rounded up, they interrupted Payton and Adriano's reunion to get details of her capture. Adriano insisted they move outside, away from Sherman's body.

Outside, Ethan was waiting. Lisa Hail came blazing down the street. Before her car came to a complete stop, she was pounding the pavement toward Adriano and Payton.

"Arrest these men!" Hail yelled at the officers standing closest to the stolen taxi.

Adriano drew Payton into the protective barrier of his chest.

Perplexed—these men were heroes—the two officers stood by and waited for the confrontation to erupt between Hail and the men.

Lisa's finger poked Jake's chest. "I told you to stay out of my way or I'd have you arrested. Well, you did it. I'm throwing you all in jail, and you'll be lucky if you're released this time next year."

"Listen, Hail—"

"And you." Lisa pointed in Payton's direction. "What's your problem? We're trying to *protect* you. These officers put their lives on the line, and you go running off. I have a mind to throw you in jail with your boyfriend!"

Adriano had had enough of the short, stocky, big-mouthed assistant district attorney. "Back off! Don't say another word to her."

Lisa looked around at the officers. "I said arrest them."

"Just a minute." A man dressed in a dark suit and long coat interrupted Lisa's tirade. "Stand down, Lisa." He pulled her aside and said something that didn't leave her happy. She huffed back to her car and took off with screeching tires.

Payton leaned into Adriano. "I really messed up, but I had to see you."

He kissed the top of her head. "We'll talk later." The way he said "later" let her know he was not happy with what she'd done.

The well-dressed man walked into their circle. "District Attorney Palmer."

Jake, Ethan, and then Adriano shook his hand.

"I hear you are heroes. Ms. Vaughn, we need to get you back to the safe house. We were able to stop the van, but the man Ethan and Adriano scuffled with fled the scene before we could apprehend him."

"Carter," she offered.

"Excuse me?" Palmer's eyebrow quirked as if he'd hit the jackpot.

"Carter is the man who grabbed me." She tilted her head up to Adriano. "I thought he was my friend."

The DA scratched his head in confusion. "Ms. Vaughn, we need to spend a lot of time together. I'd like to know how a woman like you got mixed up with some of the biggest criminals in Mecklenburg County."

"Not tonight," Adriano interjected. "Payton has had enough tonight. I'm taking her back to the hotel. You can ask her all the questions you want—in the morning. Tonight, she's staying with me."

District Attorney Palmer read the unwavering resolve on Adriano's face. He had to pick his fights, and this one he wouldn't win. Not without strong-arming his key witness, and Lisa Hail had already proven that could be disastrous.

"Doesn't look like we've done a good job protecting her, does it? Take her back to your hotel, but I want you to ride in a squad car, and the police will remain posted outside your door. I'll see you in my office first thing tomorrow morning."

Chapter 29

Adriano and Jake shared a moment of companionable silence in which they recalled the adventures of the past, experiences that were responsible for the close friendship they shared today. The two had been partners at the *Chicago City* newspaper for years. Adriano missed the weekly dinners at Jake's house while he was on the run with Payton. They would fondly remember their escapades undertaken in the name of "getting the story." Hanging out with Jake's family reminded him of the love found in his childhood home. Sitting together now, talking and sharing a beer, offered him a measure of comfort when he was confused about his future with Payton.

"You're staying?" Jake asked, tipping the beer bottle to his lips.

"Until the trial's over."

Jake laughed. "How'd you get Mr. Conners to float the bill?"

Adriano shrugged. "He wants the story."

Jake nodded. "Hurry up and get back. We owe a bunch of people favors over this one."

Adriano smiled, remembering the day Payton jumped into the SUV. "It's been wild."

"One of our best stories yet."

Adriano sipped from his beer, absently watching the bottle as he swirled the brew.

"What about Payton?" Jake asked, treading carefully.

Adriano's gaze instantly went to the closed door. Only feet away she was sleeping in the bed they would share. "She's not as tough as she tries to be."

"She's got a lot of heart. She did kick Grazicky's ass."

"Yeah." He didn't want to think about what might have happened.

"Patrick is going to come after you if you break her heart."

"It's the last thing I want to do."

"What's the plan?" Jake asked, watching him over the rim of his bottle.

"You know how I handle long-distance relationships." He had women all over the world happy to have a little piece of him whenever he visited. "Payton would never go for it."

Jake laughed. "No, I can't see her jumping on board for that arrangement." After a few minutes, Jake asked, "What's Plan B?"

Adriano ran a hand across his face. "What can I offer her? Am I supposed to move to Charlotte and try to make a life here? Doing what?"

"You can be a reporter anywhere. Granted, it won't have the big-city appeal, but you might be able to make a living."

"And then what? Take my just-getting-by salary and try to take care of Payton?"

Jake nodded, understanding Adriano had too much pride to offer Payton so little.

"I couldn't ask Payton to give up everything and move to Chicago," Adriano said, trying to convince himself. "Wouldn't I have to marry her first?"

"I don't know. Why don't you ask Payton?"

"Can you even imagine me married? With kids?" Adriano laughed, downing his beer. When he looked at Jake, he wasn't laughing.

"With Payton. Yeah, I could see it, A. The question is: Why can't you?" He finished his beer and sat the bottle on the table. "I have to pack."

They held each other in a brotherly hug.

"You're in a bad spot," Jake said. "All I know is when I met my wife, I knew no matter what I had to go through, I needed her with me. You should ask yourself if you can live with your pride and honor without Payton, because if you don't get it together, you'll lose her."

Adriano sat in the chair, wrestling with his conflicting feelings for a long time before he went to the phone and dialed his parents. Everyone had heard about the Grazicky case, and Adriano could feel the pride of his parents when he told them about his role in it. Payton should have the opportunity to come to one of his family's wild get-togethers. She'd like his sister, and his mother would adore her. After assuring his mother he was safe, he spoke with his father.

"Your mother misses you. When are you coming home?" his father asked.

"After the trial."

"The woman you were hiding, she's a real looker."

"You'd love Payton. She's smart, and sensitive, and a hellcat."

"Sounds like you got to know her pretty well."

He didn't want to become too emotional. "I did."

"Will we get to meet her?"

"I don't know."

His father made a reflective sound over the phone. "What's on your mind, Son?"

Adriano rubbed his eyes. "Tired. It's been a lot."

"Don't sound like you're tired. Something else going on? Something to do with the girl?"

Adriano could never keep anything from his father. "We became close over the past few weeks."

"How close?"

"I love her."

His father went silent for a long moment. "You don't want to leave her."

"No. I don't."

"Then you shouldn't."

He wished it were so simple. He knew everything Payton had gone through in the past few months, and it made his heart rip when he considered how her life had been destroyed. He knew the Grazickys had done more disgusting, sexually deviated things to her than Payton had admitted. She'd experienced more horrors in her life than she should have. He watched Payton fighting to stay strong, and he knew it would be his duty not to make her life harder by proposing unrealistic relationships on her life.

"I have to go, Dad. Tell Mom I love her."

"I will, Son. You take care of yourself. You'll do the right thing, and we'll support you. No matter what you decide."

Shutting the door on Jake, Ethan, Patrick, and the police officers, Payton stepped into a hot bath. When she finished, Adriano awaited her on the queen-sized hotel bed wearing only a pair of white cotton boxers. The material left little to Payton's imagination, but it certainly whet her appetite. He had bathed away most of the evidence of his hellacious fight with Carter. She wanted to jump on the bed and straddle him, but she treaded cautiously because she knew he held words of chastisement for her.

She stood at the foot of the bed, looking as innocent as she had the day she'd jumped into his Land Cruiser. Adriano sat up, plopping a pillow behind his bare back. He scanned the borrowed white undershirt she used as a nightgown. His eyes lingered at her breasts, and she knew by the way he licked his lips he wanted her as badly as she wanted him.

He scratched at the black bandana covering his long mane.

"Payton Vaughn, tonight you did the stupidest thing you could've ever done. You were almost killed."

"I had to see you."

"Why don't you ever listen to me? I told you to stay put. Sometimes I *do* know what's best. Have I steered you wrong yet?"

She hung her head. "No."

"If you ever do anything like that again . . ."

The room fell silent. The reality of what might have happened was too much for either of them to acknowledge.

She lifted her head and met Adriano's lustful eyes. She kneeled on the foot of the bed and removed her shirt. "I couldn't let Hail keep me away from you."

He reached for her. "Come here."

She crawled to him on hands and knees. She straddled his middle and tried desperately to kiss away all of their troubles.

"You could have been killed." His voice was husky, troubled. "Seeing me wasn't worth the risk." He rained kisses on her cheeks.

"You don't know how much you mean to me. One night away from you was too much."

"What did Grazicky and his crazy wife do to you? If he touched you, tell me—"

She answered between his kisses, bracing his face between her hands. "No one other than you will ever make love to me."

Her hands went inside his boxers, taking the full weight of his manhood in her palm. She massaged him to life, pulling his shorts down over the high haunches of his behind.

He lifted her and tossed her to the bed, covering her before she hit the crisp white sheets.

"I'm on top." He nibbled her earlobe. "That's your problem— don't know your place."

"I know my place. My place is with you."

His body went still, his hands unmoving on her breasts.

She understood the weight of her words, knew how they

caused him to war with himself. He would need to do the honorable thing, but his heart wanted what it wanted.

She pushed him with a simple declaration. "I love you."

He cupped her breast with tender care. He teased one nipple to full bloom with the pad of his thumb. His lips went to the other.

"Do you love me?" she asked, relentless.

"Of course I do."

"What are we going to—"

He pressed his lips to hers, stopping her from asking the loaded question. He nibbled at her mouth until she opened for him, and then he slipped his tongue inside. He tried to fill her with reassurances all would be okay, but she didn't have the answer she wanted. He tried to convince himself they would regain some form of normalcy in their lives.

"Angel, I know this is hard." He remained firm, despite his true emotions.

"It sounds like you've made up your mind."

"It's the only answer."

"Then make love to me like this is the last time we'll ever be together." She ran her fingers through his hair. "Because it is."

His face went slack, his eyes hazed with confusion.

She'd put it all out there. She loved him too much to be away from him. Risking her life tonight had proved it. Damn his righteousness. She wanted him to act with his heart. They could battle through the rest. They'd survived being chased by killers. They could work out the logistics of their relationship.

There was nothing in Charlotte for her after he left.

Patrick and her family were in St. Louis. Her brother had offered to take her back with him. He'd help her find a job, and she could stay with his family until she was on her feet again. She'd given him a vague answer, holding out hope Adriano would ask her to come to Chicago with him.

Without warning, a great sob accompanied by huge tears poured from Payton.

"It rips my heart to shreds when you cry." Adriano brushed the raindrops away and tenderly kissed every inch of her face. Handling her like she was made of glass, he sampled every part of her body, making her writhe in spite of her tears. "I'm sorry, angel," he whispered.

"I love you," Payton said as she bucked her hips, meeting his stroke.

"I love you too."

They fell into a rhythm that tugged at Adriano's heart. He moved inside her lush walls, willing the vanilla cream to spill. Her continued declaration of love pulled at his willpower. He tried to kiss her into quiet submission, but as soon as he pulled his lips away, the mantra began again.

"I love you. I love you. I love you," Payton screamed as her body convulsed beneath him. She wrapped her legs around his behind and sung soulfully in his ear. "I love you, Adriano."

His muscles became taut. She bucked beneath him. He plunged into a slippery heaven. "I love you too, angel."

Chapter 30

Payton wouldn't tell Adriano what Grazicky and his sick wife had done to her in the bedroom of the pink pastel house. He'd seen the perverted toys, observed her ripped clothing, and soothed lotion over the marks on her legs. The more he pressured her, the more she withdrew. She wouldn't allow him inside the courtroom when she testified about it, but he was there for everything else, sitting in the front row, offering his support. If Grazicky weren't dead, Adriano would have twisted his head off.

"Be strong, angel," Adriano mouthed from his seat in the crowded courtroom.

Payton took a deep breath.

Lisa Hail's suit said business and screamed "I'm all woman." Prosecuting the case, she looked softer, more feminine than she had months ago when she had burst into their suite. No one could have guessed at the flaring temper she unleashed when things didn't go her way. In the courtroom she spoke coolly, putting Payton at ease.

Payton testified to the court about memos, messages, and phone calls involving Grazicky's illegal activities, providing a foundation for Cecily's motive in murdering her husband.

Lisa asked questions to help Payton describe the murder she'd witnessed.

Cecily sobbed loudly, garnering a reaction from the gallery. The courtroom erupted in gasps. The judge pounded his gavel. The courtroom became excited by all the nervous energy. Reporters ran for the lobby to call in the exclusive. Cameras had been banned from the courtroom, but they were set up outside on the courthouse stairs, capturing every moment.

"Your Honor," Lisa shouted over the chaos, "a recess, please."

The gavel sounded. "One-hour recess."

The bailiffs cleared the room of Cecily and the jury before allowing Payton to step down from the witness stand.

Adriano pulled her into his arms. "It's almost over, angel. You were great up there." His own testimony had gone much quicker, having only discovered Grazicky's body.

Adriano, Payton, and Lisa adjourned to a private office.

"This is going well, Ms. Vaughn," Lisa said, clutching the handle of her briefcase.

"It's almost over," Adriano told Payton again, resting his arm on her shoulders.

"Now comes the hard part."

Adriano knew what she meant. His business would be concluded soon, and he would have to go back to Chicago.

"Do you want to go over what to expect again?" Lisa asked, assessing Payton's demeanor. She didn't want her star witness to fall apart under pressure.

"No. We've been over it again and again. I'm ready."

Lisa glanced at Adriano.

He answered her silent question. "She's ready if she says she's ready."

"The marshals will bring you lunch." Lisa turned to leave, but stopped suddenly. "You're doing a good thing here," she said before leaving them alone.

Adriano pulled two chairs together and had her sit facing

him. "I'm proud of you. Stay strong. This will be over soon, and you won't ever have to say the name Grazicky again."

She'd insisted before taking the stand that Adriano not be present for the portion of her testimony about what the Grazickys had done to her. After some argument, he'd agreed, waiting anxiously outside.

A few hours later, Lisa announced, "Mrs. Grazicky's lawyer has asked for a meet."

"What does that mean?" Payton asked.

"She probably wants to make a deal."

"Will you?"

"If she'll tell me what I want to know about her father and her husband's businesses."

"After everything this has put Payton through," Adriano asked, "it ends this quickly?"

Lisa's face twisted. "Does it have to be harder? The good guys won."

"It's over?" Payton asked in shock, not able to process the information.

"The attorneys will iron out the details and give the offer to the judge for final approval, but yes, it's over." Lisa turned to Payton, not a little relieved to be finished with the entire mess. "You're excused, Ms. Vaughn."

From all reports, Cecily was now isolated in the mental ward at a federal holding station, waiting to be transferred to jail, under suicide watch. She was despondent over her father's death.

The police had not apprehended Carter, but Hail assured them the threat was waning. Carter was a paid assassin, and there was no one to pay his salary.

Kellie, Hiram, Marvin, and Dan were all caught and made deals with the D.A. so that they could avoid some of the worst charges against them. However, they were all sentenced to long stretches in prison for kidnapping and assault.

Franco Cimino's body had been found by a vagrant in a

Dumpster two counties away. The body had been stripped of identification, but the medical examiner had been reluctant to release the body because of the expensive shoes it was wearing. He figured no homeless man could afford a one-thousand-dollar pair of loafers. He'd eventually been forced to release the body, but he'd kept what he needed to make a matching identification of the dental records. The body had been exhumed, and the man was confirmed to be Franco Cimino.

Not many people mourned Franco's passing. Once the news hit, people oppressed by his cruelty began to surface, turned brave by what Payton had done. Cecily's family's wealth had been built on international crimes, going back thirty years. When Cecily married, her father had allowed her to step in and run portions of the criminal organization. She'd branched off in so many different directions that retracing her steps was the government's greatest headache. Her father had taught her well, and they were having trouble tying any illegal activities directly to her. The kidnapping charges would stick, but the government wanted more—drug trafficking, white slavery, embezzlement—so they kept digging.

Grazicky wasn't as clever as Franco, and in his haste to put together an escape plan, he'd left behind a thread of evidence Hail was currently unraveling. Connections were being made between the Grazicky and Cimino families. Skye Charlotte was closed permanently, and Skye Miami would never complete construction. Hungry up-and-coming drug lords were scrambling to claim Grazicky's territories. It would be a while before they could rebuild, and hopefully Hail's new task force would be able to stop them.

District Attorney Palmer was flashing his smile on every news station. Lisa Hail stood in the background, brooding. Ethan's television exclusive had given him the fame he sought, and he was making plans to relocate to Chicago. Mr. Conners was reluctant about having another hothead on his staff, but he was considering it. Especially when Adriano informed

Mr. Conners about not wanting to take any big assignments for a while. Mr. Conners was okay with it; after all, Adriano had a multipiece story and book to write about taking down the Grazicky empire.

Adriano handled his anxiety about the trial by churning out page after page of the memoir exposing Sherman Grazicky as told by Payton Vaughn. She wouldn't let him include anything about the sick bedroom games in the book.

"Why do you want to write about all those gruesome details?" she'd ask when he questioned her about it. "If I were going to write a story about what happened, I'd make it a romance and I'd call it *All The Way.*"

He planned on the romance being his next project.

The publishing industry buzzed about the exposé, and the book was expected to debut at number one on the *New York Times* bestseller list. Adriano donated half of the advance payment for the book to a drug-rehab center in Chicago. Half of Payton's royalties were donated to the same center. Mr. Conners ran weekly teasers about the book, increasing the newspaper's circulation by 25 percent. Major movie producers were already swarming, trying to get their hands on an advance copy. The publishing company let the frenzy mount—the advance copies would be mailed at midnight thirty days before the book's release.

Soon Adriano would have to return to Chicago and get on with his life. He held Payton too tightly around the waist, but she didn't complain, and he didn't let go. He couldn't imagine not sharing his bed with her. How was he supposed to go back to Chicago and pretend she hadn't stolen his heart? He'd wrestled with the question for days, always coming to the conclusion that a good man would never ask a woman to uproot for an uncertain future with him.

Abruptly, she pulled away and jumped out of bed.

"Where are you going?" He propped himself on his elbow and drank up her naked body.

She swung around. "I can't believe you're doing this to me."

"Doing what?"

"You say you love me. Why are you giving up on us? I don't understand. If you truly love me, how can you walk away so easily?"

The sheet fell to his narrow waist. "Lower your voice."

"No! I want you to explain it to me."

"Lower your voice. We don't need the police or your brother hearing every word we say."

She glanced toward the door, having forgotten the police were stationed outside. At this point she didn't care who heard her frustration. "I don't care!" she shouted. She was fighting for their future. A future Adriano seemed too eager to throw away.

"I don't care who hears. Explain why you're breaking us apart . . . or go share a bed with Ethan or Jake."

"Hold up. I said lower your voice. If you want to discuss this with me, do it without the yelling." He paused for emphasis. "And you never put me out."

She hunted at the foot of the bed until she found the discarded undershirt. She pulled it over her head with angry tugs.

"Angel—"

"Don't call me that anymore."

"Okay, Ms. Vaughn. You want to talk about this now?"

"Yes!" She folded her arms over her chest, fixing her eyes on him. "Before, you said you'd rather let me go than place me in danger. Sherman's dead. Cecily's in jail."

"Think rationally. You live in Charlotte, and I live in Chicago."

"Are you making *excuses?*"

"Wouldn't it be selfish to ask you to have a long-distance relationship with me?"

"Hell, yes!"

He looked as if she'd slapped him.

"Hell, yes, it's selfish."

"Stop cursing at me. I respect you; you respect me."

She tried unsuccessfully to restrain her anger.

"Don't think for one minute I want to lose you, because I don't."

"It's not enough, Adriano. The words aren't enough."

"I don't know what you want."

She could see his resolve wavering. "Prove you love me as much as you say."

"I am." He raised his voice out of frustration. "By sacrificing what we have to make sure you're happy."

"We just found each other." She sat at the foot of the bed. "How could you think I'd be happy without you?"

His eyes moved away, unable to meet her intensity.

"Why won't you fight for us? For me?"

"Payton, please stop it. I'm trying to do the right thing here. Walking away from you will kill me."

"Then why are you going?" She watched him for a long time as a myriad of emotions played across his face.

He didn't answer.

She stood to leave.

He didn't try to stop her.

"I've made my best—and last—attempt to convince you this decision is wrong," she said, her voice reflecting defeat. She had done everything but beg him to reconsider. Tonight would be their last night together. In the morning she'd meet with the FBI and the district attorney's office, give them her final deposition, and it would all be over. She held her head up. No more tears. No matter how much her chest hurt, or the lump in her throat burned, she would not cry over Adriano Norwood.

"I'm going to share the room with my brother."

"Wait," he said, stopping her before she turned around.

"There's nothing else to talk about, Adriano."

"The first time we made love—I had to convince you what we were feeling was real. At the bus station, I begged you to tell me if you cared about me."

"Where is this going?"

"I've never been in love before, but I'm trying to get it right. I don't want to disrupt your life, but, angel, I don't think I can live without you."

Her heart swelled with hope, but she reacted cautiously. She'd heard his declarations of love before. "What are you saying?"

"You are my heart," he said, his voice roughened with emotion.

She watched him, unable to move, unable to speak.

"I might know a way to prove how much I love you. It's radical. Are you ready to hear it?"

She nodded as he moved to the edge of the bed. "I know you're the one for me. If we took time to date like normal people—you know, going out to dinner, meeting each other's families—it would only be a matter of time."

"A matter of time for what?"

"A matter of time before I asked you to marry me."

She trembled excitedly.

"How would you feel about moving to Chicago with me?"

"Chicago?" she repeated, unable to believe he'd finally asked her.

He took her hands in his, pulling her to stand between his legs. "I've been thinking this through for days. Jake and I have connections. We could help you find work. You'll stay at my place until you find an apartment—if I can stand letting you move. Chicago is much closer to St. Louis than Charlotte—you'd be nearer to your family."

"You don't need a list to convince me."

Adriano fisted her T and pulled her to him. He kissed her lips, restraining his nervous energy with a tender peck on the lips. "We could be home in a matter of hours. *Home,* angel. Do this with me."

He kissed her again, long and sensual. "What do you say, angel?"

She steadied his face between her trembling hands, watching his dancing eyes. "Let's go home, Adriano."

About the Author

Award-winning author Kimberley White resides in the metropolitan Detroit area. She is a nurse practitioner and applies her medical experience to her novels.

A budding entrepreneur, you can often find her at craft shows. Writing is her passion so she spends a great deal of time at the computer, at bookstores, or at book signings. On lazy days she plays with the dog or reads a juicy paranormal novel.